The Goddess of Weaver Street

Advance Reviews

"A compelling story of woman's mental health—or mental wealth? Set in the unprecedented Eisenhower boom, *The Goddess of Weaver Street*, nevertheless recalls the reader to a gentler time in Galway, Ireland, and rewards with an ending that affirms time and space count for nothing. Only love."

— PARRIS AFTON BONDS
New York Times bestselling author

"*The Goddess of Weaver Street* is a mesmerizing tale of one woman's belief that she is in the wrong place at the wrong time. Readers begin to understand and trust, as does Lynda Lee, Davis's protagonist, that the dreams providing relief from both physical and emotional anguish hold the answer she seeks."

— BARBARA CONREY
USA Today bestselling author of *Nowhere Near Goodbye* and *My Secret to Keep*

"*The Goddess of Weaver Street* is a work of fiction in the interpersonal drama, slice-of-life, and emotive writing subgenres. It is best suited to the general adult reading audience. This unique novel provides a poignant exploration of a woman's quest for inner peace and happiness. Lynda Lee Rogers, a former beauty pageant winner with what appears to be an idyllic life, grapples with the unseen struggles of depression and debilitating headaches. Her only solace is found in prescription pain pills that offer temporary relief and lead her into vivid, recurring dreams of a mysterious place."

—DENISE BIRT
Wild Sage Book Blog

"Author Joy Ross Davis's storytelling is a delicate dance between reality and dreams, blurring the lines between the two. The narrative is an introspective journey into Lynda Lee's psyche, unraveling the complexities of her emotions and the longing for a place she can truly call home. The book delves deep into the human condition, addressing themes of mental health, inner turmoil, and the search for identity and happiness, and in doing so, it tells a great personal story that is also reflected back on its readers. Davis's writing is evocative and thought-provoking, capturing the essence of Lynda Lee's struggle with empathy and authenticity. *The Goddess of Weaver Street* is a beautifully crafted story that resonates with readers on a profound level, reminding us of the importance of finding peace within ourselves, even when life's external trappings suggest otherwise. It's a powerful narrative that lingers in the mind long after the final page is turned, and I would not hesitate to recommend."

— K.C. FINN, *Readers' Favorites*

"Joy Ross Davis, has done it again! This time she treats readers with a lavish exploration of the magic of a woman's dreams ... dreams for a better life even when her current life is one filled with extraordinary and idyllic love, beauty, and perfection. *The Goddess of Weaver Street* is a delightfully thoughtful story with a conclusion as surprising as the question it asks—can our dreams in the night truly become reality?"

— AUBURN MCCANTA
author of *All the Dancing Birds*

"*The Goddess of Weaver Street* is a novel steeped in magical realism and mental illness quandaries, and presents a story of challenge, empowerment, and change. Joy Ross Davis creates an uplifting sense of discovery and achievement, weaves magical encounters with mental examinations, and deftly portrays how Lynda navigates such dilemmas as her friend's secret, the politics of medicine and her husband's achievements, and her own revised place in the world. Libraries seeking women's novels replete with atmospheres of change, magical thinking, and realistic life pivot points will find *The Goddess of Weaver Street* a thrilling acquisition. It's sure to attract women's book clubs, with its myriad of thought-provoking transformative experiences that operate on different levels."

— MIDWEST BOOK REVIEW

The Goddess of Weaver Street

a novel

Joy Ross Davis

The Goddess of Weaver Street
Joy Ross Davis

ISBN: 978-1-954332-53-9
Library of Congress Control Number: *on file*

Cover image of 1950s woman by Jorge Ferreiro | Adobe Stock.
Strings by pics five | Shutterstock.

Wyatt-MacKenzie Publishing, Inc.
www.WyattMacKenzie.com
Contact us: info@wyattmackenzie.com

Dedication

This book is dedicated to Denise Birt for her constant support, her hard work, and her unwavering faith in the success of this book.

Chapter 1

At eighteen, against her parents' wishes, Lynda Lee Brennan married a struggling medical student ten years her senior and left her family's posh New York mansion in the front seat of a new blue 1950 Ford Deluxe with a mermaid hood ornament.

Having won numerous beauty and scholastic competitions, Lynda Lee had a room full of ballgowns, trophies, ribbons, and offers of scholarships. That she was now the reigning Miss Long Island and entered in the 1950 Miss New York City pageant seemed unimportant. The cascade of dark hair flowing down her back, her striking sea-green eyes, her lithe, statuesque bearing, fine chiseled features, pearlescent complexion, and naturally rosy pink lips made her virtually unbeatable as a contestant. Everyone said so, especially her father and mother. They prepared for the day when their beautiful daughter would become the new Miss America, then Miss World, by redecorating her spacious rooms and keeping watch for the most eligible bachelors around the globe.

Lynda Lee left it all behind, married the handsome struggling medical student, and moved to a dingy studio apartment in Tuscaloosa, Alabama, and in the process, broke her parents' hearts.

She and her poor but brilliant older husband Ray—a 6'4", broad-shouldered man driven to succeed in medicine and determined to give his beautiful young bride everything she could possibly want—lived in that dark and cramped apartment for five years until Ray finished his schooling.

Lynda Lee looked forward to the day when they would move to someplace new and have a nice house and a few children, when Ray would be home for dinner most nights, and when she could use her skills in weaving, sewing, and decorating to make sure that they lived in a well-appointed home. But she most looked forward to the day when a trip to the grocery store meant bringing home fine cuts of meat, fresh produce, and enough flour and sugar to make cakes and cookies of all kinds.

She imagined herself listening to the racket of Ray playing with the children—dressed in clothes she'd made for them—sculling around in the den while she cooked a grand meal that all of them would enjoy. And when she was finished cooking, she would call them.

"Dinner's ready," she'd call, pleased with her creations.

And they would come to the table, put their napkins in their laps, and eat like ravenous little tigers. Ray would sit back and admire them.

"My family," he'd say. "My beautiful family. How I love you all."

She was determined to make it happen. It's what she'd longed for all these years, a home, a husband and children, a loving family. Her dream.

When her parents phoned each week, Lynda Lee assured them that all was well, that she had plenty to eat, hosted parties for Ray's friends, and was doing just fine. Yet each time they planned a visit, some invented catastrophe of Lynda Lee's kept them from coming. Still, every month, just like clockwork, a large box with her name on it would arrive. Inside would be some gorgeous swatches of fabric wrapped around a wad of cash. On her mother's instructions, Lynda Lee was to put aside the cash for an emergency. The bottom of the card always had these words: "Don't forget church."

She kept the money, uncounted, in an antique jewelry box in the top of her closet, and as soon as the lid closed, Lynda Lee forgot about the money as if it didn't exist.

Only occasionally did she regret not being able to beautify their apartment or to use her cooking skills to shower Ray with specialty cakes and sweet treats instead of trying to create new dishes of Spam, pork and beans, or ramen or to create desserts with the clear bags of no-name vanilla cookies she'd been buying.

And when, at last, Ray graduated and completed his residency, Lynda Lee exhaled and smiled ... until Ray told her that he'd decided to continue his schooling. His calling, he said, was surgery—heart surgery—which would require six more years. He'd been offered a part-time job with one of the most illustrious heart surgeons in Alabama, and he couldn't turn it down.

"We'll have more income," he said, "and I'll turn it all over to you, my love."

"But you'll still be a student?" Lynda Lee had asked. "It's been six years, Ray, and you want more schooling? I thought that when you finished medical school, you'd be done."

"I want to be the best cardiac surgeon around, but that requires more study, then three years working side by side with the surgeons."

Six more years, Linda thought and her heart sank. *It's 1956, and I'll be almost thirty by then.*

"Oh," Ray said and put his arms around her. "We'll be moving out of this dingy apartment and into a much better one closer to the medical buildings. Nice kitchen, three large bedrooms, an even larger living room and two bathrooms. Two bathrooms! It'll be lovely. You can invite your parents to visit, and you can use the spare bedroom for your sewing."

"Is there room for my floor loom?" she whispered into his jacket.

"Plenty," Ray said, "for your loom, your fabrics, and your sewing machine, everything you need."

"All right, then," Lynda Lee said. "As long as I can do my sewing and weaving and baking."

"In the new apartment, you'll have room to do whatever you want, my love."

Ray hugged her tightly, her face pressed against the broad expanse of his chest, and kissed her gently on the forehead.

"I couldn't have done this without you," he said, looking down at her with his glorious blue eyes, a stray lock of black hair hanging across his forehead. "You've been my rock, my foundation, and I'll never forget how you've sacrificed for me. I took away the most beautiful girl in New York and turned her into a poor housewife who couldn't afford to buy even a scrap of steak. And you, my dear, have remained just as beautiful and have been the very best wife any man could want."

Lynda Lee stood on her tiptoes and kissed her husband lightly on the lips.

"You've done your best, Ray," she said, "and you still treat me as if I'm a goddess."

"Ah, but that's what you are," he said with a wink, "a goddess of warmth and beauty with skills in sewing and cooking that are unsurpassed. I can't wait to see your gorgeous sea-green eyes light up when you first see our new apartment on Weaver Street. Three bedrooms, two bathrooms, a huge kitchen. You'll be pleased, darling. I promise you that."

"Weaver Street?"

He nodded.

"But that's the ritzy section, isn't it?"

"Indeed, it is."

And then he handed her a small box wrapped in gold foil.

"What is this?" she asked.

Ray chuckled.

"Just a gift, my love. Something that I hope will bring a smile to your gorgeous face. Open it."

Lynda Lee carefully tore away the wrapping paper and lifted the lid off the box.

"Well, what do you think? Do you like it?" Ray asked.

"It's a ring," she said. "But I already have a ring."

"You don't have a diamond, just a cheap thin gold band," he said as he slipped the band off her finger. "I want you to shine, my love," he said and put the new ring in the place where the old one used to be. "This is your gift from me for being such a wonderful wife. It's two full carats. Don't you like it?"

"Two carats," he repeated, "and it matches the sparkle in your eyes."

"But Ray," she said.

"No, I don't want to hear it. It's paid for and you are worth every penny. Now, can I please see a smile on that lovely face of yours?"

Lynda Lee offered a thin smile.

"Thank you," she said. "It's beautiful."

"Now then, there's my girl," Ray said, kissed her solidly on the lips, then hugged her tightly against him. "We should get to packing. We're out of this dump in three days. I've already called your mom and dad. They'll arrive for a lengthy stay at the end of next month.

I want them to know that you're all right, that your life is not ruined because you married me."

Lynda Lee stood on tiptoes and kissed her husband on the cheek.

"I'll go get some boxes so we can pack up our meager belongings," he said. "Did I mention that the new apartment is already furnished? It's so pretty, Lynda Lee. I know that you'll love it. Be back shortly."

When the door closed, Lynda Lee stood, her wavy dark hair falling to her waist. Her porcelain complexion reddened, her green eyes filled with tears. Barefoot, she sauntered into her kitchen. Slowly, she began to remove some of the lesser used dishes. And for each one she touched, a tear fell onto the counter.

"I'll miss this old place," she whispered as another tear rolled down her cheek.

Chapter 2

Lynda Lee gasped when first she beheld the huge apartment with its brick exterior, windows—lots of windows—done in white trim and a beautiful oak door. Along the front edge and beside the brick walkway ran a neatly trimmed garden with a variety of blooming flowers.

"This is our new apartment?" she asked.

Ray nodded and smiled.

"Just wait," he said as he opened the door.

Lynda Lee didn't move.

She was greeted by a wide hallway with oak floors that led to a spacious and bright room furnished with what appeared to be antiques and with a small but elegant chandelier hanging from the ceiling.

"A chandelier?" she asked.

"It's your house-warming present," he said to her. "Go ahead. Go on in and have a look around."

"Oh, Ray, it is so elegant, isn't it? It reminds me of the one in the foyer at my home in New York."

Every room, the dining room, the three bedrooms, had the same theme of antique furnishings. It gave them all a coherent look that Lynda Lee adored.

"We can buy new furniture a little at a time," Ray said, "if this doesn't suit you."

"No, no," she insisted. "It's all simply beautiful."

Ray smiled.

"Brace yourself," he said and opened the door to the kitchen.

Lynda Lee sucked in a breath.

"It's so big," she said as she took in the newly-renovated space filled with a bank of twelve new oak cabinets, a new Frigidaire refrigerator, a new four-burner stove and oven, a Belfast sink and a white stone countertop that virtually surrounded the kitchen. A new dishwasher glimmered at the corner of the countertop.

"I love it, Ray," she said. "And look, just look!"

She walked to the small round table—their breakfast table—and sat in one of the four chairs.

"Sliding glass doors! We can have our morning coffee and look out over the back lawn. Look, what is that?"

"Oh, it's a bird feeder. Every house has one. We'll have to get some bird seed if you want to watch the little birds."

"Yes, of course, I do. I'll get some at the store later."

"There's a lake not far away," he said. "On our off time, we can walk down to the lake and have picnics. Would you like that?"

Lynda Lee put her arms around Ray's neck and kissed him.

"It would be a dream come true, Ray. With a lake nearby, I can swim occasionally and get back to a healthy routine. And I very much love picnics. Even now, I'm thinking of all the goodies I could bake and the wonderful blanket I could weave. It's almost heaven."

Ray smiled.

"I want so much for you to be happy, Lynda Lee. It means everything to me. Can you be happy here in this apartment?"

Lynda Lee chuckled.

"Well, I made do in the last one, didn't I?"

"Yes, you made do, but I don't want you to have to make do. I want you to be able to relax and enjoy yourself and to look around you with pride in what we have. And when your parents visit, I want you to be able to show off our place to let them know that ... that you're happy with the choice you made in marrying me."

The two of them sat at the kitchen table.

"It's very important to me that you can take pride in our home," Ray said and put his hand over hers. "Your life path changed drastically when you married me. You gave up so much, so many chances to succeed, so many opportunities. Your parents are well aware of all you sacrificed. I want them to think you made the right decision."

Lynda Lee looked out over the lush lawn then turned back to Ray.

"I think my parents will be happy that I am a doctor's wife," she said. "Every mother wants her daughter to marry a doctor, Ray. My own father is a doctor, and all I heard growing up was that I should be so fortunate as my mother to find a doctor to marry."

Ray chuckled.

"I don't think she meant marrying a medical student and waiting five years to get a decent place to live or enough money to buy groceries. Your father was already a practicing physician when your parents married."

Lynda Lee shrugged.

"It doesn't matter, Ray. Once my parents see our place, they'll be satisfied that I made the right choice."

Ray took both of her hands in his.

"And you can be happy here for six years? Are you sure?"

Lynda Lee nodded.

"What's not to be happy about? I can watch the birds, I can swim, I can bake, I can sew, I can use my spinning loom to weave. I can garden if I choose. There's plenty to keep me busy."

Ray sat back in his chair.

"But will you be happy, Lynda Lee? Busy and happy are not the same."

Lynda Lee waved a dismissive hand at him.

"Of course, I'll be happy," she said. "I'm happiest when I'm doing what I love to do, when I'm creating."

"So, shall I sign the lease for the apartment?"

Lynda Lee smiled and nodded.

"Yes," she said. "By all means. It's quite beautiful here."

"How about we go to the grocery store, fill up the fridge and have a nice dinner tonight? A steak for each of us. How's that?"

"A steak?"

Ray nodded.

"Let's celebrate, shall we? Throw out all the cans of Spam. Now, we can afford to eat whatever we want."

"I'll make a nice salad," she said. "That would be lovely."

"And a baked potato?"

Lynda Lee smiled.

"A stuffed potato it is," she said.

"And what shall we have for dessert?" Ray asked and got up from the table. "Tell me, my lovely wife, what would you like most for dessert? Tell the truth, now."

"The whole truth?" she asked as she kissed him lightly on the lips.

"The whole truth," he said.

"A little girl," she said.

Chapter 3

Six months later, Lynda Lee and Ray sat in a doctor's office confirming what Ray had already suspected.

"Congratulations, you two," he said. "You have a baby on the way. You'll make a sweet little family. Do you have any questions?"

"Not yet," Ray said. "But I'm sure there will be plenty of questions to come."

The doctor smiled.

"Dr. Rogers," he said, "here is my card. It lists my home phone and my work number. If questions arise, please don't hesitate to call me. I'll see you in one month."

"Uh, how far along are we?" Ray asked.

"About eight weeks, I'd estimate," the doctor said. "I'd encourage Mrs. Rogers to take things easy, no lifting and such. The first three months are critical, and it wouldn't hurt to increase the calories. Mrs. Rogers is very thin. She needs a good rich diet."

Ray and Lynda Lee glanced at one another then back at the doctor.

"Thank you," he said to the doctor and stood up, offering his arm to his wife. "See you next month."

They walked out of the hospital and then out the double doors onto the brick pathway. The apartment was only half a mile away, an easy walk for them both.

"Are you frightened, Ray?" Lynda Lee asked as they walked. "I thought you'd be happy."

Ray didn't respond immediately.

"I am happy," he said finally, "but I'm also concerned for you."

"For me?"

He nodded.

"I want you to be safe, Lynda Lee. I don't want anything to happen to you, and sometimes, pregnancy can be dangerous."

Lynda Lee's eyes opened wide.

"Dangerous?"

They stood now at the entrance to their apartment on Weaver Street.

"I shouldn't have said dangerous. You're not in danger. It's just that I know ... well, never mind. I don't want you worried about anything. Just promise me that you'll do no lifting at all, that you'll eat a good diet, rich in fruits and vegetables, and that you'll rest every day."

"Rest? Do you mean take a nap?"

Ray smiled.

"Yes, that's exactly what I mean. You work hard. The house is always spotless, the floor gleaming, every nook and cranny shining. Our closets and drawers are organized to a T, the bathrooms fairly glow when you walk in. And still, you find time to sew and weave and to make the most delicious dinners ever. You've become a master housekeeper and seamstress. But now, you must consider yourself and the baby. A nap, just a short one every day, will give you the rest you need."

"Part of my dream coming true, Ray. I'll do as you ask."

"Will you promise to take care of yourself when I'm gone? Even if I can't make it home for dinner every night, will you still promise to eat a healthy meal and to rest as much as you can?"

When Lynda Lee didn't respond, Ray repeated.

"Will you promise me that you'll do whatever the doctor says?"

"I promise, Ray. I promise."

"And you remember, don't you, that I'm covering for Dr. Smith this weekend? When I leave on Friday, I won't be back home until Monday morning."

"I remember," she said, her eyes downcast. "I'm used to it by now. What about church?"

"I can't make it this Sunday. Will you be okay going by yourself? I mean, you have some friends at the Presbyterian, don't you? I'm sure they'll all be there."

As they went into the kitchen and took a seat at the table, Ray said, "I'm sorry, Lynda Lee, that I'm away so much. I know how hard it's been for you, having to do most everything by yourself. But if you can just indulge me while I finish school, then the world will be ours. We can do whatever we want."

Lynda Lee raised her eyebrows.

"No, I don't think you're sorry, Ray. I think you're happiest when you're doing what you love to do, and you love being a doctor, just as I am happiest when I'm doing what I love to do."

Ray lowered his eyes.

"But this is a crucial time for us. I promise you that I will make arrangements with the other doctors to be here more often, and as soon as I can, I'll stop these overnights. I promise you that."

"Oh, Ray," she said and stood up.

She walked around and kissed him on top of his head.

"I know you mean well, but please, don't make promises that you've no intention of keeping. Right now, you're the beginner in cardiac. You've no say at all."

"But it won't always be so, Lynda Lee. Another year and I'll move up. I won't be the beginner anymore. I'll have more authority."

Lynda Lee looked at him and shook her head.

"It won't be like that, Ray. The more you move up, the more authority you have, the less time you'll spend at home. In a year, I'll see you even less than I do now. I've been a doctor's wife too long to fool myself. I know how things work."

Ray got up and stood beside her.

"What do you want me to do? How can I make things better?"

Lynda Lee chuckled.

"Oh, Ray," she said, "there is nothing you can do, no way to make things better. You've made your choice already. You weren't content to be a doctor. You needed more. So, you chose to become a cardiac specialist. More school, more work. That's what gives your life meaning and purpose."

"But, you are my wife, Lynda Lee, and I want to make you happy."

"I am happy, Ray. I have a nice apartment, a pretty garden, a bird feeder that brings precious little birds to our window. I can do all the things I missed being able to do those first five years. And now, we're having a baby. What more could a woman want?"

"Maybe a husband who is home more often," he said.

Lynda Lee didn't respond.

"I need to go by the office for a little while," he said, "but remember that we have the church social tonight for the new recruits into the cardiac unit. It's not too formal, and we don't have to be there until seven."

"I'd forgotten," she said. "Who's hosting this time?"

"Beth and John, I think."

Ray checked his watch.

"It's only two now. You have plenty of time to get ready."

He bent and kissed the top of her head.

"No stress, no worries. Even if you wear what you have on now, you'll be the most beautiful woman there."

"And after the party?" she asked.

Ray smiled.

"I'll be yours for the rest of the night."

"Good," she said. "A whole night with you would be a welcome change."

"Now, listen to me, young lady, you promised you'd take a nap," Ray said in a stern tone. "You've plenty of time for a short nap before we go to the party."

"But ...."

"No buts about it. Make time for a short nap. You promised."

Lynda Lee sighed.

"Very well," she said. "One nap coming up. See you in a little while."

"That's my girl," he said and kissed her on the lips right before he walked out the door.

Chapter 4

Doing as her husband asked, Lynda Lee cast off her shoes, climbed onto the daybed, put her latest issues of Vogue's 1956 Special Spring Fashion Edition in her lap and lay back on her pillow for a short nap, though she didn't feel at all tired, but a promise was a promise. *When the children come, he'll be home more. We'll be a real family.*

She stared up at the ceiling until her eyes closed and she drifted into a deep sleep.

In the dream, she found herself walking down a dirt road. On either side of her stood crumbling cottages overgrown with all manner of plants. As her bare feet touched the road, little sprays of dust flew into the air. She wore one of her favorite pageant gowns, light blue with a sash of embroidered roses that trailed down the back of the dress. Head erect, shoulders back, she adopted the pageant stance she knew so well. She fluffed her dark hair and kept walking until she came to a fork in the dusty road.

And then she saw her: an old woman, her face wrinkled and weathered, weaving at an ancient spinning loom. The woman wore a white cap which hid her hair and a dingy apron over full skirts and dark button-up shoes, the soles worn through with holes.

Lynda Lee recognized the old loom and knew it to be a Saxony wheel with the sheep's wool wound around a bobbin that turned constantly as the weaver used the foot treadle. Using just the foot to turn the treadle, the weaver then had both hands free to work and smooth the woven wool.

The woman seemed entirely focused on her work, the feet and gnarled hands working in harmony with the squeaking bobbin and growling treadle to produce the worsted wool used in fabrics, her countrymen's jackets and pants.

As Lynda Lee drew nearer to her, the old woman stopped her work and turned her head.

"Yer a fair beauty," the toothless woman said. "What brings ye back to Galway?"

Unable to respond, Lynda Lee kept walking forward toward the weaver, the edges of her pageant dress dragging across the dirt road. But she didn't care about the dress. All she wanted was to touch the old loom, to let her hands wander over all the parts, absorbing the feel of such an ancient piece and running her fingers over the fabric.

"I've come to touch the fabric," Lynda Lee said. "May I?"

The old woman beckoned her.

"Tis sheep's wool," she said, "This here will be worsted wool fine for our men."

Lynda Lee let her fingers touch the wool and curl around it.

"It's very soft," she said.

The toothless old woman grinned.

"Sure," she said. "Sure, it must be now, mustn't it? It's worsted, as I said, still with some of the sheep's lanolin in it so it'll be nice and soft. And you, my girl, you're a weaver yourself, eh?"

Lynda Lee nodded.

The old woman pointed a finger at her.

"Then be content. Don't be wanting for more than yer share in this world."

Lynda Lee cocked her head.

"More than my share?"

"'Tis naught to be gained by wanting everything. Never fret about what ye lose. Ye'll have what yer meant to have."

The old weaver went back to her loom, her hands and feet working in perfect rhythm. Lynda Lee watched, almost transfixed as the old woman's bumpy fingers worked the loom, stretching and pulling as if she were a young girl.

"Doesn't it hurt your hands?" Lynda Lee asked.

The old woman stopped and looked up at her.

"It does, yes, but pain is temporary, Child. The weaver's job is permanent. Our fighting men must have warm, comfortable clothes. Now, get on back home so's I can finish. I've lots to do to turn this into something usable."

"Lynda Lee? Wake up. We've only an hour or so before the party," Ray said as he shook her gently.

Lynda Lee opened her eyes and tried to sit up but felt so heavy that she could barely move.

Ray sat on the side of the bed.

"Are you sick? You look pale. Do you feel all right?"

"Ray?"

He smiled down at her.

"I'm right here, Lynda Lee," he said and kissed her on the cheek.

"Where's the weaver?" she asked.

"The weaver? What weaver?"

"The old woman. I was just talking to her."

"Let me help you sit up. There's no one here but me, so you must have been dreaming."

"Ray, where is Galway?" she asked as her feet touched the soft carpet.

"Galway? It's in Ireland, isn't it?"

"Ireland? But I've never been to Ireland, yet I felt right at home."

"Your ancestors were from Ireland, weren't they? Your great-grandmother and -grandfather, if what you've told me is right, so you do have a smidgen of a connection."

Ray stood up and then helped her to stand.

"How do you feel?" he asked.

Lynda Lee looked around the room. Gone were the old woman, the ancient spinning loom, and the dusty road, all replaced by their grand, well-appointed apartment.

"That must have been some dream," Ray said. "Well, do you feel good enough to go to the church social tonight?"

"The church social?

"What is it, Lynda Lee? What's wrong? You don't seem like yourself."

"I'm out of place here, Ray," she said and rubbed her forehead. "I want to go back to Galway."

"Lynda Lee, honey, you look so very pale. Tell me how you feel."

He put his arm around her shoulder.

"My stomach hurts, Ray," she said and bent over with a moan.

"Here, lie back. Let me have a look."

"Oh, Ray, it hurts, it really hurts," she said as tears rolled down her face.

He picked up the receiver on the phone and dialed a number.

"Jeremy? It's Ray Rogers. I need an ambulance quickly at 625 Weaver Street. Quickly."

Lynda Lee shook her head.

"Not the hospital, Ray. Please."

"I'm just being cautious, honey."

"But what about the party?"

Ray chuckled.

"The party? No worries, love. No worries. Your health is much more important than any party."

"It hurts, Ray. It hurts," she said, her hands at her stomach.

Ray heard the ambulance's siren, picked his wife up, and carried her to the front entrance.

Two medics spilled from the back of the ambulance.

"Dr. Rogers," one of them said, "we'll take it from here. Put her on the gurney, and let's get moving."

"What's happening, Ray?"

"You're going to be fine," he said and kissed her on the cheek. "Don't worry, love. I'm erring on the side of caution, that's all. You'll be fine."

"But I'm going to have a baby, Ray, so that we can be a real family."

"Yes," he said, "and that's exactly why I want to have you checked thoroughly. I want to make sure that you and the baby are safe."

She grabbed his hand and moaned again.

"Stay with me, Ray. Don't leave."

"I'm not going anywhere," he said. "I'll stay right with you."

Her breathing labored now, Lynda Lee looked at Ray and asked, "Will the ambulance take me to Galway?"

Ray closed his eyes and shook his head.

"Not today, my love. But when you're better, you and I will go to

Galway. Deal?"

Lynda Lee nodded her head, moaned again, and closed her eyes.

Chapter 5

Three weeks later, Lynda Lee was released from the hospital. As she and Ray pulled up to their house on Weaver Street, Ray took her hand.

"I love you," he said, "with all my heart. I'm so thankful to have you."

Lynda Lee smiled and patted his hand.

"I can't have children," she said. "How can you love me when I can't give you children? Every man wants a son or daughter to carry on his name."

"Not every man, Lynda Lee. Some men are content with what they've been blessed with. A beautiful and talented wife, a good career, and a nice home, a job I love. That's quite enough for me, and if the career and home were taken away, I'd still have you and you are the most important part of my life. I can do without a lot of things, but you're not one of them. I love you, and you're quite enough for me."

Ray opened the car door and climbed out. Then he went around and opened the door for Lynda Lee. He was struck immediately by how pale she was, how thin she'd gotten, the luster gone from her hair and eyes.

He held out his hand.

"Come along, my lovely," he said. "We're home, and because I failed to do it the first time, I'll do it now."

He scooped her into his arms and carried her over the threshold and into the kitchen. She took a seat at their table and looked out over the lawn. Almost instantly, several little birds appeared at the feeder: chickadees, nuthatches, warblers, sparrows, all greedily going for the seed.

"Just look at all the little birds, Ray. I love watching the little fellas."

"Yes, and the flowers have begun to bloom," he said. "I'll put the kettle on and you and I will sit here and enjoy the view."

"But I didn't plant anything," she said.

Ray smiled.

"I took the liberty of asking a few of the students to create a lovely garden for you. See? Some of the sprouts are already shooting out of the ground."

"How very kind of you," she said with a thin smile.

"In another few months, you'll be seeing beautiful pink roses, lilies, and a few hostas. Not too much, but just enough to make your view lovely. Oh, and on the other side, just out of your line of vision is a small vegetable and herb garden. Potatoes, tomatoes, peppers, thyme, basil, and sage."

Lynda Lee sighed.

"Well, I guess I'd better learn more about gardening. But ...."

"But what, my love?"

"I've shown that I'm not very good at growing things. I couldn't even grow our baby."

Ray squeezed his eyes shut and wondered what he could say to make her feel better, but he couldn't think of anything to say or do. He simply walked over to her and kissed her gently on the mouth.

"We have each other, Lynda Lee, and perhaps we can learn to be content with that. Perhaps we shouldn't dwell on what we can't have but rather what we can have."

Lynda Lee looked at him, her mouth open.

"What did you just say?"

Ray took the whistling tea pot off the heat.

"I said that maybe we shouldn't dwell on what we can't have."

Lynda Lee rubbed her forehead.

"That's what the old weaver said to me in my dream, Ray."

Ray poured them each a cup of hot tea, set it on the table, and sat across from her.

"What do you mean?"

"The old weaver," she said. "Those are almost exactly her words to me in the dream. Could she have known what was coming? Could she?"

"You've lost me, honey. What dream?"

Lynda Lee took a sip of her tea.

"The one about Galway and the ancient weaver. She told me that I shouldn't grieve over what I couldn't have. I couldn't imagine what she was talking about, or maybe I thought she was talking about us, that we spend so much time apart. But no, Ray. I think she knew about the baby and she knew that I'd miscarry and that there would be complications. She was trying to help me prepare for it."

"Did you know this woman?"

Lynda Lee shook her head.

"It was in a different place, a different time, long ago. She asked me what I was doing back in Galway."

"Ah," Ray said. "Galway. I remember that name."

"Do you think we might be able to go there some time? I know it won't be the same now because the dream seemed to take place ages ago, but for some reason, I feel pulled to go there."

Ray finished his tea and sat back in the chair.

"You know, one of doctor's wives, Beth, dabbles in genealogy. Perhaps she could help, as well. Shall I ask her about it?"

Lynda Lee smiled.

"Yes, I'd like that."

"Then consider it done. I'm not sure she can help, but it's worth a try. You'll speak to your mother, then, and try to get some information? I'm sure she'll need specific names. Do you remember any of their names?"

Lynda Lee shook her head.

"When are my parents coming? I've forgotten."

Ray chuckled.

"You've forgotten about your parents' visit next week?"

"Next week? Oh, there's so much to do, Ray. Can I possibly have everything ready by then?"

"Now, explain to me exactly what has to be done, please. The house is spotless. The bedrooms are beautiful. The guest bathroom hasn't even been used, and you can see that the kitchen is practically pristine. Even the master bedroom and bath are both beautifully appointed and immaculate."

"You cleaned the master? By yourself?"

Ray shrugged.

"Maybe I had a little help," he said with a smile. "Maybe I gave a couple of the grad students an extra assignment, and maybe one of them needs a side job, and I've hired her to come and clean twice a week until you're in tip-top shape."

"I don't need a housekeeper, Ray. I can handle things on my own, thank you."

"I know you can, Lynda Lee, but for now, please humor me. Let me try to help with the chores, at least until after your parents leave. Oh, and I've taken my vacation time for that week so that I'll be here to help, as well."

"Since when have you taken vacation time? You're hoping to be Head of Cardiac, Ray. It's time. A promotion is coming up, and you deserve it. You can't take time off now, not when you've worked so hard. If you take time off work, you'll just have to work doubly hard when you go back. No, that's not a good idea."

"I thought you'd be happy," Ray said.

"It doesn't make me happy to know how hard you will have to work once you return from your time off. No, that doesn't make me happy, but what would make me happy is for you to get what you want from your job. You're an asset to that company and you deserve the promotion."

Lynda Lee got up and took their cups to the sink.

Ray followed her and put his arms around her thin frame. He kissed the back of her neck.

"I've missed you so," he whispered.

"Nonsense," she said and turned to him. "You've seen me every day."

He kissed her softly on the lips.

"But that's different," he said. "I've seen you but I haven't had you in our bed, haven't been able to hold you or kiss you, haven't been able to watch you puttering around the house in your bare feet. I haven't sat with you while you're taking your bubble bath. I've missed all of that, Lynda Lee."

"Well, whatever shall we do about it?" she asked. "I'm here and perfectly healthy now."

As Ray unbuttoned her blouse, he said, "How about a quick nap?"

"I have a better idea," she said as she dropped her skirt and unbuckled his belt. "Why don't you just sit down in the chair and we'll admire the view together."

As he slipped off his trousers, he said, "You're already making me weak-kneed."

Lynda Lee stood naked in front of him.

"Better?"

"Heavenly," he whispered as he reached for her. "Heavenly."

Chapter 6

Sometime later, as they were getting ready for another party, Ray confessed to her.

"Why did you do it, Ray? And without telling me?" Lynda Lee asked as she dug through her closet to find her new shoes. "How on earth could you make a decision like that without talking to me first? I'm your wife. Shouldn't we at least have discussed it?"

Ray sat on the edge of the bed and hung his head. "I thought ...."

"No," Lynda Lee screamed. "No, it wasn't right. All of your thinking in that marvelous brain of yours benefits everyone else around you except me! I might never forgive you for this, Ray," she said as she stomped off to the bathroom and slammed the door.

Ray winced from the sound of it. He slipped on his dress socks, pulled his best black Oxford lace-ups from under the bed, and grabbed the cloth from inside one of them and began to shine them up.

He could hear Lynda Lee screaming at him.

"I can't believe you'd do such a thing without even telling me!" she yelled from behind the door of the bathroom. "Without even asking what I thought! How dare you, Ray. How dare you!"

He winced again at the high-pitched screams.

"It was for the best," he whispered.

Lynda Lee slung open the door.

"What did you say?" she yelled.

"Nothing, Lynda Lee. I'll explain when you calm yourself. You're too angry now to listen to me."

"You bet I'm angry, and I'll stay angry for a very long time," she said and slammed the bathroom door again. "You had no right," she screamed from beyond the door. "NO RIGHT AT ALL."

Ray closed his eyes and imagined the two of them at tonight's gathering. He'd never seen her so angry before, and of course, it was his fault, all from a single decision he'd made independently when she was in such critical condition in the hospital. To him, it was a decision that had to be made, something that had to be done. It was, after all, his job to protect her.

Lynda Lee slung open the door again.

"You think you're so smart," she yelled, slinging her arms. She got right in his face and hissed, "Did it ever occur to you to discuss it with me? Did I ever once cross your mind while you were having yourself permanently fixed? I guess my mother was right when she said that marrying you was the wrong thing to do. I should have listened to her."

She slammed the door again.

Fully dressed now except for his tweed Ferragamo suit coat, Ray paced the room. He had no idea what to say or do to calm her down.

When Lynda Lee opened the door again, she appeared in her long slip and her stockings with her makeup and hair impeccable. She walked to the closet without saying a word, but he could tell by her straight back and the set of her shoulders that she wasn't a candidate for a conversation. She wouldn't even look at him.

Instead, she plucked her blue shimmering gown from the closet, grabbed the matching heels, and went back to the bathroom, slamming the door one more time.

A few minutes later, she emerged looking like a goddess.

Ray stood transfixed at her beauty, and before he could stop himself, he said, "I shall call you the Goddess of Weaver Street. No one can match your beauty."

She looked at him, finally, one eyebrow raised.

"Every goddess needs a god, and you're not there yet, but perhaps if I try hard enough, I can find one who could meet my needs. Perhaps there might even be an eligible one at the party tonight. I'll keep my eyes open."

Ray would have felt better if she'd simply plunged a knife into his heart then twisted it back and forth to make sure it was a killing blow.

"Come on, then," she said, her voice sending shivers down his spine. "Let's not be late. We don't want to deny any of those students or professors the chance to grovel at your most distinguished feet. You are such a master at taking care of other people's hearts."

"Lynda Lee, please," he said moving toward her and grabbed her by the shoulders. "I don't know what else to say or do except to ask your forgiveness. I thought you'd be okay with it. Otherwise, I'd never have done it. A vasectomy will keep you safe, Lynda Lee. Don't you realize that you nearly died in that hospital? I watched you slipping away, and I swore I'd never do anything else that harmed you. It was the only decision I could make."

He put his hand on her cheek.

"I love you," he said, "and this way, you'll never have to go through the pain of a miscarriage again or worse, be at death's door because of it. I can't lose you, Lynda Lee. I just can't."

"And I'll never be able to have children," she said and turned from him. "That was my dream, Ray, to have a husband, a home, a family ... children scampering around. It was my dream."

She wiped an elegant hand over her forehead.

"Lynda Lee, you couldn't have had children, honey. Remember what the doctors said? No more trying. It's just too dangerous for you. The vasectomy just ensures that you'll be safe from ever going through that again."

"But, but, I had hope, Ray, hope that the doctors were wrong, hope that by some miracle, I'd be able to have a little girl someday. But now, you've shattered that hope, and you did it without even mentioning it to me," she said. "How could you?"

Ray's heart seemed to dive bomb to the pit of his stomach.

"Forgive me," he said. "I made the decision when you were so ill, when I knew it was my fault that you were suffering. I'm the one who made you pregnant. Me. And I felt that I was the only one who could remedy the situation for good by never, ever having you go through that life-threatening situation again."

Lynda Lee just stared up at him, a single tear slowly trickling down her cheek. She blotted it away quickly with the hanky in her hand.

"I don't want to ruin my makeup," she whispered. "You betrayed me, Ray."

She turned away from him, then, and walked to the door. "Come, let's not be late for your church social."

"Stop," he said in a voice louder than he intended.

Lynda Lee turned and looked at him.

"I didn't betray you, Lynda Lee. I protected you. That's my job, to make sure you're safe and protected. I did what I thought was right for your safety."

Lynda Lee chuckled.

"Really?" she said and opened the door. "You didn't want children, Ray. They'd interfere with your illustrious career. No, you didn't do that for me. You did it for yourself and for that damnable job of yours. So, don't try to tell me that you were thinking only of my safety. You were thinking of yourself. Having yourself fixed was your choice, a choice you made without telling me, a choice that affected both of us and took my hope right along with it."

Lynda Lee opened the door and walked down the staircase that led to the foyer, the hem of her formal gown billowing around each stair.

"Are you coming?" she called back. "You don't want to miss the celebration, do you? All those energetic, devoted students just waiting to grovel at your feet. Oh, goodness, no. You don't want to miss that."

Ray closed his eyes, took a deep breath, and exhaled slowly.

Someway, somehow, he had to fix this.

Chapter 7

The crowded room hushed as Lynda Lee and Ray walked in.

For a moment, no one spoke.

They simply gazed at the magnificent beauty standing before them.

"Oh, just look at you! Why, you're a vision of loveliness. Ray, why didn't you tell us what a beauty you were married to? I'm Janine Masters," she said. "My husband, John, works with your husband in the cardiac unit."

"I'm Lynda Lee," she said and smiled.

Don't show too much teeth, her mother's voice reminded her.

"Come along," Janine said and took her hand. "Let me introduce you to our guests."

Lynda Lee replayed the routine she knew so well.

Head up, tilted slightly to the side. Lift from the ribcage. Back straight. Core tight. Shoulders down and pushed back. Arms loose at the sides. Chin up. Neck long. Show only the front teeth.

For the majority of her life, these instructions had been her mantra. She was a pageant queen, after all, and had been since she was four and won her first beauty pageant. Now, in her late twenties, she missed the thrill and discipline of that pageant life, the one she'd exchanged for marrying Ray.

"Lynda Lee," Janine said, "I'd like to introduce you to a few of our members and guests."

She pulled Lynda Lee in front of her.

"Just look at this beauty," she said. "This is Lynda Lee. She's the wife of our new Head of Cardiac, Ray Rogers. Isn't she gorgeous?" This is Dr. Raymond and his wife, Sarah. This is Dr. Bentley and his wife, Laura. And this is Dr. Martin and his wife, Beth. Beth's our genealogist in the group. All of them work with your husband in the cardiac unit, so they're all brilliant. Geniuses! So, say hello to our lovely Lynda Lee."

Lynda Lee adopted her pageant pose and smiled.

"It's lovely to meet you," she said. "Forgive me, but I'm terrible with names. I can barely remember my own sometimes."

Everyone chuckled.

"Beautiful and clever," one of the men said. "Hello, Lynda Lee. I'm John Masters, Janine's husband. Why haven't we seen you before?"

Lynda Lee lowered her eyes.

"I'm very much a homebody," she said.

"Well, there's certainly nothing wrong with that," one of the wives answered. "What do you do to keep yourself busy now that you're a resident of Weaver Street?"

Lynda Lee looked surprised.

"Oh, honey," one of the wives said, "we all live on Weaver Street. We've come up in the world."

A huge burst of laughter filled the room.

"We girls don't see our husbands often, so we all have hobbies. We all go to church on Sunday, the Presbyterian just down the road, and all of us girls play cards during the week, specifically Canasta. Do you play?"

"No, I'm afraid not," Lynda Lee said. "I don't know anything about card games."

"Pity," the wife said. "We all meet one day a week to play. If you'd like to join us, we'd be happy to teach you."

From behind her Ray said, "You might like it, Lynda Lee. Would you like to try it?"

"Oh, please say you will," another wife said. "We can always use another player, and we'd be delighted to have you join us. It's an easy game. You'd catch on in no time."

"Perhaps I could try it," she said, "the Canasta."

"Oh, that's delightful," another wife said. "You see, we gather once a week to keep each other company. We serve light refreshments and just have ourselves some girl time. We meet right here every Wednesday at 9:00, so it would be just a short walk for you."

Janine said, "If you'd like to join us, I'll come by on Wednesday morning and bring you back here for the day. Does that sound all right to you?"

Ray interrupted. Lynda Lee glared at him.

"I think she'd love getting to know all of you," he said. "With such demanding hours on all of us doctors, I'm sure she gets lonely at times. She is a former beauty pageant queen and spent her childhood entering and winning beauty contests. Then, I swept her off her feet and for the last few years, she's spent a great deal of time alone. It wasn't quite what she bargained for, but ...."

"I'd very much like to join you," Lynda Lee interrupted. "At least, I can try it."

All of the wives shouted with glee.

"That's just wonderful," Janine said and walked to a shelf behind the bar area.

"Be right back," she said and grabbed something off the shelf. She handed a pamphlet to Lynda Lee.

"We can always use another convert to Canasta, and to start things off right, here's a little booklet I made years ago when we started our group. It just outlines the basic rules of the card game."

Janine handed her a pamphlet with the word Canasta written in bold type on the front.

"I was the editor at a newspaper when I married John. So, whenever I can, I use the skills I learned at that job to help out my friends on Weaver Street."

"She also makes posters, pamphlets, and booklets for the hospital," John Masters said. "She's quite handy at it. Her skills at calligraphy have helped her create some wonderful posters for the hospital. There's even talk of hiring her to produce the newsletter."

Janine smiled and patted her husband on the arm.

"Thank you, my dear," she said to him, "but let's not get ahead of ourselves. It's only talk for now."

"But that would be wonderful," Lynda Lee said. "You'd be contributing your time and efforts to a worthy cause."

Janine laughed.

"Well, I certainly wouldn't do it without a little compensation," she said. "I'm not that unselfish. I'd expect to be paid for my time, and speaking of that, I'd really like to know where you found that gorgeous dress. I've searched the dress shops around here, and I can attest to the fact that there is nothing comparable anywhere."

Lynda Lee looked down at her dress and then at Janine.

"It's one of my old pageant dresses, but it was out of style, so I did what I could to make it look all new."

Janine's mouth dropped open.

"You made that dress? By yourself?"

The other women gasped.

"Surely not," they said in unison. "How on earth could you do that?"

Lynda Lee shrugged.

"I like to sew. I even like to use my loom to weave different types of cloth."

Beth Martin, the hobby genealogist, moved closer to her.

"You have a loom?"

Lynda Lee nodded.

"It belonged to my great-grandmother," she said, "so it's old, but I love using it. I taught myself how to use the loom and then how to weave the wool into fabric. It's a lengthy process, but I've done it twice all the way through."

"I'd love to see it when you have time to show it to me. Would you mind?"

Lynda Lee smiled.

"Of course not, but don't expect too much. It isn't a new one. As I said, it's very old, but somehow, it works for me."

Beth spoke again.

"I'm a seamstress myself, but a weaver? No, I've never used a loom, only needle and thread and my Swing-Needle Singer Automatic, but I would absolutely love to see your loom. What kind of sewing machine do you have?"

"It's a Singer, too, like yours, a gift from my mother when Ray and I married."

"So," Janine said, "it seems that in our beautiful Lynda Lee, we've found a true sister. Imagine that. Oh, I can't wait for our first card game. We'll have so much to talk about."

Beth said, "Well, I for one, can't wait to go to her house to check out that loom. Could I come early Wednesday morning before our card game? I'll bring some of my specially brewed coffee, and we can have a cup together. How would that be?"

Lynda Lee smiled.

Three hours later, after they'd returned from the social, Ray hugged her and said, "You were a hit tonight, honey. Everyone loved you, and just look at the new friends you made. Wasn't it wonderful? Your face just lit up when you were talking to those women."

"I didn't realize how lonely I was for company," she said. "I've had good friends all of my life. Until I married you."

Stung, Ray stepped back.

"I know you don't believe this right now, but I'd do anything for you. My love for you burns as brightly as it always has. I'd be lost without you, Lynda Lee."

Lynda Lee smiled at him and began to remove her gown.

"You are Dr. Ray Rogers, Head of the Cardiac Unit at Westwood Hospital. You have patients, students, doctors who practically worship you for your incredible genius, and nurses who admire and respect you. You wouldn't be lost without me, Ray. Far from it. You have a hospital full of people who adore you."

"But those people are not you, Lynda Lee. They don't have my heart or my love."

"I'm tired now, Ray. I think I'll get some sleep."

"But can't we talk about the argument we had earlier? Can't we clear the air, so to speak?"

Lynda Lee looked at him.

"What's done is done," she said. "The old weaver told me not to want what I couldn't have but to be content with what I do have."

"So, you forgive me?" Ray asked as he removed his clothes.

"I hope to dream of the old weaver again," she said. "She'll tell me the right thing to do."

"So, you don't forgive me? The battle still rages within you?"

"Like a violent storm," she whispered and pulled the covers around her.

Chapter 8

In the dream, she climbed a short hill, her long pink gown shimmering in the sunlight, the hem of it gathering dust and tearing on the nettles and brush. In her hand she carried a bolt of bright blue fabric, silken and soft but heavy. In only a moment, she topped the hill and saw the dirt road ahead. Barefoot, she wriggled her toes in the soft dirt, adjusted the weight of the cloth and went forward toward the sunlight, toward the old weaver busy at her task.

"You've come back now, have ye?" the old woman said.

Lynda Lee nodded.

"I couldn't stay away," she said. "I've brought you a gift."

"What is this, now?" the old woman asked. "Cloth?"

"Yes, for your weaving," Lynda Lee said. "It's dyed wool, ready to be woven."

"Flimsy," the old woman said as she felt it. "Not fit for our fighting men."

Lynda Lee knelt in the dirt beside her. In a tree beside the cottage, she could hear birdsong. A tiny chickadee stood at the edge of a branch and sang away.

"Look," Lynda Lee said. "My favorite wee bird."

"They're all around us here, Child."

"I thought you could make something soft for yourself, maybe a night garment or a robe. It has a heavy backing that will keep you warm."

The old woman stared at her with rheumy eyes, those gnarled hands running back and forth over the cloth.

"And what kind of warmth is it that you seek, my little one?"

Lynda Lee lowered her head.

"Speak up, Child, so's I can hear ye."

"Children, a family," Lynda Lee said.

"Are ye alone in this world then?"

"No, ma'am, I have a husband, but ... he did something terrible. I'm still angry."

The old woman remained silent for a few minutes. Then she said, "Here, we believe in the power of forgiveness to heal and in the power of love to strengthen. Forgive and ye will be healed. Love and ye will be strong."

"I cannot," Lynda Lee said.

"Oh, but ye must and ye will."

The old woman reached toward her and put a twisted hand on her shoulder.

"Do as Maman commands ye."

"Maman?"

The old woman thought for a second.

"Granny," she said. "Away with ye now."

A loud buzzing sound pulled her from the dream.

"Sorry, I forgot to turn it off," Ray said, slapping his hand on the alarm. "Go back to sleep, love. It's early, too early for you to get up."

"I dreamed of Galway again and the old weaver."

"Yes, I know," he said. "You mumbled in your sleep."

"Ray, would you hand me a sheet of paper and a pencil?" Lynda Lee asked as she sat up and moved the covers away from her. She rubbed her eyes. "Please?"

He shuffled to the desk, opened a drawer and pulled out a piece of paper. As he got to the bed, he took the pen from the nightstand.

"Will these do?"

Lynda Lee smiled at him.

"Yes, thank you."

"I like that smile on your face," he said. "I haven't seen it in a while."

Lynda Lee shushed him as she wrote the lines before they escaped her.

"Believe in the power of forgiveness to heal and the power of love to strengthen."

"What's that you have there?"

"Wise words from Maman," she said and showed it to him.

"Wise words, indeed," he said. "And who is Maman?"

"No, Maman, like mama but it ends in an 'n.' Maman."

"And who is this Maman?"

"Well," she said as she got off the bed. "It's the old weaver. She told me to call her that. It means Granny in English."

She held out her arms to her husband.

"But what about your violent storm?" he asked.

He stood close to her and ran a hand through her long dark hair.

"The anger in me is gone now."

Chapter 9

Lynda Lee went into the kitchen, opened the sliding glass doors, and walked out past the garden towards the lake. As she walked, her steps suddenly quickened. Something compelled her to get into the water, yes, get into the water.

She'd long loved the water. Swimming was an essential skill for a beauty queen. It exercised the body, toned the muscles, and got rid of excess fat. At her home in New York, her parents had an indoor pool specifically for her and her mother to use as exercise. From the time she was but four years old, she swam every day, she and her mother racing to a finish line. It became a routine for them, and as they swam more and more, Lynda Lee discovered another talent. She became an excellent underwater swimmer, able to hold her breath far longer than her mother could. But then, her mother smoked cigarettes, a habit Lynda Lee never picked up. She wanted all the strength in her lungs to go unhindered so that she could practice swimming under water, using her body to propel her, to allow her to begin at one end and make it to the other without having to surface and breathe.

She fancied herself a bit of a mermaid and even wore a pastel blue and green dress in her first pageant to symbolize the mermaid in her. She'd won that pageant without anyone ever knowing how much she adored the water or rather, being under the water. She swam with her eyes wide open in their family pool, swam and swam ... until she met Ray.

She wondered now if she'd lost her ability to swim. But maybe it was like riding a bicycle. Once you learned, you never forgot how to do it. She was older now, though, older and more sluggish. Still, the lake called to her, so she spread out the towel she'd brought and sat looking into the lake, the water dark with tiny ripples, certainly not what she'd been accustomed to. She put her hand in the water and allowed the cold ripples to brush across it.

Nothing.

So, she turned and dangled her bare feet in the lake.

"I was once a mermaid," she whispered to the water. "Once upon a time, I could swim the length of this lake without ever coming up for air."

As if in response, a tiny fish swam across her feet.

Lynda Lee gasped at first but then relaxed.

"Yes," she said to the fish, "long ago, I could swim as well as you."

For a reason she could quite understand, she stood and let her dress fall to the ground. She removed her slip and stood in her undergarments.

And then she did it.

She put her arms above her head, hands just so, used her toes to push off, and dove head first into the lake in a perfect slice of the water without making a single sound. Underneath the surface in the cold water, she used her legs for speed, slowly at first, but gradually, the skills she had had when she was younger came rushing back and before she knew it, her fingers felt the bank.

She popped her head out of the water and looked around.

A smile crossed her face when she realized she'd swum the width of the lake. She took a couple of deep breaths to fill her lungs then dove under again. It took several broad strokes, but at last, she made it to the bank, climbed out of the water and saw her towel and clothes.

"I can still swim," she murmured. "I am still a mermaid."

She took a deep breath and relaxed.

"I haven't lost everything," she whispered. "I haven't."

And then she dried herself off, dressed, and spread out the towel again.

"I haven't lost it all," she said as she plopped down on the towel. "Some of me is still in there somewhere."

And then she lay back on the towel and the tears rushed out in a flood of despair. Her shoulders heaved, her breath came in short gasps, her nose ran, and she simply let loose, all the pent-up emotions that had kept her captive for these last years.

She sobbed until all her energy was gone. Sobbed until her eyes burned, until she could barely breathe, until she felt so weak she wondered if she could stand.

"Where did my life go?" she mumbled through her tears. "Where did I go? Who is this woman who pretends to be happy? Who am I now?"

Still, she sobbed, and as she did, she drew up her knees and scrunched down into a fetal position and as the images of her former life as a beauty queen, as a beloved daughter and granddaughter, as a girl who had everything came flooding back, she sobbed all the more for the young woman she used to be and the life she had left behind, the opportunities she had missed, what she could have been.

And then suddenly, she sat up, dried the tears from her face and said, "Ray was right. Busy and happy are not the same at all."

And the voice of the old weaver came back to her.

"Never fret about what ye lose. You'll have what yer meant to have."

Lynda Lee pilfered through her bag and found a bottle of pills the doctors had given her for pain in her stomach, cramps for the miscarriage. She twisted the cap, poured out two pills, and popped them into her mouth, washing them down with a bottle of soda she'd put in her bag in case she got thirsty.

Then she lay back on the towel.

"What is wrong with me?" she whispered, "Why can't I simply be content?"

And then she closed her eyes and drifted into a drugged sleep.

Ray stood nearby behind a large oak. He'd seen and heard everything, and though his instinct was to run to her, to grab her up and care for her, to make things right, he stood very still, hidden from her view, his heart shattering into tiny pieces.

He walked quietly to where she lay, draped her bag over his arm, and picked her up, towel and all, carried her inside, and gently laid her on the bed. He had the urge to put her into a warm shower. He imagined himself gently washing her, then drying her, brushing out her clingy wet hair, and putting her into her silk pajamas. Then he'd take her back to bed, cover her, and wait until she woke. He'd be there. Waiting for her eyes to open, for the pills to wear off.

Instead, he reached inside her bag, took the pills, and hid them in his medical bag, a place she'd never look. Then, he sat in the big chair by the bed and watched her sleep. He'd taken the afternoon off as a surprise, thought they could go on a picnic or drive to a restaurant and have a casual, intimate dinner. He thought she'd be pleased, and until that moment when he heard her by the lake, he thought they were happy, that she'd adjusted to being the wife of a doctor/med student.

Sometimes, when he found her barefoot in the kitchen preparing a meal or baking a pie, she'd be humming to herself. Or when he peeped in on her as she was sewing or weaving, he'd hear her humming and occasionally smiling.

She never complained, his Lynda Lee, not about anything. But then he remembered her reaction to his having a vasectomy without telling her.

Was that it? Had that violent storm she mentioned stayed bottled up inside her?

He got up then and walked to the bay window.

I'm a doctor. I should know the signs of a breakdown. I should have known she was unhappy. Why didn't I? Am I so wrapped up in my medical career that I can't see when the woman I love is in pain? She's hurting, you idiot. She's in pain. She's unhappy and resorting to drugs to help her sleep through it.

"And her parents will be her tomorrow," he whispered, then looked back at his wife, enrobed in her drugged sleep, oblivious to and protected against the life she'd chosen.

He walked to the bed, took one of her small, cold hands in his and kissed it.

She moaned and turned over.

The blanket slipped off her shoulders, so he pulled it up again, and tucked it in beside her. Then he got out an extra blanket and put that around her, as well. He bent and kissed her wet head.

"Sleep now, my love," he whispered.

Chapter 10

A few hours later, Lynda Lee shuffled into the kitchen and found Ray in his tee shirt and shorts at the table, obviously going over notes.

"Ray?"

He looked up at her.

"Would you like some tea?" he asked.

Lynda Lee shook her head.

"What time is it?" she asked as she adjusted the belt on her robe.

"Close to four, I guess."

She went to the refrigerator and pulled out a carton of milk, poured a half glass and went to the table. She moved Ray's papers aside, gulped down the milk, and put the glass on the table.

"Why are you home so early? It's still light outside."

Ray put his arms on the table and looked at her.

"I came home to surprise you, to take you out to dinner, but when I came in, you were out by the lake. I watched you swim and then lie back on your towel."

Lynda Lee's eyes widened.

"You were watching me? Why didn't you say something?"

Ray shrugged.

"Didn't seem appropriate at the time," he said and got up. "I think I'll put on a pot of coffee."

Lynda Lee stared out the sliding glass doors, her mind a blur of images. She saw herself swimming and laughing, heard herself sobbing, saw her hands on the bottle of pills. Her heart raced. Had he seen her take the pills? Had he heard her talking to herself? Did he know what she'd said?

"Ray?"

"Um?"

"Please sit down and tell me what you heard and what you saw. Please."

She adjusted her robe again and ran her hand through her drying hair.

"I'd rather not right now," he said. "Let's have some tea or coffee instead."

Lynda Lee got up, then, and turned to him.

"I'll just go take a shower and wash the lake out of my hair," she said.

Ray sat at the table with his cup of hot coffee.

"Don't forget that your parents will be her tomorrow," he said as she walked toward the door. "Maybe it would be a good idea for you to consider going back with them and staying a few days."

Lynda Lee stopped at the door and turned to him.

"Go back with them? To New York?"

Ray nodded and tried to smile.

"Never hurts to revisit your old stomping grounds, does it? Besides, your folks would like nothing better than for you to come and stay a few days."

"I don't think so," Lynda Lee said and ran her hand along the door frame. "They pretend that they want me with them, but I know from experience that what they really want me to do is to obey their every rule. Besides, I'm married now. I won't let them ruin that for me. If I go back with them, I might stop having my wonderful dreams. I won't risk that for anything."

Ray finished his coffee, put the cup in the sink, then washed and dried it.

"I didn't mean to imply that I wanted you to go, Lynda Lee. It's just that sometimes, you don't seem very happy here, and I thought a short stay back at your beautiful home in New York might be a welcomed change."

Lynda Lee shrugged and dug in the pocket of her robe.

"That just tells me that you don't know as much about me as

you think you do. The answer is no. I won't go back to New York."

"Then, perhaps, we could take a short weekend vacation, just the two of us. It's not out of the question," he said as he walked toward her.

"A vacation? The two of us?" she asked as she checked the other pocket.

"If I work at it, I know I can arrange a few days off," Ray said. "I'll take you anywhere you want to go."

Laughing so hard that she could barely utter the words, Lynda Lee said, "Right now, I want to go shower. Did I leave my bottle of medicine in here? Have you seen my pain pills?"

"I have them," he said.

"I'd like to have them back, please," Lynda Lee said and held out her hand.

"You shouldn't be in pain, Lynda Lee. You've had plenty of time to recover from the miscarriage, so if you're in pain, we need to see the doctor."

He turned on the coffee pot again, got his cup from the drainer, and waited for a response.

"The doctor said that I might have intermittent pain for several months, Ray. And I do. I need those pills."

Ray walked to the counter where his medical bag stayed, opened it, and got the bottle of pills. He opened the top and counted six pills.

"How many do you take at one time?"

"Just one," Lynda Lee said. "Or if I'm in extreme pain, I take two."

He checked the bottle again and saw that there were no refills left, so he handed the bottle to his wife.

"These pills are addictive," he said. "They have the power to make you want them whether you're in pain or not, just for the high they produce. Lynda Lee, once this bottle is gone, there are no refills. So, whatever you're getting from them will be gone, too. You can't get more."

"I can't?"

"No, these pills are a one-time prescription. The more you take them, the more you'll want them. And then, you'll be addicted to them. I can't stand the thought of you becoming addicted to these pills. Please, let me throw them out."

"I'll be very careful, Ray. I promise you. Once the pain goes away, I won't need them at all. The pills are mine, Ray, prescribed by my doctor. They're keeping me healthy."

"No, my love, they are not keeping you healthy," he said and knelt beside her. "They are keeping you drugged so that you think you're doing fine, but actually, you're becoming addicted," he said as he held out his hand. "Just let me keep them. If you're truly in pain, then something is terribly wrong, and we need to see about it."

Lynda Lee lowered her eyes.

"You want me to suffer?" she asked. "You want me to be in pain?"

"No, no, Lynda Lee. I adore you. I don't want you to suffer at all. Never would I want that. But if you are really and truly still having pain, then we need to go back to the doctor. These pills might make the pain go away, but the point is that you shouldn't be in pain at all. You've been cleared by the doctor. You're healed completely. You shouldn't need the pills."

"I promise to be very careful, Ray. If I think I need a doctor, I'll tell you," she said, and slipped the bottle into the pocket of her bathrobe.

Chapter 11

"Mother!" Lynda Lee said as she opened the door. She smoothed the jacket of her most expensive Dior two-piece suit, one that she was certain would impress her mother. "Come in. Don't stand out there in the rain."

"There was nothing about rain when your father and I checked the weather last night," her mother said.

"You never know what to expect in Alabama," Lynda Lee said. "Take their coats, Ray."

Ray obliged and hung their coats on the coat rack beside the doorway.

"Please, have a seat," he said and motioned to the living room. Neither of her parents had so much as glanced his way.

"Well, how was the trip?" Lynda Lee asked. "It was a long flight, I know, but were you comfortable?"

"We flew first class, so yes, we were comfortable," her mother said as she walked around the living room running her gloved fingers over the tables and checking them for dust.

"I'm impressed, Lynda Lee. Your living room is well-appointed and clean. I like your choice of antique furniture, but I'm not really fond of those drapes. They're colorless. I think we could find some much better ones to complement all the lovely furniture."

"Would you like some tea or coffee, Mother? I baked an apple pie this morning. Would you and Daddy like some?"

"No, not really, dear," her mother said. "We had plenty to eat on the plane. Didn't we, Daddy?"

Her father nodded.

"Maybe later," Lynda Lee said.

"You really should try her apple pie," Ray said as he sat. "She's an excellent baker."

"A baker," her mother said. "Our beautiful daughter spends her time in the kitchen?"

"I quite enjoy it, Mother."

Her mother rolled her eyes.

"With all your talent, you ended up being a baker? Working in the kitchen like a common servant?"

"I'm not a servant, Mother. I'm a housewife who loves to bake."

"I see," her mother said. "Shattered dreams for all of us. And what committees do you chair? What medical groups are you a member of?"

"Well," Lynda Lee said.

Her mother interrupted.

"Goodness gracious, hasn't all your training taught you that you never begin your sentences with the word 'well'? Have you forgotten everything I tried to teach you? You were the front runner for Miss World, for heaven's sake. And you begin a sentence with 'Well,' like some uneducated moron!"

Ray stood up.

"My wife is not a moron, and you will not speak to her with such disrespect in our own home."

Her parents ignored him.

"Lynda Lee," her mother said. "Why don't you consider coming back with us for a few days. Get to know your old friends again. Commune with the people of your same class. Go to a few church socials. We'd have a good time, I promise. The Hamby's Ball is only a week away. I can't imagine that you'd want to miss that, and you still have beautiful gowns at home. You can surely take a few days off from your household duties, and we'd love to have you, wouldn't we, Daddy?"

"Of course," Daddy said. "I'd like nothing better than to spend time with my little girl again. And don't worry about the Ball. We'll find a worthy escort."

"You can still fit into your ball gowns, can't you?" her mother asked.

Lynda Lee nodded.

"I think so," she said.

"So, there's no sign of any grandchildren yet? If you can do it, I'd love to have three perfect little grandchildren. It would be so nice to see their smiling faces whenever they came to visit. I've already bought a world of toys for them, fit for boys or girls. And we've renovated our second spare room into a child's room. You should see it, Lynda Lee. You'd be so happy with what we've done."

"Mother, please, please just be quiet for a moment," Lynda Lee said worrying her hands together. "I got pregnant earlier but miscarried. My doctor says I can't have children, so I'm afraid there won't be any grandchildren."

A tear rolled down Lynda Lee's cheek.

"I'm sorry, Mother, so very sorry."

"Don't cry, Lynda Lee. I'm certain the doctors are wrong. We'll take you to a specialist, a good one in New York. He'll tell you that your other doctor was simply incompetent."

Ray interrupted, this time in a more forceful way. He sat beside Lynda Lee on the sofa.

"She's not wrong, Mrs. Brennan, and her doctor was a specialist, one of the finest in Alabama. Lynda Lee can't have children. It would kill her to give birth to a baby. I'm afraid there will be no grandchildren."

"None?" her mother asked.

"No ma'am," Ray said. "None."

Her mother took a deep breath.

From her chair, her mother looked at the collection of magazines on the coffee table: Vogue, Vanity Fair, The Southern Lady, Ladies' Home Journal.

"Well, Daddy," she sniffed, "it's time we were leaving. Our flight leaves in a few hours, so we'd better run along."

Lynda Lee sat primly with her hands folded in her lap.

"But Mother, why did you come for only one day? I thought we planned on three days. Your flight doesn't leave for two more days."

"I must not have mentioned that we're staying with my Aunt Cornelia for a day or so before we head back to New York. I thought I'd told you. She's a Brennan, too. Imagine that. I do wonder how that happened since Brennan is from your father's side."

"No," Lynda Lee said, "you didn't tell me."

"Oh, cheer up, Lynda Lee. We'll be back to visit in a few months," her mother said and hugged her. "I promise."

"Ray, would you help them with their coats?" Lynda Lee asked.

Ray did as he was instructed.

"Have a safe trip home," he said as they left.

Perhaps they didn't hear him because he got no response.

Chapter 12

Lynda Lee fell into a deep sleep and dreamed that night.

In the dream, she walked barefoot along a dirt road for a very long time, her ball gown dragging in the dirt, but she saw no sign of the ancient weaver.

"Where are you?" she called. "You're supposed to be here, Maman. Please, be here."

"Of course, I'm here, dearie. I didn't expect ye at this time of night."

When Lynda Lee looked at the place the voice came from, she saw the ancient weaver, but she was not at her weaving loom. Rather, she stood, wearing the same clothes, at the entrance to an old cottage as worn as she was wrinkled. Ivy grew all around it, almost hiding it from view. Part of the roof was missing.

"What is this place?" Lynda Lee asked.

"It's me home, Child. Come in and we'll have a spot of tea."

Lynda Lee followed the old weaver inside and was surprised at its interior. It was a tiny place but clean and orderly with one small bed, a small sink, a table with two chairs. At the back of the cottage, a large fireplace stood. The old weaver pulled a piece of iron forward from which a large pot hung. She removed the large pot and replaced it with a smaller one. The fireplace, seemingly on its own, roared to life.

"Sit," she said. "Tea is on its way. Are ye cold, dearie? There's a blanket beside ye. It'll warm you up."

While Lynda Lee covered herself with the blanket, the ancient weaver fiddled with the small pot on the fireplace, removed it and took it to the tiny countertop. She took the two cups from their cupholders and poured the steaming liquid into them. Then, she dusted the tops with something Lynda Lee couldn't see.

"There now," the old weaver said. "Tea with a bit of cane sugar on top."

"Thank you. It smells delicious."

"I'm fairly well known 'round here for my tea making. It's the sugar, of course, but I keep my secrets to myself."

"Maman, where are we?"

"Child, where do you think we are?"

"Galway? In Ireland?"

Maman smiled.

"Indeed," she said. "Where else would we be?"

"Do you know what year it is here?"

"Oh, I've lost the years, Child. So many have passed. But it's likely seventeen something, maybe early eighteen. Years are of no consequence anymore. Now, tell me what's a botherin' ye."

"Maman, do you remember your mother?"

"Of course I do, though sometimes I have trouble remembering the details of her face. But I remember her smell, her gentle touch, her long hair."

"She was a kind mother, then?"

"Yes, very kind. And yours?"

"I displease her always. She isn't kind. She berates me and has done so since I was a child. As a little girl, I thought she was beautiful. But over the years, when I look at her, all I see is disdain. Never a smile or a kind word. As hard as I try to please her, I always fail. And she tells me that I've failed."

"And how does that make ye feel?"

"Think, Maman, of your beautiful mother. How would it make you feel to know that you would never be good enough for her? That to her, you were not lovable because you would always be a disappointment."

"Take a sip of your tea, Child, before it gets cold."

Lynda Lee sipped the tea and smiled.

"It's delicious. Thank you for sharing it with me."

For the very first time, Maman smiled at her.

"Did you know, Maman, that I live in Alabama in the United States, yet here I am sitting with you in Galway, Ireland."

"Miracles happen, Child, when we least expect them."

"Maman, what is your name?"

The old weaver looked toward the sky.

"I've been called Maman for so long that I can hardly remember, but I think it used to be Hattie, Hattie Brennan."

"Oh, we must be related somehow. My last name was Brennan, too, before I married. Could it be that we're related?"

"Perhaps so, though there are lots of Brennans in Ireland."

Lynda Lee frowned and worried her hands.

"And what did you do when you were younger, Hattie Brennan?"

"I've always been a weaver, Child. Even as a young girl, I was taught the loom. We Irish seem to have had to fight for our lands. Other kingdoms admired it for its beauty. My job is and always has been to help keep our people clothed as best my mother and I could. We had a gift with the loom, for we were able to turn our warm clothing faster than any of our other weavers."

"And did you ever fall in love with any of those fighting men?"

"Child, I was too busy at the loom to think of love."

"So, in all the years you worked, you never loved anyone?"

Maman turned her eyes toward the sky again.

"Aye, 'twas one," she whispered. "His name was …."

"Lynda Lee," the voice came. "Wake up, Lynda. It's time for work."

Lynda opened her eyes.

"Ray, what are you doing? Why are you shaking me?"

"Lynda, did you forget? Beth Martin is supposed to be here in an hour to talk to you about the genealogy."

"I don't feel well, Ray. Please call her and tell her not to come. I'm not getting out of bed. I feel terrible, and I'm freezing. I need one of my pills."

Ray placed one of the pills in her palm.

"As I said, Beth will be here in an hour, so please get up and treat her as a guest. You can do it, Lynda Lee."

"Go away, Ray. Leave me alone."

Chapter 13

An hour later, after she'd shaken off the dream and wiped the sleep from her eyes, and relaxed with the effects of the pill, Lynda Lee was dressed in casual wear and ready to receive her guest. She'd made both tea and coffee and uncovered the apple pie she'd made a day or two before. She sprinkled the top of the pie with a mixture of powdered sugar, nutmeg, and cinnamon.

Getting the two Spode Botanical saucers and cups from the cabinet, she arranged them neatly on a silver tray, ready to serve. She adored this porcelain pattern. Soft white with a flower print in the middle and gold edging. Of her two sets of good dishes, her Johnson Brothers Blue Willow, and the Spode Botanical, the floral was her favorite. These things she did from rote memory, because on her mind weren't the trays or the cups or the pie. Occupying her thoughts was only one thing: Hattie Brennan, the old weaver.

The knock on the door startled her a bit, but she knew that it was Beth Martin, come to tell her what she'd found about her family.

She opened the door and greeted Beth with a warm smile and a perky hello.

"Come in," she said. "I have tea and coffee ready and an almost-fresh apple pie."

"Thank you, Lynda Lee," Beth said. "What a gorgeous home you have! I've never seen such beautiful antiques before. I've been in almost all the houses on Weaver Street, but yours is the first I've seen that is so well-appointed with fine antiques. May I see the loom before we get started?"

Beth put her large folder on the dining room table.

"Sure, it's right this way. As I said, it was a gift from my great-grandmother, a gift given to her by her own mother, so I'm certain it has a history of some sort. Did I mention that it's a Leclerc?"

"Yes, and I've spent a good deal of time researching those old looms. They're not made any more, and the design has been updated, but you can buy them used in their store in Canada."

"Canada?"

"But where would my great-grandmother have gotten hers? I don't think any of our family lived in or visited Canada, especially during my great-grandmother's time."

"If you don't mind, I'd like to take a photo of your loom. I'd like to forward it to Canada to the Leclerc store to see if they can tell me the exact years it was made. It's too much to hope for a name of a buyer, of course, but at least they might be willing to give me some dates to go by."

"Follow me," Lynda Lee said. "The loom is right in here. Take as many photos as you like."

"Ah, there it is," Beth said. "What a beauty! I don't think I've ever seen one before. And you're weaving now, I see."

"Yes," Lynda Lee said. "I'm making new drapes for the living room. My mother visited and said the drapes lacked color and didn't suit the antique décor. So, I'm making new ones to replace the ones that were here when we moved in. Do you like the color and fabric?"

Beth fingered the smooth blue material.

"Is it velvet?"

"Yes, a thin velvet, especially for draperies. I thought the cobalt blue color might accent the antique furniture in the living room."

"I can hardly believe that you're making your own draperies!"

"I use that loom all the time," Lynda Lee said. "Remember our first walk downtown together? While we were in town, I stopped in at the fabric mill and picked up some bundles of dyed wool, and a few patterns. I've never made draperies before, but I'm willing to try. The lining will be a sateen white. I got a couple of bolts of it when we were in town."

"And are you putting sheers behind them?"

"Yes, of course. I've chosen an intricately decorated milky white tulle. I think they will be lovely. What do you think?"

"I think that you are truly the goddess of Weaver Street."

"It soothes me to weave and sew."

"Lynda Lee, you could make a small fortune in this area if people knew how skillful you are at weaving and sewing. Weaver Street houses all the classiest people, and all the women want to out-do the others. If they could see your draperies and the plans you have for them, they'd be dumbfounded and greedy to have some just like them. You should think about having a home business."

"Business? But I'm just an ordinary housewife. I know nothing about business."

"Perhaps the Fates have smiled on us, then. I have a business degree. The genealogy is just a hobby. My forte is business, mainly helping people with new businesses. Will you think about it?"

"I'll ask Ray to see what he says, but I don't fancy myself a business woman."

"I, personally, think you have everything it takes to be successful. You were in beauty pageants, right?"

Lynda Lee nodded.

"Then, you certainly have the discipline and the skills to present yourself in the very best manner. Presenting yourself well in front of an audience is a skill that you already possess."

"I hadn't thought of it that way. But yes, I've had years of training in showing my best self to an audience, but it's been a long time since I've done it."

"Well, we'll start small. When your draperies are finished and hung, we'll call several of the women from Weaver Street and invite them to a 'drapery party.' It will be the first in the neighborhood. How would that suit you?"

Lynda Lee smiled.

"I think it would be just fine. I've never displayed my work, well except in the home, but I like the idea of others giving me credit for a job well done. It's certainly more than my mother's ever done. Sorry, I didn't mean to get all gushy on you."

"No worries. Speaking of your mother, let's have some tea and look at what I've discovered in your family tree. Shall we?"

Chapter 14

When she and Beth had finished going over the genealogy chart, Lynda Lee thanked her, saw her out, and then sat at the little table in the kitchen with a cup of tea. She hadn't found anything on the chart that interested her except that both sets of her great-grandparents immigrated to America from Ireland, and both sets knew each other.

It was the complete opposite of what her mother had told her. She claimed that her parents had no ties to Ireland, that it was only Papa's people who'd immigrated, but Lynda had known her maternal grandparents. It was her grandmother who'd given her the loom. Her grandmother had insisted she'd come here with her parents when she was a girl, a little girl from Ireland.

Lynda Lee was stymied by this. Why would her mother intentionally lie about her heritage? What difference could it possibly make in their lives? Did her mother find some shame in being the daughter of Irish immigrants?

As she sat at the table, she dismissed all thoughts of her lineage. She sipped the last of her tea and went back to her draperies. After an hour or two, Ray came in the door with a big smile on his face.

"Hello, my beautiful goddess," he said and hugged her. "How has your day been?"

"Interesting," Lynda Lee said and kissed him on the cheek. "Beth was here today, as you know, and I learned all about my history, though I admit that I wasn't really interested. But, I did learn that my mother has lied to me all my life about it. She's insisted that we are not Irish, but my grandmother was an Irish immigrant. I wonder why she would lie to me about it?"

"No one knows why your mother does anything," Ray said. "Now, you know the truth, so that should make you happy. How are you feeling, Lynda Lee?"

Lynda Lee shrugged.

"Cold, dizzy every now and then, thirsty."

"You'll be over this in no time," he said. "I promise you."

Lynda Lee just looked at him, a pitiful expression on her face.

"I have a little surprise for you."

"For me?"

"Of course, who else would I want to surprise? It's nothing fancy, just something I saw when I was at the home repair shop today. I thought you might like it," he said and grabbed her hand. "Come along. Follow me."

"Wait, did I hear that right?" she asked as she stood, her hand in his. "You were at the home repair shop today? What on earth could drag you away from your beloved hospital to a home repair shop?"

"You," he said and smiled, "only you."

As she followed him outside, she noticed a delivery truck in their driveway.

"Over here, fellas," Ray shouted. "We're going into the back yard."

The driver and his crew climbed out of the truck and opened the back of the cargo hold. They each carried boxes and made several trips. After thirty minutes or so, Ray took Lynda's hand.

"Let's go look at your surprise," he said. "The neighbors will be envious! It's a good thing that our outdoor patio is big."

"Well, it's only big because you had the contractors almost double the size of it. I hated it at first, but now that the flowers have grown up around it, it's pretty and big enough for all of my potted plants."

"Are you ready to see the surprise?"

"Since it's already here, I don't think I have a choice," Lynda Lee mumbled. "Okay, I'm ready."

Ray led her to the large back patio.

"Well, what do you think? Do you like them? Come on. Let's try them out."

Lynda Lee walked up the steps to the patio and stared at the two large chaise lounges with extra thick cushions covered in pink, blue, green and yellow flowered fabric.

"The fabric is waterproof," he said as he stretched out on one of the loungers. "Go ahead. See if it's comfortable."

Lynda Lee lay on the lounger and rested herself on the cushions.

"It's comfortable," she said, "but the sun is shining in my eyes."

"Watch this," Ray said and smiled, as he reached the top of the chaise lounge and pulled. Out came a sturdy matching shade. He pulled it forward to shade his eyes.

"Go ahead. Reach for yours and pull it out."

Lynda Lee did as she was told and to her delight, found that the shade worked and kept the sun out of her eyes.

"The cushions are beautiful. I love the flowered pattern, and the shade is perfect, and I can see the little birds as they fly to the feeder."

"I thought that on good weather days when you want to take a break from your weaving and sewing, you could bring a cup of tea or coffee, come out here, stretch out, and enjoy the nature around you."

"Yes, what a good idea," she said and smiled. "I know there's an extra side table in the guest bedroom. It will fit between the lounges and be big enough for both of us. Remind me to get it."

"I love seeing you smile, Lynda Lee," he said and put his hand on her arm. "It brings me such joy, and speaking of that, we're going out for dinner tonight. If you've already cooked, then just put it away for tomorrow night. Does that suit you?"

"Where are we going?"

"I made reservations at The Relay House," he said and sat up. "Is that all right?"

"But that's a private club, Ray, and membership is not cheap. I know that a lot of your doctor friends go there, but I think it's out of our price range."

Ray chuckled.

"You're right, my love, it was out of our price range, but the private practice at the hospital combined with the surgical teaching for incoming students led to something I've been waiting for. I got another promotion, Lynda Lee. I'm now Assistant to the Administrative Director of Cardiac Care Unit, Intensive Care Division. That's a step up from being the Director. It's a new position, new responsibilities and twice the pay."

Lynda Lee sat up.

"What does that mean, Ray? What does it mean for your career and … and for us?"

Ray took her hands in his.

"First of all, it means a considerable raise in pay. Second, it will be another promotion that I can add to my resume. And third, it means I'll be recognized for the contributions I make to the Intensive Care Unit. Finally, it means that I can take vacation time like all the other senior doctors."

"Vacation time?"

"Yes, a week whenever I want. Maybe we can go to Italy, or maybe, well, we could go anywhere you might want to go. A full week by ourselves. Does that make you happy?"

Lynda Lee smiled a thin smile and patted his cheek.

"Of course, it makes me happy, Ray. Why wouldn't it? I'm proud of you. You've come a long way since your early days, and that's been your dream, to advance into recognition. I'm extremely happy for you."

"So," Ray asked, "where would you like to go when I get my first vacation?"

Lynda Lee chuckled.

"I think you already know the answer to that question, Ray."

Ray nodded.

"Ireland," he said. "Am I right?"

"You are exactly right. Is it all right with you?"

"But wherever we go, we'll need passports, so both of us need to apply for one and mail in our applications."

"Where do you get the applications?"

"Montgomery," he said. "I'll get my secretary to write two letters of application, one for each of us. Once we apply, we have to wait six to eight weeks for the passports to be mailed to us."

"That will be exciting, Ray, to have passports that allow us to travel all over."

"Then, it shall be done," he said and kissed her cheek. "Our reservation is at 6:00, so maybe we should think about getting ready for our big night out. The Relay House is in for one stunning surprise. As soon as you walk in, the crowd will hush, the waiters will freeze in their places, and the whole room will think of only one thing: the beautiful goddess of Weaver Street!"

"And perhaps her handsome, newly promoted companion," Lynda Lee said. "You've risen in the ranks so quickly, Ray. I'm proud of you."

"I'll be the envy of every man in the room," he said and chuckled.

Chapter 15

As soon as the two of them entered, all of the guests turned, looked, and said not a word. Then, suddenly, a soft, "She's breathtaking," could be heard coming from one of the tables. A moment later, the guests turned back to their tables.

The Relay House was all that Lynda Lee had hoped it would be. The restaurant was magnificent with beautiful five-tiered crystal chandeliers, gleaming hardwood floors, waiters dressed in tuxedoes, and each table positioned so that the diners could see out the plate glass windows that surrounded the restaurant. City lights shone below, and in the misty rain, seemed alive, like living creatures greeting each guest.

"You like?" Ray whispered to her.

"It's magnificent," she said, patting her chignon to make sure every hair was in place. She smoothed her new formal gown, a green apple-colored sheath that fell almost to her ankle and topped with a daring green, pink, and blue floral jacket.

"You look beautiful," Ray said. "And that sparkling barrette beside that up-do is simply magnificent."

"It's called a chignon," she whispered.

The host, a tall, black, tuxedoed gentleman, greeted them at the door.

"Follow me, please," he said in a thick British accent.

He stopped in front of a round table covered with a beautiful white tablecloth. In the center of the table was a gold and black lettered sign that said, "Dr. and Mrs. Rogers." Alongside their cutlery were two matchbooks, green with gold lettering, one that said, "Ray Rogers." The other, "Mrs. Rogers."

The host pulled out Lynda Lee's chair.

"Would you care to sit now?"

Lynda Lee sat and the host scooted her chair to the table. Then, he picked up the large white linen napkin and placed it into her lap. A waiter appeared with two pitchers.

"Water or coffee?" the host asked.

"The lady will have water," Ray said. "Coffee for me."

The host nodded as the water glasses were filled, tiny chunks of ice floating in them. Then, the waiter filled Ray's coffee cup, a beautifully designed cup, solid white with gold trim along the edges.

"That's beautiful porcelain china," Lynda Lee said. "I've never seen that pattern before."

"It's Haviland, exclusively made for The Relay House," the host said in his British accent. "It's a favorite of mine. If you need anything, just ask for Bugg," he said.

"Bug?" Lynda Lee asked.

"Yes, Bugg, two 'g's."

"Thank you so much, Bugg. It's been a pleasure meeting you."

"Likewise, Madame Rogers."

He turned and left, all the while using his hands to signal instructions to various waiters.

"What a nice man," Lynda Lee said. "I love his British accent."

"Very nice," Ray said. As he looked up, Bugg appeared again and handed them two small menus, one with the prices on it, the other without.

"Our specialty tonight is rib-eye steak with salad, scalloped potatoes, and haricot vert, but you are free to order from the menu if you'd like. I'll give you a few minutes to decide."

With military precision, he abruptly turned and left.

Lynda Lee perused the menu.

"Would it be awful of me to order from the menu?" she asked.

"You don't want a rib-eye? I've never seen you turn down a steak before," he said as he took a sip of coffee.

"Actually, Ray, I'm not in the mood for steak. Since your first promotion, we've had steak quite a lot. I'm just in the mood for something different, something we wouldn't normally eat at home."

"Ah, you're aiming for an adventure," he said and smiled. "What would you like?"

"This tuna filet sounds good," she said. "It's served with a baked potato and green beans ... uh, haricot vert and comes with a salad of fresh Romaine lettuce, cherry tomatoes, radishes, and cucumbers. It also comes with a plate of French cheeses: Camembert, St. Nectaire, and one I've never heard of called Pave d'Affinois. It sounds so exciting!"

Ray smiled and summoned Bugg.

"We're ready to order," Ray said. "I'll have tonight's specialty."

"Two?" Bugg asked.

"No, my wife has decided on something from the menu. She'd like the tuna filet and all the trimmings. She's especially excited about the cheese plate that comes with the salad."

"Excellent choice," Bugg said. "The cheeses are absolutely delicious. They're French and one of our best sellers."

Lynda Lee smiled.

"I've never had French cheeses before. I can't wait to try them."

"French cheeses are extremely rich, so the best way to eat them is with a cracker and a small amount of cheese," Bugg said. "Otherwise, you'll be stuffed. Now, how would you like your tuna? Baked, broiled, or fried?"

"What do you recommend, Bugg?

"The baked is particularly flavorful," he said.

"Then I'll have mine baked," Lynda Lee said.

"Very good," Bugg said. "And you absolutely must leave some room for our very special dessert. It's magnificent."

He turned and was gone.

In only a few moments, the waiters arrived carrying several trays.

In front of Lynda Lee, they put a plate with her tuna steak, a salad plate, and a small porcelain bowl filled with different cheeses, each one with a toothpick sticking out with the name of the cheese on it.

"Delightful," Lynda Lee said. "Utterly delightful."

Immediately, she got a cracker and tried the Camembert.

"Mmm," she said. "It has a nutty, earthy sort of flavor. Would you like a taste?"

Ray shook his head.

"Eat up," he said.

Then, she tried the St. Nectaire.

"Oh, this is nice," she said. "More robust than the Camembert, but very good."

"Don't eat too much. Your fish awaits you."

"I'll get to it. Only one cheese left, Pave d'Affinois."

She took just a bit and put it on a cracker.

"Oh my," she said. "This is my favorite. It's silky, smooth, and very light. It's wonderful."

Ray chuckled.

"You're becoming a cheese connoisseur," he said. "If we can buy these cheeses, you could have a tasting party with the women of Weaver Street. Now, please try to eat some of that delicious looking tuna before it gets cold."

After dinner, when both of them thought they could not eat another bite, Bugg showed up at their table carrying a white platter filled with a beautiful red concoction.

"For you, a special dessert," he said and lit the dish afire.

"Oh," Lynda Lee said. "Oh, my!"

"Cherries Jubilee," he said and put the platter on small table beside him. The flames grew smaller until only a tiny blue one appeared throughout the dish. Carefully, he scooped it over bowls of vanilla ice cream and served it.

"I hope you enjoy it," he said and walked away.

Ray ate every bite of his.

"This is the best dessert I've ever had," he said and wiped his mouth with his napkin.

Lynda Lee took only a few bites of hers.

"It's delicious," she said, "but I'm so full that I don't have room for anymore."

"I can remedy that," Ray said and swiftly changed bowls with her, scooping up the last of the melted ice cream and cherries.

He sat back in his chair and sighed.

"What a meal," he said. "I've never tasted better. I guess we'll have to start a new bank account and bit by bit put money in it so that we can enjoy another meal here soon."

"Are you ready to leave?" Ray asked.

Lynda Lee nodded and as they walked to the car, she could see herself putting away the money her mother had given her many years ago when she leaned over and whispered, "your escape money." She remembered putting it inside the secret compartment on her jewelry case. Ten thousand dollars sleeping all this time in her jewelry box.

"Galway," she whispered softly.

Chapter 16

"Ray," she said as she slipped off her sequined dress, hung it in its proper place in her large closet and changed into her nightgown. She put her heels side by side in her built-in shoe rack, and turned to her husband.

"Ray," she said again. "There's something I need to tell you."

Propped on his pillows reading over the latest medical journal, Ray put it aside and held out his arms.

"Then, come here, my beautiful wife, and talk to me."

Linda Lee climbed into bed.

"Do you remember when we first married?"

"What kind of question is that? Of course, I remember. It was one of the scariest days of my life."

"Scary?"

"Yes," he said and sat up. "I was taking this beautiful New York City beauty queen away from all that she knew: her wealthy socialite parents, her pageants, her scholarships, her friends. I feared that I was kidnapping you and putting you into a life of poverty and struggle. I was afraid that after a year or so, you'd hate me, and I'd lose you back to the life you loved."

"You never told me that," she said and brushed a stray hair from her face.

"I couldn't, Lynda Lee, for fear that if I said those words, I'd lose you for good. The first two years of our marriage, it was all I thought about. I was terrified that you'd go back to your parents, and honestly,

I wouldn't have blamed you. I took you from wealth, status, and social prominence into something no better than a hovel, tiny dark rooms far away from everything you knew and loved."

Lynda Lee put her hand on his.

"You've always treated me well, Ray. Even in our worst times, you made sure that I had what I needed."

"I was only able to do that because of the small inheritance my father left me. It paid for my schooling, thank goodness, but there was never much left over for the things we needed."

"Ray, when I left to follow you, my mother gave me an envelope. She said it was my escape money, and over the years, she's kept sending me money, but I never counted it until recently. I've always kept it in the secret compartment in my jewelry box. I had no idea how much was there since I didn't even think about it."

"That's okay, Lynda Lee. Whatever is there belongs to you. It's yours, not mine. To tell the truth, I'm grateful to her for sending it. Every woman needs money to fall back on in case of ... well, any kind of emergency."

"A few days ago, I remembered that money, so I counted it. Then I put it back into my jewelry box and didn't think of it again until tonight after we'd had that wonderful dinner at The Relay House. I thought of something you said, something like if you could eat there more often, you would and that it was the best meal you'd ever had."

Ray cocked his head.

"I'm not following you, sweetheart. The Relay House is quite expensive. I've managed to pay the membership dues, just as most of the other doctors have done, but I didn't mean that I'd want to eat there all the time. And I also didn't mean that the dinner was more delicious than the meals you fix all the time for me. You're a wonder in the kitchen."

"I know what you meant, Ray. But I need to say this and get it out. Just listen, okay?"

Ray nodded.

Lynda Lee leaned over and pulled an envelope out of the drawer of her bedside table.

"This is what I'm talking about," she said. "It's the money my mother has given me over the years, my escape money."

"Okay," Ray said. "It's yours, my dearest, to do with as you please. Buy a new dress, get some new furniture. Do whatever you want with it. That money is for you, Lynda Lee. You can use it however you want."

"You're not going to ask me how much money it is?"

"No," he said. "Even if it's a small fortune, like two thousand dollars, you could use it to redecorate the house. Buy some new appliances. Whatever you want."

Lynda Lee handed the envelope to Ray.

"Count it," she said and smiled. "Just count it."

"Why?" he asked.

"Please count it, Ray."

Ray sighed and opened the thick envelope.

As he counted, he said nothing.

Finally, he said,

"Lynda Lee, there's ten thousand dollars in this envelope."

Lynda Lee nodded.

"Ten thousand dollars!" Ray exclaimed. "And it's been with you all this time?"

"Yes, but I didn't know how much was there until a few days ago. For some reason, I thought of the money in my jewelry box, and I was curious about how much was there."

"I'm dumbfounded," he said. "We could have used this to help make life easier. You wouldn't have had to scrimp and save, make do with hardly anything at all. I wouldn't have had to work so many overnights just to pay the bills. Our lives would have been different, Lynda Lee. Why didn't you ever use it?"

"I didn't think of it. Honestly, Ray, I didn't know how much was there. I just knew that it was my escape money from a mother who literally finds nothing lovable about me. It was her bribe to get me back to New York City, and I wanted nothing to do with it, so I just put it out of my head."

"I see," Ray said. "But what about now? Isn't there something you want to do?"

"No, but there's something I want you to do," she said and sat up straight. "I want you to take the money and put it into some sort of savings account in both our names. Ask your friends about how to get the best return on the money. It will give us a healthy nest egg for the future. That way, neither of us will have to worry in case of a financial emergency."

"Lynda Lee, are you sure? Isn't there anything you want to buy for yourself?"

She shook her head.

"You make decent money now, Ray. We don't worry as much as we used to about paying bills and buying groceries. We have everything we need, don't we?"

"I'll make a deal with you," Ray said. "I'll ask around to see how my friends invest their money, but only $9,000 of it. We'll keep out a thousand for "house money," which will be yours to spend on anything you want or need. You can fill that weaving closet with all sorts of yarns, wools, patterns, whatever you want. How's that?"

"That seems fine," she said and smiled. "And Ray, I haven't been totally honest. There is something I want, but I know it will be expensive."

"Name it, sweetheart, and it's yours."

"You might not agree, Ray."

"Okay, tell me about this mysterious gift you want."

Lynda Lee hung her head and whispered in his ear.

Ray's jaw dropped open.

"What?"

"I thought we might go to Galway, Ray," she said. "Take a trip to Ireland."

Ray got up and paced the room.

"You don't want to go to Ireland, Ray?" Lynda Lee asked as she worried her hands.

"I know why you want to go to Ireland, but I fear you'll be disappointed. You tell me about those dreams you have, but those dreams aren't real, Lynda Lee," he said and knelt in front of her. The Galway we travel to won't be the same as the one in your dreams. Things are more modern now. And you'll never find your old Irish weaver."

"But what if you're wrong, Ray? What if everything is just as it is in my dreams? I can find her and talk to her, see her home."

Ray shook his head.

"I don't want to go to Ireland, my love. To me, it's a risky venture with no good to come from it," he said and pushed a few stray hairs from her face. "You're expecting something that you can't find."

Lynda Lee got up and went to the kitchen. She poured a glass of milk and drank it down.

"You can't be sure of that."

Ray put his arms around her shoulders.

"What year did the old weaver tell you it was in the dream? Didn't she say early 1800s?"

Lynda Lee nodded.

"It's the middle-plus of the 1900s now, Lynda Lee, 1957. That's more than a hundred years. Common sense should tell you that she won't be there. The old Galway doesn't exist anymore, my love. It's been replaced by the new Galway. Ireland has changed just as our country has changed."

Lynda Lee sat down at the kitchen table and looked out at the water.

"I don't care about that, Ray. I'm not stupid enough to think that she'd be there. But all of my ancestors came here from Ireland, and I'd love to see if it is as beautiful as everyone says it is. I really want to go, Ray."

"I'll do some checking, then, and see what I can come up with."

"Ray, where does your family come from?"

"England," Ray said. "The first recorded Rogers was a tax collector in Cornwall in the 1600s, but I don't have a genealogy for my family. All I know is that my ancestors came here from England. When they settled in America, they stayed."

"Oh," Lynda Lee replied.

"But, I do have one famous relative."

Lynda Lee brightened.

"You do?"

"Yes. My family refers to him as Frontier Pete. He was an immigrant, poor, with nothing to his name except his much beloved wife. In Oklahoma, the government gave away large plots of land to whoever could win a race to stake a claim. Frontier Pete ran faster than any of the other men and staked his claim at a beautiful spot that bordered a river. It took him two years to finish his lovely home, but when it was done, it became his home place and all of his relatives were able to move close by. They even established a community of Rogers."

"How exciting!" Lynda Lee said. "What a brave man. Is the community still there?"

"It is, a whole town, in fact, named for him."

"That's a wonderful story, Ray. Why have you never told me?"

"It was a long time ago, and of course, I never knew him. He was a great-great-great-uncle or something. I hear that he and his wife lived to a ripe old age and raised children, grandchildren, and even great-grandchildren there. The plot of land was more than six acres, and his business thrived as the community grew. The more money he made, the more he invested in buying land."

"And what was his job? How did he make money?"

"Frontier Pete was a doctor, registered as Dr. Peterson Gaylord Rogers."

"Would you like for Beth to help you do your genealogy and find out more about Frontier Pete?"

Ray shrugged.

"Maybe. But I have all sorts of tales and stories right up here," he said and pointed to his head.

"But you never tell them. You're always working."

"I'll call Beth, I promise, and tell her about Frontier Pete. She'll be delighted, and we can talk about it at dinner with her and Johnny."

Chapter 17

Dinner at the Martin's house was much better than either of them expected. Beth could hardly keep still with her new project in her mind. The other couples giggled at her enthusiasm and were fascinated by Ray's story about Frontier Pete. They talked on and on until Ray glanced at his watch, saw that it was close to midnight, and bid them all goodbye.

"Now, don't forget the dinner here at the beginning of the week," Beth said. "We have a special guest."

By the time they got home, both of them were exhausted.

"I might just sleep in my clothes," Lynda Lee said, but decided against it and changed into her pajamas.

"Good night, my love," Ray said and kissed her on the cheek.

Lynda Lee smiled as her eyes closed and she fell into a deep sleep.

In the dream, Lynda Lee wore a different sort of gown this time, a sheath covered in sequins. Barefoot, she walked along the dirt road and looked for the old Irish weaver.

"Are you here, Maman?"

When no answer came, Lynda Lee's heart began to race. There was no sign of her. Lynda Lee spied the ruined cottage and moved aside the ivy so that she could step in.

"Maman?" she called as she made her way inside, but when she entered, she was sure that she was in the wrong place. The cottage, bright with sunlight, smelled wonderful, everything clean and sparkling. The sun's reflections shone off the bright surfaces around her.

"Maman," she called in a louder voice. "Maman, are you here?"

"I'm here, dearie," a voice came from behind her.

"The cottage looks so nice, Maman. What has happened since my last visit?"

"The years, dearie. Just the years. Sometimes, change comes in unexpected ways."

"Are we still in Galway? What's that I hear, Maman? It sounds like a horse."

"Tis," she said. "Come."

Lynda Lee stepped out of the cottage and saw a man on horseback. He wore a white shirt and dark pants, a beret perched neatly on his head. When he saw Lynda Lee, he jumped down off the horse, bowed and said, "Hello, you must be Maman's friend, Lynda Lee. My name is O'Reilly. Folks around her call me O'Reilly the Scaylee."

Maman chuckled.

"He's a storyteller, Scaylee is. He travels around and tells stories to anyone who'll listen and if they are entertained, he asks only for a meal and a drink."

"What kind of stories do you tell, Scaylee?"

"Whatever suits the audience whether it be lessons or histories or tales of fun and laughter. I have a wealth of stories stored right up here," he said, and pointed to his head. "And I learned them all from my father, who was a Scaylee, too, and his father before him and his before him. 'Tis our family's calling. My great-great-great-grandfather told stories to the Ard Ri, the High King of Ireland."

"Then you have a noble profession," Lynda said, and smiled. "Do you never ask for money as payment for your stories?"

"Money? No, no. We tell our stories to as many as we can, not to make money but to teach and entertain. The good people of Ireland see fit to reward us with a wonderful meal afterwards."

"I want to hear one of your stories, please, Scaylee, when you have time. Is that proper, Maman, to ask to hear a story?"

"Of course, Child. Always ask for what you want. Otherwise, no one will know. You shouldn't make people guess at what you want. Tell them straight out and you'll never be misunderstood."

"Tell them straight out what I want," Lynda Lee repeated.

"Yes, Child. It is the best way in this world of ours."

"Lynda Lee, come on. Wake up. It's time for me to go to work."

"Ray, quit shaking me. I don't want to wake up. I'm tired. Leave me alone and let me sleep."

Lynda Lee shook off her sleepiness and glared at Ray.

"Why can't I just sleep in this morning? Leave me alone, Ray. Just leave me alone."

"Sorry, I thought you had plans for lunch today with the other women."

"That's tomorrow, and now, you've ruined my dreaming. I wanted to listen to a story."

Chapter 18

Lynda Lee felt out of sorts when she finally climbed out of bed. Her hair was a mess, her mouth had a bitter taste in it, and her head throbbed.

She looked into the drawer of her nightstand and found her bottle of pain pills, newly-filled by a doctor friend of Beth's. After a short visit with him, he was glad to refill her prescription and even told her to call when she needed a refill.

"Maybe just one," she mumbled to herself as she put the pill in her mouth and shuffled to the bathroom and stopped in front of the large mirror above the countertop. She ran some water, filled a cup, and took the pill. Then she turned on the shower and by the time she'd finished, she felt much better.

She stood in front of the mirror and combed through her wet hair while she imagined the storyteller, Scaylee, sitting atop his horse, his beret cocked to the side. Though he must have been poor, he had an elegance about his carriage, and a very handsome face to go with it. Perhaps he'd come from wealth and lost it somehow. Maybe during one of the rebellions, though he didn't seem much like a man who fought.

She remembered his deep, melodious voice and wished she could have stayed long enough to hear one of his stories. She imagined how nice it would be to sit beside him and listen as he spun tales, all sorts of tales about the people he'd known.

She toweled her hair until it was almost dry, then ran a brush through it. With nothing much on her to-do list today, she dressed casually in capris and a button-up blouse, and even though she had no real plans for the day, she decided that a dab of make-up wouldn't hurt.

Lynda Lee opened her make-up drawer, put on a bit of mascara, though her thick eyelashes and brows demanded not much of anything. She dabbed on a bit of Elizabeth Arden foundation, some brow color, and last, she added a little blush, a peachy pink to highlight her coloring and match her fingernail polish. She turned her head this way and that then stood back for one last look.

She toweled her hair one more time, brushed it, and as she walked out the door, she stopped. Lipstick, she'd forgotten her lipstick, so she hurried back into the bathroom, pulled her gold tube of Pink Violet lipstick out of the drawer and slid it carefully over her lips. She smiled, blotted her lips, and whispered, "Yes, you look presentable."

As she stepped into the kitchen to get a cup of coffee, she heard a knock on the door and was surprised when she opened it to see Janine, Sarah, Laura, and Beth, all of them dressed to a T.

"Good morning," Janine said and pushed past her with the others following right behind. "I thought we'd do some shopping before lunch."

Lynda Lee stood frozen in place.

"Are you all right, honey? Did you forget about our luncheon today?" Janine asked.

"I thought it was tomorrow," Lynda Lee said. "I've just gotten out of the shower."

"Yes, I can see that," Janine said. "But we have plenty of time. Why don't you go change and we'll go into town, do some shopping and then have lunch."

"Please, help yourself to coffee," an embarrassed Lynda Lee said. "I'll be back shortly."

Lynda Lee chided herself as she walked back to the bedroom mumbling.

"What's wrong with me? I was certain the luncheon was tomorrow. Am I losing my mind?"

She walked to her closet, pulled out one of her twenty or so two-piece suits. She shrugged off her clothes, pulled a pair of shoes from one of the many boxes in the closet, and sat on the bed while she pulled on her hose, fastened them to the garter belt, let her slip drift over her shoulders, and finally, finished the look in an aqua-colored suit and matching shoes.

She stepped into the bathroom and noticed her partially wet hair. She did her best with a towel to dry it. She didn't have time to sit under her portable dryer, so she decided that her hair would have to dry on its own.

"I need to have this long hair cut," she whispered as she brushed. "It's too much trouble, but Ray would have a fit."

She took a deep breath, a last look in the mirror, a last fluff of her hair, a dab more lipstick, and closed her eyes.

"This is not where I want to be," she whispered and walked back toward the kitchen.

"Ah, there she is. Look at that. Even with partially wet hair, she looks and walks like a goddess of beauty," Janine said.

"Thank you, Janine," Lynda Lee said. "I apologize for my hair. I didn't have time to use my portable dryer."

"Did you put a brush in your purse?" Beth asked. "I mean, for later, when your hair dries."

Lynda Lee smiled.

"Yes, I'd never go anywhere without make up and a brush in my purse. Those are essentials, aren't they?"

"Indeed, they are," Janine said. "Now, what sort of shopping will we do today, Ladies?"

"Something adventurous," Lynda Lee said. "Something we've never done before, but wait just a moment. I've forgotten something. I'll be right back."

Lynda Lee walked into the bedroom, opened the drawer in her nightstand, and took out her bottle of pain pills. The headache was better, but what if it came back while they were shopping?

She put the bottle in her purse and joined the others.

"I'm ready," she said. "Let's see what we can find."

"If we can find one by Laurent, I need a new sun hat," Janine said. "Something elegant and attractive that will keep the sun off my face and draw attention from adoring fans!"

All of them giggled.

"I try to avoid the sun if at all possible," Lynda Lee said. "It's something I've been taught all my life."

"There's little way that we Southerners can avoid the sun. Oh, that's right, though. You grew up in New York City, didn't you?"

Lynda Lee nodded.

"But we have sun there, too. It's just that there are so many buildings around that we really don't have to worry about too much sun. Still, my mother insisted that I either stay indoors or wear a sun hat. Mostly, I just stayed indoors."

"Mercy," Beth said. "I was making mud cakes outside with my brothers when I was four. We didn't care at all about the sun. We cared about playing."

"I'm with you there, Beth," Janine said. "I loved being outside, playing tag, making mud pies, swinging, playing hide and seek. We went outside as soon as it was light and stayed until the sun started going down. We had a whole neighborhood filled with kids. We had a secret playhouse, girls only, and we all had our special hiding places to outdo the boys."

"I've never heard of these games," Lynda Lee said. "I wasn't allowed to play with other children, although once a week, my mother arranged for a tea party with neighboring girls, but only those in our neighborhood, and only those whose mothers didn't work outside the home."

As soon as she spoke the words, Lynda Lee realized, for the first time, how shallow they sounded.

"I'm very sorry," she said. "I didn't mean to sound so hateful. It's just the way I was raised. But now that I've said it, I see how hurtful it could have been to the other little girls in the neighborhood."

Janine patted Lynda Lee's arm.

"It's not your fault, honey. You were obeying your mother. It wasn't a conscious decision on your part."

"But wouldn't you think, Janine, that at some point, I would have realized how hurtful it must have been for my other neighbors?"

"No, Lynda Lee. Your mother was in control. Didn't you tell us that you'd had a strict schedule to follow every day? That your mother commanded every second of your time?"

"Yes, she did," Lynda Lee said and lowered her head. "Why didn't I ever question her decisions?"

"Don't be silly, Lynda Lee," Beth said. "Children really don't think to say no to their mothers, even if they don't like what she makes them do. I was a bit of a rebel. I talked back. I questioned, but probably, if I hadn't had older brothers, I wouldn't have been such a pain for my mother. My brothers were always arguing about something. They rebelled against rules and we caused our mother a great deal of pain as children."

"You did?" Lynda Lee asked.

"Oh, worlds of pain. At one point, I overheard my mother tell our father that she couldn't take it anymore. She said she'd had it being a full-time wife and mother and that she wanted more from her life than bratty children and a demanding husband.

"My father told her it was her job as a woman to raise children and take care of her husband. It's what women were meant to do. He told her it was clearly laid out in the Bible and that she shouldn't be questioning God."

"Oh, how did your mother react to that?" Lynda Lee asked as she pulled a tissue from her purse.

Beth said very quickly, "She left us and went to stay with her sister."

Janine gasped.

"She left you?"

Beth nodded her head.

"Yes, she left us and found a new life in Texas. She got a job as a secretary somewhere and stayed with her sister for six months."

"What on earth did you do?" Sarah and Laura asked simultaneously.

"I cried a lot," she said, "but after a few weeks, my brothers and I decided that there was work to be done and we had to do it so our daddy could work. We took over the household duties. We all knew about cooking and cleaning. Our mother had set us up well with the skills she taught us. So, my three brothers and I took care of the house, did the washing, the ironing, the cooking, and the cleaning."

"How old were you at the time?" Lynda Lee asked.

"I was five when she left. My brothers were older, 10, 13, 15."

"I'd love to go in one of these shops, but I'm mesmerized by your story, Beth," Janine said. "Why don't we stop for a coffee and a bun and you can finish telling us about your life."

They found a table at a nearby restaurant, ordered coffee and honey buns, and listened to Beth's tale.

"After a while, my brothers and I paid little attention to our duties.

We just did what we knew we had to do so that Daddy could work. We kept each other company. We laughed and sang and kept our spirits up. We had a routine and we followed it every day, and eventually that summer, we all became closer. We didn't fight or argue, and we didn't mention our mother. Sometimes, at night, though, I'd break down and cry, but my brothers always came and did some silly thing to make me laugh. They were good boys and they took good care of me."

"Honestly, I can't say that I would have handled it as well as you did," Sarah said. "My mother was my best friend. She still is."

Beth shrugged.

"I didn't have that choice, Sarah. By the time my mother left, she was outdone with all of us, with her life and ours."

Lynda Lee leaned forward.

"I hate to ask, but when did you last see your mother?"

Beth laughed.

"My mother came back to us eight months after she left. She had no money and asked my father if they could somehow rekindle their relationship."

Janine gasped.

"You're kidding," she exclaimed. "After all that time?"

"Yes," Beth said. "And my father let her come back and live with us. But he insisted on separate bedrooms. Two of my brothers had to bunk together so that my mother could have her own room."

"Did you all resent her?"

"No, she was still our mother. She took over the cooking, but the boys and I kept up our own chores. Dinner time was always quiet after that. My father refused to speak to her, and my brothers and I kept quiet. It was tense after that. Once she came back, everyone was on edge. The house took on a different feel, and our happy times disappeared."

"What a sad story, Beth," Lynda Lee said. "I had no idea that your life had been so tragic. I'm so sorry you had to go through that."

"Oh, Lynda Lee, don't worry about me. As it turned out, our mother left again after a few months and went back to Texas. Her sister's husband had died and she moved in with her. She found a job and another husband. My father signed divorce papers, and that was that. She married again. She kept in touch with weekly letters, always addressed to my dad, but as soon as one would arrive, he'd hand it to me or my brothers to read."

"Was that better for your brothers and for you?"

"Much better. We went back to our routine and shortly, our house was filled with laughter again."

Lynda Lee smiled.

"I've never lived in a house filled with laughter. I've always wanted to, but ...."

"Lynda Lee, my goodness. You have everything a woman could want, beauty beyond compare, a rich husband, a gorgeous home and if you'll do as Beth instructed, you'll be a very rich business woman weaving drapes for all the wealthy women of Weaver Street."

Lynda Lee smiled, reached into her purse, took a pill from her bottle, and swallowed it.

"You're right, of course. Beth, we must come up with a plan to spread the word about the draperies. We've so many friends and connections here that I might be able to have some women who might want my draperies."

In just a few minutes, the pill began to take effect. It took away the sadness in her heart, the yearning for children, the unhappiness that plagued her, and most of all, the idea that she was not where she was supposed to be.

Chapter 19

After a full day of shopping, Beth and Lynda Lee walked toward their homes.

"Do you ever feel that you're not in the right place?" Lynda Lee asked Beth as they walked to her house together.

"What do you mean?"

Lynda Lee went into the kitchen, Beth following right behind.

"Sometimes, I feel that I'm not where I'm supposed to be, sort of like the life I'm living now is not the one that was intended for me. Is it awfully silly of me?"

Beth took a glass of water and sat at the table.

"It's not silly, but I've never had that feeling. I've always felt that I was doing what I was supposed to be doing. Or maybe I've just never thought much about it."

"It's probably just my wacky brain," Lynda Lee said. "But sometimes, Beth, I have dreams that seem so real that I don't want to wake up. I want to stay in the place forever. But this is our secret, okay?"

Beth smiled.

"Okay, I promise not to mention it to the others. Tell me more about this place you dream of."

Lynda Lee sat across from Beth at the table in the kitchen. She ran her fingers across her forehead.

"Headache?" Beth asked.

"No, I was just trying to think of what to say."

Beth took another swallow of her water.

"Why don't you tell me where you think you are in the dream."

Lynda Lee smiled.

"Now, that's a question I can give a clear answer to. I'm in Galway, Ireland, 1800s or so. And with me is an old Irish weaver sitting at her loom. She said that the Irish are always fighting for freedom from attempts at takeovers by one country or another, and her job is to make clothes to keep the soldiers warm."

"She talks to you?"

"Oh yes, she does. Her name is Hattie Brennan, but everyone calls her Maman, similar to our word *granny*. She says the wisest things, Beth. I'm very comfortable around her. I listen to every word she says." Lynda Lee moved closer to Beth. "The first time I saw her, she was in the middle of a dirt road weaving away. I've visited often since then, and each time, her little cottage changes. It was in ruins on my first visit, but now, it seems to have new life."

"That's quite a realistic dream, Lynda Lee. There's so much detail to it."

Lynda Lee smiled.

"I feel so at home there. In fact, when Ray wakes me from a nap, I'm angry at him for pulling me away from the old Irish weaver."

"And what does Ray think of these dreams?"

"He thinks they're foolish. At first, he feigned interest, but now, he gets angry when I want to talk about them. I can't blame him. After all, I'm his wife. He gives me everything I want or need. He treats me like a queen and never wants me to work too hard, especially since the miscarriage."

Beth slid her hand across the table and took Lynda Lee's.

"I had no idea you'd had a miscarriage. I'm so sorry."

"It was a long time ago when we first moved into our apartment. We were both excited about bringing a baby into the world, but our hopes were dashed. Afterwards, Ray had a vasectomy. I was furious, but the doctor said I couldn't have children, that I'd risk my health if I did. So, Ray took it upon himself to make sure I'd never be pregnant again."

Tears rolled down Lynda Lee's cheeks.

"I'm so sorry," Beth said. "I can't have children, either."

Lynda Lee looked at her, a surprised look on her face.

"You?"

Beth nodded her head.

"But Johnny is okay with it. He says we can always adopt later if we want to."

"Ray's never mentioned adoption, and I hadn't even thought of it."

"You might be surprised at the couples in our community who have adopted children. There are so many without homes, so many needy children here. I'd rather adopt some that need a mother and a father, really, because I know how it feels to be abandoned by a parent. Someday, Johnny and I will look into it, as soon as he finishes school and finds a job in a place that he likes."

"My mother would have a fit if I adopted some homeless child. She's all about breeding. If I ever went on a date, the first thing she'd ask is 'Who are this boy's people? Where are they from?' She's a snob, and she's always thought that we are better than 'common folk,' as she calls them."

"Common folk, what a term! I'm glad she doesn't know about my life," Beth said. "She'd be horrified if she knew we were friends."

"I don't care about your life story, Beth. I care about who you are now and how nice it is to have you as a friend."

Beth smiled.

"I'd better go," she said. "It's not long before dinner time, and Johnny will be starving. Thank you for a lovely day today. Next time, let's talk more about your dream. It's so very interesting."

Lynda Lee walked her to the door and waved goodbye.

Chapter 20

When Ray came home that night, Lynda Lee was already reading a Southern Lady magazine in bed.

"How was your day?" she asked, but barely looked up from the magazine.

"Long," he said as he put his scrubs in the laundry basket and changed into his pajamas. "The new supervisor is a slave driver. He wants thorough details on every visit we make, every patient we see. It's not enough that we complete the information on the charts. Now, we have to do an additional written report with the charts. It's a waste of time."

"But you're the assistant director now. In many ways you carry more weight than even the director, " Lynda Lee said. "Can't you complain or something? I thought that's what your assistants were for, to do the endless paperwork. Otherwise, what good are they?"

"I don't want to cause trouble," he said as he sat on the bed. "Complaining about it would just make me seem uncooperative, and I certainly don't want that on a resume."

"No, of course not," she said and flipped a page in the magazine. "Things aren't working out the way you planned here, are they? You have the recognition you've wanted, the job title that meant so much. Is it time to move on, Ray?"

"Move on, as in leave the hospital and our home on Weaver Street?"

"No, I didn't mean it that way. I meant is it time for you to consider another position in the hospital? You know, I've watched you all these years, Ray. You started in 1948, now it's 1958, and you're not where you want to be. You've given most of your life to the hospital. Don't they appreciate that? I'm not saying I know anything about your business because I don't, but I do know that you can do whatever you want to do. You're a respected cardiologist."

"There's not a position higher than Head of the Cardiac Intensive Care Unit."

"Of course there is. Again, I know nothing about your hospital business but it seems to me that everyone has a boss, so there must be someone who's above you who could help you. I think that with very little effort, you could become a supervisor yourself, say, the supervisor of Cardiac Special Care or something like that, a different position but still doing what you love."

"There's no Cardiac Special Care division, Lynda Lee."

"Oh, well, then, perhaps there should be, Ray," she said and flipped another page in her magazine. Then, she put it down and said, "There's absolutely nothing standing in your way, Ray. Couldn't you talk to your director or something? Couldn't you stress the need for better cardiac care, maybe even a special unit? Don't most of the big hospitals have them now?"

Ray leaned back on his pillows.

"The director would never go for it. It takes money to start a new unit, lots of money and cooperation from our financial supporters. You can't create something from nothing, not here, anyway."

Lynda Lee put her magazine on the night stand and turned off the bedside lamp.

"You could try, Ray. Get some sleep."

In the dream, Lynda Lee made her way up an overgrown hill, pushing aside various branches that seemed to spring from nowhere until she came upon a beautiful red wild rose bush. The blooms sent their aromas into the air. Lynda Lee inhaled their sweet smell. She hadn't noticed the wild roses before, but now they sprang wildly beside her, the heady scent intoxicating. There were reds, white, corals, as far as she could see. At the top of the hill lay the dusty road she sought and springing to life beside it was an enormous rose bush with roses in a vibrant blue.

"Maman," she called. "I've found something most unusual."

"I'm here, Child. What have you found?"

Lynda Lee saw the old weaver at her loom working the loom and sheep's wool. She walked toward her, the edges of her sequined gown kicking up dust behind her.

"Maman, have you seen them?"

"What Child? I'm busy. I've no time to waste. Our soldiers need warm clothes. It'll soon be winter and winter in Ireland is cold."

"The blue roses, have you seen them?"

"Of course, I've seen them. They grow wild here. They're everywhere."

"No, I mean the blue ones. They're so vibrant and with such a heady aroma that I felt almost intoxicated by them. In all the time I've been here, I've never seen roses, especially blue ones. How did that happen?"

"I'm afraid you'll have to ask Mother Nature herself," she said as her feet pushed the treadle back and forth. "Those blue ones are new, perhaps only fifty years old or so, if my mind judges correctly. 'Twasn't me who planted them, Child. They came on their own, but my guess is that they symbolize change, some form of change."

"But before when I was here, there were no roses."

"It's been a long time since ye've been to see me, Child. Much has happened and part of our landscape has changed. Beyond the hill you climbed are roses as far as ye can see."

"But it's the blue ones that are so fascinating. Where I'm from, there is no such thing as a blue rose."

Maman chuckled.

"Sometimes, we just don't see, Child. And sometimes," she said as her hands smoothed the wool, "there are no answers, simply mysteries. Nature can do that. She can create something where there was nothing before."

Ray's words ran through her mind: "You can't create something out of nothing."

"What is it, Child? You've gone pale of a sudden."

"Nothing, Maman. I just remembered something my husband

Ray said to me recently. 'You can't make something out of nothing.'"

"Pish tosh," Maman said. "Nature does it all the time."

"I hate to take you from your work, but could we go inside the cottage and have some tea?"

The ancient weaver gave her a stern look.

"I've clothes to make, Child, but we'll sit a spell if you'd like."

Lynda Lee watched as the weaver slowly got up from the loom.

"Well, go on," the weaver said and motioned her forward.

When Lynda Lee turned to go inside, she stopped. Her eyes widened.

"The cottage," she said. "It's so different, so bright and big and clean."

"The old one's gone," Maman said, "went up in a blaze it did. But we Irish stick together. Neighbors from all over Galway came and rebuilt it for me."

"Hattie! Hattie Brennan!" the deep voice called. "How're ye keeping today?"

Lynda Lee looked up and saw Scaylee trotting toward them on his horse. When he jumped down beside them, he dusted himself off, removed his beret, and bowed.

"We're just going inside for a spot of tea, Scaylee. Care to join us?"

"I'd be honored. Lynda Lee, I trust you are well."

Lynda Lee nodded and felt her heart beat faster.

"I'm well," she said. "I'm afraid I've kept Maman from her work. I've been talking since I've been here."

"And what topic of interest have you two been discussing?"

"This and that," Maman said.

"Blue roses, actually," Lynda Lee said. "Where I'm from, there are no blue roses, yet right over there is a bush with the most vibrant and fragrant blooms."

"Ah, one of Nature's many gifts to the Irish."

"Scaylee," Maman said, "I've some hot tea and scones, and I've made tomato jam."

"I can't wait to try them. Ladies first," he said as a big smile spread across his lips.

Lynda Lee gasped when she entered the cottage.

"Maman, it's so lovely in here, so bright and beautiful. Just look at all the colors."

The ceiling allowed them all room to stand comfortably and the walls were white with bright blue trim. The once-crumbling fireplace had been rebuilt of stone and inside was the same black iron pot that could be moved back and forth for cooking.

"Take a seat," Maman said. "Tea and scones coming up."

"May I help?" Lynda Lee asked. "I'm a good baker."

"Are ye now?" Scaylee asked.

"Yes, I love being in the kitchen and cooking, baking. The kitchen is where I'm most at home."

"Hattie Brennan. Did you hear that? We have a cook in our midst," Scaylee said.

"Well, maybe next time, she can make the scones while I finish my weaving."

Lynda Lee smiled as Maman served the hot tea in pretty porcelain cups and placed a scone on each saucer, followed by a spoonful of her tomato jam.

"It smells delicious," Scaylee said. "What a feast for the eyes, the noses, and our mouths. We are grateful and send our blessings for these gifts."

"Thank you, Scaylee. We are, indeed, grateful for this bounty. Try some jam, Child," Maman said as she took a scone and slathered a bit of tomato jam onto it.

Lynda Lee inhaled the wonderful aroma, the scent of it causing her mouth to water. She gingerly brought the scone to her mouth.

"Lynda Lee, wake up," Ray called to her. "Lynda Lee. I'm home, and we're late for the dinner at Beth and Johnny Martin's house. I told her we might be a few minutes late. Lynda Lee," he said as he shook her shoulder. "It's time to get up. We're supposed to meet the Martins in a little over an hour."

Lynda Lee blinked her eyes and looked around the room.

"Maman?" she called. "Where are you, Maman?"

Tears rolled down her cheeks.

"Maman, please, I want to come back. Please, Maman, help me come back."

"What are you going on about?" Ray said. "You're ranting like a madwoman. We need to get ready for dinner at Beth's house."

"Just go away and leave me alone, Ray. I don't want to be here. I want to be with Maman and Scaylee. I wanted just one bite of that scone. Don't you understand? I don't want to be here. So, you go to dinner by yourself."

"No, Lynda Lee, an absolute no. They were kind enough to invite us, and we'll be gracious enough to accept that invitation," he said as he changed his shirt. "Besides, someone very special has also been invited, Dr. Lucius Grant, the state's leading cardiologist. He's a genius of a thinker and an inventor. He's working on creating a device that will regulate a person's heartbeat, and he's asked me to look at his designs and offer my input."

Ray finished his shirt and tie and slipped on his black dinner jacket.

Lynda Lee wiped the tears from her face and sat up.

"So, the night will be devoted to you and Dr. Grant," she said as she stood, "another symposium on cardiology."

Ray stood beside her.

"What's wrong, sweetheart? Why do you look so sad? I thought you'd be happy about the advancements."

Lynda Lee looked up at him, her face tear-stained.

"When have you ever been right about what would make me happy, Ray? And when have you ever asked me what I wanted?"

She walked to the closet, picked out a proper suit with matching heels, and went into the bathroom to change.

Ray stood silently in the middle of the room. No words came to him. She'd said it herself. She didn't want to be here. So, he stood helplessly in the same spot until his head began to throb as words burst from his mouth.

"What do you want, Lynda Lee?" his voice loud, his arms waving. "How have I failed you?"

Then he walked to the bathroom and banged on the door.

"Answer me, Lynda Lee. Answer me. What do you want?"

Lynda Lee opened the door, a look of shock on her face.

"What are you talking about, Ray? We have an important dinner to attend. Now, go and let me finish getting ready. I still have my makeup to put on."

"Do you still love me, Lynda Lee?" he said as he stood in the doorway. "Do you?"

Lynda Lee dabbed on a bit of foundation.

"Don't be silly, Ray. Now, go and let me get ready."

Ray turned but looked back, "You said you didn't want to be here anymore. That means you don't want to be with me anymore, doesn't it?"

Lynda Lee powdered her face then looked right and left in the mirror to make sure there were no gaps.

"Oh, you look like a sad little puppy dog," she said. "Brighten up, Ray. I'm here with you, aren't I and we have an important dinner to attend. So, stop your sulking and put on a professionally happy face. You don't want that famous doctor to see you looking so grim, do you?"

"That famous doctor means nothing compared to you, Lynda Lee. Nothing."

She laughed out loud and carefully brushed her hair.

"That famous doctor means everything to you. You'll have a chance to be remembered for a great contribution to medical science if you make a good impression. So, wipe that frown off your face."

"All I can think about is what you said. You don't want to be with me anymore. That outweighs everything else."

As she walked out of the bathroom, she said, "Ray, please, just drop it, okay? I didn't mean it. It's just that I get bored sometimes, tired of the same routine over and over."

"What can I do, Lynda Lee? What can I change to make things better for you? I'll do anything. If I lose your love, I don't think I can go on."

Lynda Lee kissed him on the cheek.

"You're not going to lose me, Ray. I'll be right here with you always."

Ray sat down on the side of the bed.

"Do you want a divorce?" he asked. "Will that make you happy?"

Lynda Lee turned on him then, furious.

"Don't you *ever* mention that word to me again," she said and bent close to his face. "I mean it. If you ever say that again, you'll find yourself living with a mean and hateful woman who'll do everything in her power to make your life a living Hell."

She shocked herself with her tone and her rampant anger. The man had never done a single thing to hurt her, yet she'd yelled at him as if he were some brute. He'd given her everything she wanted. He'd taken care of her. But something inside her broke loose and spilled onto him. She regretted it immensely.

Ray leaned away from her.

"I'm sorry," he said softly. "I'm so sorry. I won't mention it again. I promise."

Lynda Lee knelt in front of him.

"No, Ray. I'm the one who's sorry," she said as she stroked the side of his face. "I didn't mean a single thing I said. I don't even know where all that rage came from. You've been so good to me all these years. You've treated me with love and kindness and given me everything I've ever wanted. I do love you, Ray. I'm so very sorry I yelled such hateful things at you. Can you forgive me?"

Ray stood and brought her up with him. He wrapped his arms around her and hugged her close to him.

"I can forgive you anything, sweetheart, anything as long as I know you love me and that you don't want to leave me."

"I'll never leave you, Ray. If there's leaving to be done, you'll be the one to do it."

Ray chuckled.

"You don't have to worry about that. You're my one and only true love. I'd never leave you. Never."

Lynda Lee took his face in her hands.

"Are we okay then?" she asked.

Ray kissed her lightly on the lips.

"We're okay, my love. We're better than ever."

She slipped back into the bathroom, grabbed a bottle from the drawer, popped two pills in her mouth and took a sip of water.

She held out her hand to Ray.

"Come along, my dearest, we've a party to attend."

"The Goddess of Weaver Street has spoken," he said and grinned.

Chapter 21

Beth Martin opened the door and found the beautiful Lynda Lee with her husband beside her.

"Sorry we're a bit late," Ray said.

"No bother," Beth said. "The others came a little too early, but it's fine. The guest of honor has just arrived."

"Guest of honor?" Lynda Lee asked. "Oh, I assume you mean the new doctor."

"Yes, of course," Beth said. "Johnny insisted that we have Dr. Grant for a welcome dinner. Johnny is thrilled, naturally. He thinks of that man as a god of cardiac medicine."

"We all do," Ray said. "And to have him here is a great honor. There's so much he can teach us about his specialties and his current technologies."

"Come, Lynda Lee, and meet the others. You know most of them, our bunch, but there are new people here that you haven't met yet, and I'd hate to deprive them of a meeting with the beauty!"

Beth stood at the top of the three stairs leading into the living room and cleared her throat.

"May I have your attention, please," she said and took Lynda Lee's hand.

When she was sure that everyone had turned to face her, she spoke.

"I'd like to introduce you to Lynda Lee Rogers, wife of Dr. Ray Rogers. Isn't she simply stunning? She's a former beauty pageant queen from New York City. Lynda Lee fits right into our little group, and we all love her dearly. But we can't help but see how very beautiful she is, and in our little group, we refer to her as the Goddess of Weaver Street. Lynda Lee Rogers, everyone. Please say hello."

A crush of people came toward her. At first, she backed away, but then someone said, "Lynda Lee, I'd like to shake your hand for putting up with that bull of a husband of yours!"

Lynda Lee chuckled and held out her hand as the people backed away.

"He's not so bad," she said with a smile.

"Hello," he said, took her hand, and kissed the top of it. "I'm charmed."

"Thank you," she said. "And you are?"

"Dr. Lucius Grant," he answered. "I've done many things in my life, but I've never come face to face with a goddess before. May I get you a drink?"

Lynda Lee smiled.

"I'd love a small glass of Coke if Beth has some."

"I'll just go and see. You'll be here when I get back?"

Lynda Lee nodded and looked around for Ray. As usual, he was surrounded by students listening carefully to his every word. Some were even taking notes.

"One glass of Coke for the goddess," Dr. Grant said as he handed her a glass. He, too, looked around the room and saw Ray and his students.

"He's a great doctor with a very bright future in cardiac care. You should be very proud of him."

"I am, of course. His work means everything to him," Lynda Lee said. "He works hard, but to him, it's not like work at all. It's where he feels most at home."

Dr. Grant finished his drink and put his glass on a silver tray.

"I might have another," he said. "I don't have to work tonight, so I can indulge a bit."

"Help yourself," Lynda Lee said as she watched him walk to the drink table. She mumbled to herself, "so the great doctor is a drinker."

When he came back, he asked, "Care to take a spin around the room with me?"

Lynda Lee frowned.

"I don't think so. Why don't you stay where you are and enjoy your drink? I'll just go check in with Beth."

"I'm crushed," he said.

"Mingle with the other brilliant doctors milling about. I'm sure you'll enjoy that. You can talk about your work."

Lynda Lee left in search of Beth and found her talking to Janine.

"There you are," Janine said. "I've never seen you look more beautiful, Lynda Lee. How do you do it? I'm gaining weight and now, most of my clothes are too tight. And just look at my hair. I can't do anything with it anymore. But you, you are as beautiful as you were the first time I saw you. Honestly, I don't know how you do it."

"I really don't do anything," Lynda Lee said.

"It's all in the genes," Beth said. "We're all programmed to be exactly who we are: short, tall, beautiful, elegant, pudgy, bad hair, good hair."

"I need to be dieting," Janine said. "Seriously, I don't want to be a pudgy, middle-aged, frump of a woman. I've seen and criticized too many of them."

"Just don't go on that crazy cabbage soup diet that's all the rage now. Cabbage soup for every meal? It's absurd," Beth said. "Or the Cream of Mushroom soup diet. Besides, you should be concentrating on keeping your pantry stocked. There are threats of war, you know. Eisenhower says we should keep our pantries stocked, just in case. This is no time to be worried about gaining weight, Janine."

"You look perfectly fine," Lynda Lee said. "To me, you look healthier than I've ever seen you. You've been too thin, Janine. Enjoy adding a bit of weight. You'll feel better and have more energy."

"You're beginning to sound just like my mother, Lynda Lee," Janine said with a chuckle.

"My mother would have heart failure if she could see me now," Lynda Lee said. "Of course, there's little chance of that."

"Let's go into the kitchen," Janine said. "There's too much going on here. I can barely hear myself think."

The three of them slipped into the kitchen.

"Ah, that's better," Janine said. "Now, tell me, Lynda Lee, what's the deal between you and your mother?"

"I've never been good enough for her," Lynda Lee said and lowered her head. "Nothing I've ever done has pleased her. She cares only about winning pageants and being rich."

Janine scooted a chair out from the table.

"Sit," she said and adjusted her chair. "But you've won beauty pageants, and your family is rich, so why isn't she happy?"

Lynda Lee shrugged.

"I guess she dreamed of a different life for me. It broke her heart when I married Ray and moved here. She spent all of her time and a lot of money preparing me for pageants and scholarships to prestigious universities. She put her whole life into it. Now, she wants nothing to do with me. She thinks I ruined my life and hers when I left New York and married Ray."

"I'm so sorry," Janine said. "But your mother is wrong, Lynda Lee. You didn't ruin anyone's life by moving here."

"She wouldn't agree. She came for a visit a while back and was supposed to stay for a few days, remember? But after only an afternoon with me and Ray, she hurried back to New York. She hated the house. She wouldn't even talk to Ray, and she and my dad left without so much as a hug. She's still very angry at me for giving up my life in New York. She considers me an utter failure at everything."

"But couldn't she see how happy you are? How could she not love your beautifully appointed home?"

"I betrayed her," Lynda Lee said and wiped a tear from her eye. "I took all her dreams and wishes and threw them away. After she devoted her life to making me a beauty queen, I broke her heart. She will never forgive me."

"But she's your mother," Beth said. "Mothers love their children. It can't be so bad that she'll never forgive you."

"Trust me," Lynda Lee said and blotted her cheeks with a handkerchief. "My mother will never forgive me. Never. She believes that I destroyed her hopes and dreams. I'm a failure as a daughter."

Janine got up and fixed them all a shot of whiskey in one of her green water goblets.

"Here, take a sip. It won't hurt you, but it might make you feel a little better."

The three of them sat, clinked their glasses together and knocked back the shot.

Lynda Lee coughed.

"That is some strong stuff," she said. "I might not be able to walk to the car."

"But it tasted good, didn't it?"

They all laughed at that.

"It warms you all the way down," Beth said.

"Want another?" Janine asked. "It's the hubby's secret stash. Of course, I use these green water goblets to disguise what we're drinking."

They all laughed again.

Lynda Lee held up a hand.

"No more for me, thanks."

"You know what I think we should do, girls?" Beth asked.

They both shook their heads.

"I think we should plan a weekend getaway, just us girls. We could do it. We could leave food for the husbands, clean our houses before we go, and then take off to a place where we could be alone with ourselves, no men to bother with."

"I have a passport," Lynda Lee said. "Do you have one?"

"No, I've never even thought about one," Beth said. "Travel isn't something I thought would be available to me, with Johnny's work schedule. But it's an intriguing idea."

"I wouldn't even know how to get one," Janine said.

"It isn't hard," Lynda Lee said. "You just fill out some papers and send them to Montgomery then wait a few months and voila! You'll get your passport in the mail, and if we all had passports, then we could go to Ireland."

"Ireland?" Janine asked. "Why would we want to go to Ireland? Aren't they always fighting over there?"

"Janine's right," Beth said. "I know you'd love to go, Lynda Lee, but it's no place for us until the fighting stops."

Lynda Lee sighed.

Chapter 22

When the phone rang, Lynda Lee dried her hands on a dishtowel and answered.

"Hello," she said.

"Hey, let's go for a walk downtown," Janine said. "Beth and Sarah are up for it. How about you? We're not shopping. We're just walking and looking. If I spend any more money on clothes, I'll be in the dog house. When can you be ready?"

"What's everyone wearing for this big walk downtown?"

"We're all casual. I'm wearing pants and a floral blouse. Beth is in jeans and a nice tee shirt. Sarah's wearing a shirt-waist dress with her tennis shoes."

"My hair needs a wash, but I'll just do the best I can with it."

"Your hair is always perfect, Lynda Lee, although I can't imagine how you deal with all that long hair every single day."

Lynda Lee chuckled.

"I just brush it a lot."

"We'll come by in about thirty minutes, okay?" Janine said.

"Yes, that will give me time to finish the dishes."

"You have a dishwasher to do that for you, you know."

"I don't mind doing it."

The four of them walked side by side down Main Street in Tuscaloosa watching for the right turn that would take them to the shops that lined the tiny mall. To their surprise, they saw an enormous building under construction.

"Look," Beth said. "We're getting a Sears! Won't that be wonderful?

Sears has everything!"

"We will still do our clothes shopping at our great little boutiques, though. I wouldn't want to buy clothes from Sears," Janine said. "The quality is strictly for those who can't afford better."

"Janine!" Lynda Lee said. "That's so snobbish of you."

"Well, would you buy clothes from Sears?"

Lynda Lee shook her head.

"If I need clothes, I make them or have them done by my tailor."

"Exactly," Janine said. "You need to face the fact that we are in a class above most everyone else in this town. How many families live on Weaver Street? Ten in all, out of this whole town."

As they browsed outside the shops, something across the street caught Lynda Lee's eye. It was a green sequined gown hanging on a rolling hanger outside. Taped onto one sleeve was a sign that read "Ten dollars."

"I'll be right back," Lynda Lee said to Beth.

Lynda Lee hurried across the street and stood close to the gown. It wasn't made well, but it had a striking appearance among the assorted dresses, blouses, and pants crowded next to it on the hanger.

"May I help you?"

Lynda Lee turned around and saw a little girl of about ten.

The girl held out her hand.

"I'm Julie," she said. "I'm in charge of the sale today."

"The sale?" Lynda Lee asked.

The girl coughed several times then spoke. "Yes, Ma'am. I live here at the orphanage," she said as she turned and pointed to an enormous white house with a sign on the top: Broadhurst Orphan's Home. "We have sales every month to raise money for the Home."

"I see," Lynda Lee said. "I'm Mrs. Rogers, but you can call me Lynda Lee."

"You're very pretty, Lynda Lee," Julie said as she brushed a stray blonde hair from her face.

The girl was clean and dressed in clean but worn clothes. She had pretty blonde hair, blue eyes, and chiseled features. Though she was extremely thin, she presented herself well and her posture was beyond reproach.

"Did you want to buy something? The money will go for a good cause."

"What sort of cause?" Lynda Lee asked.

"The Home needs repairs and the smaller children need proper food and clothing." Then she leaned toward Lynda Lee and whispered, "Even in summer, the house is cold. The small children need blankets and coats." She coughed several times again.

In that moment, Julie's words touched her heart. The thought of the children being cold was something she just could not abide.

"Well, Julie," she said as she wiped a tear from her eye, "what shall we do?"

"Maybe you could buy this gown," Julie said. "It's very expensive, but it's pretty."

"And who gets the money from the sale?"

"Oh, all the money goes to Mrs. Miller. She runs the Home."

"And if I give some money to the Home, will Mrs. Miller make sure the children have proper food and clothing?"

Julie lowered her head.

"I can't say, Lynda Lee. The Home needs many repairs."

Lynda Lee opened her purse.

"How many children live here at the Home, Julie?"

"I think we have close to fifty right now."

Lynda Lee frowned.

"Fifty children?"

Julie nodded.

"Okay, Julie. I'd like to buy this gown and everything hanging on the rack with it."

Julie's jaw dropped.

"I beg your pardon?"

Lynda Lee ran her hand across the clothes hanging on the rolling rack.

"All of these," she said. "Just add them up and tell me what I owe."

Lynda Lee watched as the girl carefully added the price of each piece to her list.

"And what are you doing here, Lynda Lee?" Beth asked.

"Oh, Beth. This little girl is Julie. She lives here at the Home. Today is a sale to help with expenses, upkeep, food. These children are in need."

"But Lynda Lee, this is the Broadhurst. I'd think that family would provide well for all the children's needs. Who's to say where your money goes? The Broadhurst family is loaded, the wealthiest in all of Alabama."

Lynda Lee cocked her head.

"I'm sure that it will go for the repairs and for food and clothing for the children."

Beth smiled.

"Perhaps you're right."

"Miss Lynda Lee, the total is forty dollars."

"Forty dollars!" Beth exclaimed. "What on earth did you buy?"

"All the clothes that were hanging on this rack. I'm glad to donate."

"Don't you need to ask Ray about it?"

"No, this money is from my private stash. I'll tell him about it, but he won't mind."

Lynda Lee handed over the check.

"Now, you keep those clothes and give them to any of the children who need them. I saw several nice jackets. Be sure that the children get them."

"I can't do that. Mrs. Miller is in charge of it, but we're all very grateful to you, Lynda Lee."

Lynda Lee handed Julie a calling card.

"I want to hear from you if the children are not properly fed and clothed. Just call me and let me know. My phone number is at the bottom of the card."

"This says you're a weaver and a seamstress. Is that right?"

Lynda Lee nodded.

"My grandmother was a weaver," Julie said. "I used to watch her when I was just a little thing."

"What happened to her?"

Julie lowered her head and wiped at her cheek.

"She died. All of my family died when our house caught fire. My little brother and I were the only ones to get out."

Lynda Lee could not find the words to speak, so she hugged Julie.

"What is your last name?" Lynda Lee asked.

"Kramer," Julie said. "My little brother is Mark."

"And how old is Mark?

"I'm ten, and Mark is eight."

"Well, Julie Kramer, I'm very glad I got to meet you."

Chapter 23

"Ray, I need to tell you something," Lynda Lee said as she prepared for bed that night.

"Is it something good or something bad? Do I need a shot of whiskey before I hear it?" But then he smiled. "Tell me," he said, as he patted a place on the side of the bed.

"I did something today that Janine thinks you'll disapprove of, but I told her she was wrong. I told her that I used some of my private money."

"Lynda Lee, that is your money, sweetheart. It's yours to spend as you want, no matter what. I have no say in it."

"But I want to tell you anyway to get your reaction."

Ray smiled and kissed her softly.

"My reaction or my approval?"

"Both, I guess."

"I'm listening," he said and lay back on his pillow.

Lynda Lee took a deep breath.

"You see, the girls and I took a walk downtown this morning. On our walk, I saw a little girl standing beside a rolling hangar that held a sequined ball gown, so I walked over to inquire about the gown. I could tell instantly that it was crudely made, as were most of the clothes she was selling."

"She was selling clothes on the street?"

"Yes, it was a monthly sale to earn extra money for the orphans at the Broadhurst Home. She was a sweet little girl named Julie, about ten, clean but thin and she had a persistent cough."

"The Broadhurst Home? Yes, I know of it. The hospital has a volunteer group that sees after the children, I think."

"Anyway," she said and worried her hands, "I bought some items and donated forty dollars to the Home."

"I see," he said. "That's a lot of money to donate, especially to a private institution. The Broadhursts are among the wealthiest families in the South. Why would the children need to have sales?"

"I'm not sure, Ray, but it's a monthly thing there. All the money goes to a Mrs. Miller, the woman who runs the orphanage. She decides where the money should go."

Ray chuckled.

"That's an easy one. I'd be willing to bet that it goes right into her pocket."

"Really?" Lynda Lee asked and leaned closer to him. "You really think so?"

Ray stroked the side of her face.

"I'm afraid so. The children probably never see a dime of that money."

"But Julie said that the house needed extensive repairs and that no matter what temperature it was outside, the house was always cold and the children always sick. They never got warm."

"Do you know what your next job will be?"

"I have to get a job?"

"Not what I said. Your next job will be to investigate the Broadhurst Home. Some of our doctors volunteer their services there. If there are sick children, they haven't been seen."

"But how do I start, Ray?"

"First of all, go to the courthouse and ask for records on the place. Some will be public, and that's where you start. Perhaps Mrs. Miller is listed as an employee. Then, you go and talk to Mrs. Miller. Don't tell her that you're investigating. Just ask for a tour and hint that you're looking for an investment opportunity."

"But if I invest, she will get the money."

"That's my point. You invest, and we'll track that investment to see how it is used. One of the senior doctors in Pediatrics in on the board that oversees the Home. He's a friend. Maybe we should ask him to dinner."

"That's a wonderful idea. Yes, we'll have him over for dinner. You're the best, Ray!" she said and kissed him on the lips.

Chapter 24

At a little after nine the next morning, Lynda Lee called Beth.

"Good morning," she said when Beth answered.

"Well, if it isn't our Goddess of Weaver Street calling lowly me!" she said and giggled. "How are you this morning?"

"I have a mission in mind," Lynda Lee said, "and I need your help."

"A mission? Now, that sounds interesting. Tell me all about it. Why don't you come for a cup of coffee. We can talk better face to face."

"I was hoping you'd ask," Lynda Lee said. "I'll be right over."

Lynda Lee checked her hair, makeup, and wardrobe in the antique cheval glass mirror in the foyer. She ran her hands through her hair to fluff it, put on a bit more lipstick, and smiled at her reflection. Her new shirt-waist dress—white with a bold floral pattern—and matching belt fit well. White pumps completed the look.

She arrived at Beth's home only a few minutes later.

"Wow," Beth said, "you look spectacular. I adore your outfit. It's perfect for you."

Beth, a little plumper now, wore a new shirt-waist dress, too, but in a dark striped pattern.

"And yours," Lynda Lee said. "I've not seen it before. Is it new?"

Beth nodded.

"As you can tell, I've gained some weight, so I've had to buy a few new pieces. I hate being this fat, and I can't figure out why I've gotten that way. My diet is the same as always. And I've already checked. I'm not pregnant, so I can't use that as an excuse."

"Perhaps you should see a doctor, Beth."

"I'm married to a doctor," she said. "He barely notices that I've gained any weight at all. Or if he has, he never mentions it."

"But I mean a doctor who isn't your husband. There are all sorts of reasons why women gain weight suddenly. You need to find a doctor who might help you."

"Let's sit at the table and have some coffee," Beth said as she walked toward the kitchen. "You can tell me all about this secret mission!"

Lynda Lee followed right behind and took a seat.

"The coffee smells good," she said. "Is this another of your exotic blends?"

Beth smiled.

"It is," she said. "I bought it from that new coffee shop that's opened in town. It's from Costa Rica. Try it."

"I need sugar and cream."

"I know," Beth said and slid the creamer and sugar bowl toward her.

After Lynda Lee had "doctored" her coffee, she took a sip.

"Mm," she said. "It's rich and smooth, none of that bitterness. Nice, Beth, very nice."

"Okay, tell me," Beth said and took a sip of her coffee. She got up, took something from the bread basket and put it on the table. "Have a croissant. They're only a day old, but they're still quite tasty."

Lynda Lee took a croissant, cut it in half, and put the other half back in the basket.

"Remember, Beth, when we were all walking in town, I saw a little girl on the sidewalk across the street. What caught my eye was a sequined gown that hung on one of those rolling racks."

"I remember," she said.

"Anyway, she said that the Home has a sale every month and that the money goes to Mrs. Miller, the woman who runs the Home."

"Okay," Beth said as she chewed her croissant, "I'm not seeing a mystery yet."

"The thing is that Julie, the little girl I met, said that the Home needed lots of repairs and that the children were always cold, no matter the temperature outside. Apparently, Beth, there's no heat inside that place. But how could that be?"

"The Broadhursts are loaded, aren't they?" Beth asked.

"Ray says they are among the wealthiest families in the South. So, why don't they keep the building safe and why are the children always suffering from the cold?"

Beth shifted closer to Lynda Lee.

"Maybe a better question is what does Mrs. Miller do with the money from the sales?"

"That's exactly what I want to know," Lynda Lee said.

Beth got up and took her cup to the sink.

"I love a good mystery," she said. "You and I will find out exactly what happens to the money and why those children are cold all the time. But I have to warn you. I won't stop until I'm satisfied that we've done all we can do."

"I agree," Lynda Lee said. "Ray suggested that I call and ask for a tour as a possible investment opportunity."

"That's a great idea," Beth said. "And with two of us, Mrs. Miller might think that both of us are willing to invest money ... money for her pocket!!

The two of them laughed.

"So, you're up for this?" Lynda Lee asked.

"Ready, willing, and able," Beth said.

"You know, Beth, I haven't felt this good in a long time. I haven't even had a headache this morning."

"I didn't know you were plagued with headaches. Do you take anything for them?"

"They're terrible," Lynda Lee said. "Sometimes, they're so bad I can hardly see, and they're not getting any better. In fact, they're getting more frequent and more painful. And yes, I have a prescription for pain killers. I keep them with me most of the time, just in case. But this morning, I didn't even think to get them."

"Maybe your thoughts were occupied by all those children who need your help," Beth said. "How many did you say lived in that home?"

"About fifty," she said.

"Mercy, all those children, cold and maybe even hungry. You and I are going to investigate this and make sure that those children are taken care of. Right? We'll start today by calling Mrs. Miller and asking for a tour. Is that okay with you? I'm dying to talk to the old bat," Beth said and chuckled.

"Make the call," Lynda Lee said.

Chapter 25

A week later, everything arranged, Lynda Lee and Beth walked the three blocks to the Broadhurst Home to begin their "investigation."

When they knocked on the door of the enormous house, a woman dressed in solid black came to the door. Her white hair was done in a tight bun atop her head with not a single hair out of place. She wore no makeup and did not smile.

"Mrs. Miller?" Beth asked. "I'm Beth Martin and this is my friend Lynda Lee Rogers. We set up an appointment to see the home and possibly make an investment."

"So I've heard," Mrs. Miller said. Still, she did not smile. "Follow me, and I will give you a short tour of our orphanage."

"The Broadhurst family owns this building. Is that correct?"

Mrs. Miller nodded.

"Are you the only worker here?"

Mrs. Miller frowned.

"Of course not. We have two live-in cooks, two housekeepers, two nursery keepers, and a full-time nurse's aid. The older children also have jobs within the Home to help with the younger children."

Lynda Lee stepped in front of her.

"I met Julie yesterday at the sale. She seemed to be about ten, and she was very polite. I bought a few items in hopes that it would benefit the children. I'm sure they need clothes, shoes, jackets, and everyday outfits."

Mrs. Miller stopped.

"This is not a state-run institution, Ladies. This is a privately-funded home for orphans. Mr. and Mrs. Broadhurst see to it that everything is in order and that the children are warm, clothed, and fed a nutritious diet."

Lynda Lee slipped on her sweater as did Beth.

"Begging your pardon, Mrs. Miller," Beth said, "but it seems a bit cold in here. Do the children complain of being cold?"

"Complain? Our children? Nonsense. They've nothing to complain about. We keep the heat turned low to ward off infection. Our doctors have stressed the benefits of a cool house."

"Do you provide the children with warm clothes and jackets?"

"Certainly," Mrs. Miller said. "These children are all well cared for. Mr. and Mrs. Broadhurst visit personally once a month to make sure everything is in order and that the children are safe and well."

"It's very quiet in here," Beth said. "Where are the children?"

"Most of them are in school where they should be. The youngest are upstairs in the nursery rooms."

"Can we see them?"

"I'm afraid not. Strangers always create havoc when they visit. We want to offer our children a strict schedule. Schedules keep them calm because they know what to do."

"But what about the youngest children, those who can't yet follow a schedule?"

Mrs. Miller scowled at them.

"Are you implying something, Mrs. Rogers? Your questions seem as if you believe the children here are not cared for properly."

"Not at all," Lynda Lee said. "But, if we are to make an investment, we need to know that the money will help the children."

"Who else would it help?" Mrs. Miller asked, the frown visible on her face. "Would you like to see the kitchens?"

"Yes, please."

"The younger children are having the morning snack. They won't be able to see you, but you can see them."

They followed Mrs. Miller to the entrance of the two large kitchens. The first held a long wooden table with long benches on each side. Several high chairs were stationed at intervals along the table. Though the children couldn't see them, Lynda Lee and Beth watched as some were spoon fed and others sat on the benches and ate oatmeal and drank milk. Lynda Lee counted twenty youngsters, yet not a single child said a word. The kitchen was as quiet as a sanctuary.

"See," Mrs. Miller said. "Our children are content here. While they're eating, would you care to see the nurseries? Since they're eating, your presence won't disturb them."

They followed Mrs. Miller up a flight of stairs and into two large rooms, both with wooden floors, cots dispersed throughout, and several boxes of toys along the walls. Several high chairs sat undisturbed along another wall. The wallpaper was bright and cheerful and depicted several caricatures of different kinds of animals.

Lynda Lee walked over to one of the cots and found clean sheets with two blankets folded at the end of the cot. She ran her hand over one of the blankets. They were soft and smelled nice.

"I could weave blankets if they're needed," she said to Mrs. Miller. "I do a lot of weaving."

"Orphanages always need blankets," Mrs. Miller said. "If they are soft and warm, that would make a nice donation."

"I can make sweaters and jackets, as well, if they are needed. It would be a pleasure to make warm sweaters and jackets for these little ones."

"That's kind of you," Mrs. Miller said. "Mr. Broadhurst and his wife insist that the temperature stay at a certain degree, so I'm sure that some of the children think it's cold. But they don't complain, and I'm always putting in orders for more blankets and jackets for them."

"I would be very happy to take care of that for you, Mrs. Miller," Lynda Lee said. "My favorite activities are weaving and sewing. It would be something I could contribute to the children."

"I will mention it to Mr. and Mrs. Broadhurst," she said. "If he and his wife approve, then I'll get in touch with you."

"That sounds wonderful," Lynda Lee said. "I'll write down my name and phone number before I leave."

"Shall we go, then?" Mrs. Miller asked.

As they walked toward the entrance, Lynda Lee stopped for a moment.

"May I leave a message for Julie? You see, when I was younger, I was in several beauty pageants, and I have ten or so gowns that I would be honored to donate if they would bring any money. But I have one in particular that I would like to give to Julie. It would have to be altered, but perhaps, someday, she would have need of it."

"A beauty pageant dress?" Mrs. Miller asked and knitted her brows. "Why on earth would she need such a thing?"

"Perhaps she won't always have to live at the orphanage. Some family might adopt her and she could have a normal life. Did you see to that cough she has? It worried me a bit."

"The nurse gave her some cough medicine. It's nothing contagious and nothing to worry about, but I will mention it when the doctors come."

"Thank you, Mrs. Miller. We can see that you're doing a wonderful job. We appreciate all the work you do and we're grateful to you for letting us see what a great place this is. I'll be sure to mention it to Mrs. Broadhurst when I see her," Lynda Lee said.

As they walked down the steps, Beth said quietly, "What do you think?"

"I think I want to help. I can make sweaters and jackets for the children and perhaps weave some soft blankets for them. What did you think?"

"I think that Mrs. Miller is a master manipulator," Beth said. "None of the children said a single word when they ate. The place felt like a mausoleum. There is something going on that Mrs. Miller is trying her best to hide."

Chapter 26

Mrs. Miller, after speaking on the phone with Mrs. Broadhurst, who seemed delighted about the donation, called Lynda Lee to tell her that her donation and volunteer efforts greatly pleased Mrs. Broadhurst and that yes, her donation would be welcomed. Lynda Lee spent the next few weeks at her loom and her sewing machine. She'd told Ray what she intended to do for the children and he agreed that it was something positive that would help the children and give her a sort of purpose.

"That's what you need, my dearest. You need a purpose. Making jackets and sweaters for these children is a marvelous idea. I'm almost sure the Broadhursts would agree. Apparently, on their last visit some of the children seemed to be sickly and underfed, malnourished."

"Just as I thought, Ray. The little girl I met, Julie, is such a dear, but I could tell that she hadn't had adequate care. She was far too thin. Her face was pale, and she coughed almost incessantly. I think she is sick and needs attention. Would you be able to see her?"

"Me?"

"Yes, you, Ray, or someone you know. I'm talking about a private visit. Is that at all possible?"

"Give me a minute," he said. "I'll call one of the doctors who handles the children and see what he says."

As Ray talked, Lynda Lee listened and while she listened, she smiled. She had faith in Ray to be able to pull his weight at the hospital.

He hung up and put a hand on her shoulder.

"Dr. Patterson is their doctor. The children are due to come in next week. I told him about Julie, the age, symptoms, and such. He said he'd have one of his interns see her personally and give her a thorough exam. Happy?"

"Yes," she said and stood to hug him. "I knew I could count on you, Ray. I'll feel much better when I know that Julie is okay."

"Do you know her last name? It would help us to know that. I'm sure she's not the only Julie in the bunch."

"I found out that Julie's last name is Kramer. Julie and Mark Kramer."

"Great, let me just give the doc a call and let him know. Be right back."

Lynda Lee sighed and went back to her weaving.

"Ray will fix this," she whispered to herself. "He'll see that Julie gets the care she needs."

In a few moments, Ray came back to her weaving room.

"We're all set," he said. "I've given her name to Patterson. He'll see that the intern gets it. Now, can you stop your weaving and sewing for a while? I'd like to treat you to dinner at the new restaurant that's opened in town. I took the liberty of making reservations for four. We'll take Beth and John with us."

"How nice! What kind of restaurant is it?"

"It's Chinese. The first in town. Are you willing to try it?" he asked as he held her close to him. "I love my evening hugs."

Lynda Lee kissed him lightly on the cheek.

"I really don't know much about Chinese food, but if Beth and John are going along, I'm willing to try it, but I need to change clothes and pretty myself up a bit. I've been at this loom and the sewing machine all day," she said as she straightened the materials around her into a neat pile.

"Go ahead," Ray said as he removed his jacket, took off his tie, and laid them both carefully across a chair back. Then he sat at the kitchen table where Lynda Lee had placed today's newspaper for him. He poured himself a shot glass of bourbon and called to Lynda Lee.

"Take a shower and relax. It's not a formal place, I don't think, so just wear whatever you want."

Lynda Lee ran her bare feet over the plush carpeting in their bedroom. She stood in front of the closet and chose the new blue and beige polka-dot dress she'd bought last week at Beth's insistence. The slim blue belt at the waist gave it a formal touch. She had no matching shoes, so she decided on her beige pumps.

Since she didn't have time to wash and dry her still-long dark hair, she bundled it up with several hair clips and a headband to hold it off her face. She felt the beginnings of a headache tapping at her skull, so she got her pill bottle out of one of her old purses, took two of the pain pills, and slipped the bottle back into the old handbag. A pang of guilt stabbed through her, but she felt she had no other choice but to keep them hidden.

She hadn't told Ray that she'd seen a new private doctor in town, one who had no affiliation with the hospital, who'd prescribed her a fresh bottle of pills with refills. She hadn't lied to Ray. She'd simply not mentioned it. If he found out about the pills, he'd have a fit and throw them away. He just didn't understand how much they helped her.

The new doctor had said she could be having migraine headaches, but he couldn't be sure. There was not much to do for them except take the pills at the first warning sign.

She showered quickly, dressed in record time, and added a bit of makeup, just enough to enhance her facial features. Her new lipstick, Elizabeth Arden's Red Cherry, gave her the finishing touch. She blotted her lips and smiled.

She let her hair back down and gave it one last brush, saw the sheen of it, and called, "I'm ready, Ray."

The doorbell rang just as she walked downstairs.

Beth and John stood outside the door.

"Come in," Lynda Lee said.

"I didn't know we were supposed to dress up," Beth said. She wore a pretty white blouse, a black skirt, and black flats.

"Oh, you look fine, Beth," Lynda Lee said. "This is the dress you insisted I buy on our shopping trip the other day. Do you like it?"

Lynda Lee turned in a circle to show off the blue and beige polka dot dress with a belted waist and flowing skirt.

"Of course, I like it. You look absolutely smashing in it. No matter what you wear, you're still the Undisputed Goddess of Weaver Street!"

"Will you stop with that goddess business already? I'm no goddess. I'm just an ordinary wife like you are."

"Spoken like the true goddess that you are. Whether you like the title or not, it's true. There isn't another woman in this town whose beauty comes even close to yours, and you stay exactly the same while the rest of us are battling our weight and our wrinkles! But you? No, you look just as young and slim and beautiful as the first day we all met."

"I agree," Ray said and kissed her lightly on the lips. "Now, who's hungry? Let's go find out how much we like or dislike Chinese food."

Lynda Lee smiled up at Ray, the effects of the pills beginning to make her feel much better.

"Let's go," she said.

Chapter 27

The restaurant called The China Doll looked like nothing Lynda Lee had ever seen before. The décor was a bit overdone for her taste, but it was interesting nonetheless. The wallpaper featured small Chinese figures battling dragons, battling each other, and then there was a lovely scene of a lavish Chinese garden, an ornate archway in front, being tended by many workers. The shelves behind the check-in counter were filled with red dragons and objects of all kinds, all of them Chinese.

The four of them savored the aromas that wafted from the kitchen. They inhaled the scents of exotic spices, hot oil, searing meats and vegetables, and what must have been different sauces. It was like a banquet of scents.

"What is that amazing aroma?" Ray said.

Beth sniffed the air.

"I can smell hints of ginger, garlic, anise, maybe some cinnamon."

"That's a good nose you have, Beth. The taste of the food must be wonderful."

The hostess seated them at a table with a bright red tablecloth with silverware and napkins. In the middle of the table was a basket filled with fortune cookies. Ray and John were handed menus, while Beth and Lynda Lee focused their attention on the hundreds of decorative vases and other objects scattered about the room.

"What would you suggest?" Ray asked the waitress as she put a glass of ice water in front of each of them.

The waitress looked at him and said in a very broken English, "Mongolian Beef and Happy Family," she said, "both cooked in sesame oil."

"Then, that's what we'll have. One of each."

"White rice or fried rice?" the waitress asked.

"White rice," Ray said. "All of this goes on one ticket. I'm treating us all to dinner."

The waitress nodded.

"Drinks?" she asked.

"Sweet tea," Ray said. "Is that okay with everyone?"

"I'll just have water," Beth said. "No sweet tea for me."

"Has anyone ever had Chinese food?" Ray asked as the waitress left.

They all shook their heads.

"Never," John said. "This should be interesting."

Lynda Lee put her napkin in her lap.

"I've never had it, either," she said. "What about you, Beth?"

"No, I'm not sure what to expect."

"Several of the doctors at the hospital have tried it and recommended it highly," Ray said. "We'll consider it an adventure."

Lynda Lee smiled.

The waitress brought their tea and said, "Your food is almost ready."

Ray's eyebrows shot up.

"Already?" he asked.

She nodded and put four paper-wrapped sets of chopsticks in the middle of the table.

"Chopsticks," Ray said and opened his.

"Do you know how to use those?" Lynda Lee asked. "I hope she brings us some forks."

At that moment, the waitress appeared with their dishes on a large tray.

She set two platters, each one brimming with food, in the middle of the table.

"Mongolian Beef," she said and pointed at one platter. "Happy Family," she said and pointed at the second platter. She reached behind her toward another stand that held various things.

The waitress set a large white plate at each their places and spooned white rice onto each one. Then, she reached behind her and grabbed silverware. She put a fork, knife, and spoon beside each of their platters.

"Thank you," Lynda Lee said.

"Enjoy," the waitress said, reached into her pocket and took out several packets labeled Soy Sauce and Duck sauce, something Lynda Lee had never seen before. Finally, she set the last dish on the table.

"Eggrolls," the waitress said. "Very good." Then she turned walked away.

"I think I'll just use my fork," Beth said. "I'm not sure how to use these chopsticks."

"I feel the very same, but if the food is good, we'll each learn how to use them," John said.

Beth smiled at him.

"Fork for me," Lynda Lee said. "How about you, Ray?"

"I'm taking the safe way and using my fork. But if this food is as good as the doctors say, you and I can learn how to use chopsticks, too. Okay?" he said to Lynda Lee.

"You first, Lynda Lee," Ray said. "Try a bit of each."

"I'd like an eggroll," she said. "And some of that Duck sauce.

"What is Duck sauce?" Beth asked.

"I've no idea, but I'm willing to try it," Lynda Lee said as she opened the little packet and squirted some of the sauce onto the eggroll. She picked up the eggroll and took a bite.

"Mm," she said. "You have to try the Duck sauce. It's fruity sweet but with a sour note to it. It's delicious."

"Yum," John said. "That's the way to do it. Just hold it and eat it."

"They are delicious," Beth said.

The waitress appeared again and asked them if everything was all right.

They all nodded. Then passed the two platters around. They settled in to try the food, cautiously at first, but with gusto after the first few bites.

"This is delicious," Ray said as he squirted some of the soy sauce over his food.

"I'm going to be brave and try a bit of everything," Lynda Lee said.

As she chewed her food, she said, "Oh, this is wonderful. Ray, we're going to have to learn how to use chopsticks! Surely a cardiac surgeon can figure out how to use them."

After a few moments of eating non-stop, Lynda Lee said, "Did you get a chance to talk to Dr. Patterson about Julie?"

Ray wiped his mouth.

"I did," he said. "She's coming in next week for an exam."

"Oh, I'm so grateful for that. I know the child is sick, so maybe Dr. Patterson can help her."

"Pass me some more of that Mongolian Beef," John said. "It is yummy."

"I prefer the Happy Family," Beth said. "But everything I've tried is delicious. I've heard that they use something called a wok for cooking, and they cook so hot that it takes only a minute or two."

Lynda Lee took another bite of the Mongolian Beef and savored the sweet, spicy taste of those morsels of beef mixed with green onions. When she finished chewing, she said, "I asked Ray to talk to some of his doctor friends to see if they'd agree to see Julie privately. Dr. Patterson has agreed to give her a thorough exam. Isn't that wonderful?"

"It is, yes. Are you still making clothes for them?"

"Every day I make more," Lynda Lee said. "It's fulfilling to know that my weaving and sewing might help these children stay warm. It won't be long until winter is upon us. So, I work every day to make sure they'll have warm jackets, the zippered ones that they can easily put on themselves."

"What a great idea. You're simply amazing, Lynda Lee. What can I do?" Beth asked as she finished another of the egg rolls with duck sauce. "These are delicious."

"Whatever you can think of to keep the children warm," Lynda Lee said. "I was going to weave some heavy blankets, and I still might, but I'm focusing on jackets and sweaters. I can't stand the thought of those little children being cold."

"You know what I think I'll do? Do you remember that second-hand store downtown?"

Lynda Lee nodded.

"I think I'll browse through it and see if I can find some heavy blankets. They'll be discounted, so maybe I can get several if I can find them."

"That's wonderful," Lynda Lee said. "I talked at length to Mrs. Broadhurst. She was shocked to hear of the sale they had out front. She's under the impression that the children are in very capable hands with Mrs. Miller and that if they need anything at all, Mrs. Miller would tell her."

"Did you tell her we visited?"

"Yes, I did. I commended Mrs. Miller on keeping a clean and very quiet place. I even mentioned that while the children were eating, we didn't hear one word out of them. I also said that they all were unusually pale. I don't have children, but I surely didn't think that young children and babies should be so quiet. And I did tell her that I was concerned."

Ray spoke up.

"Does anyone want this last egg roll? I just can't resist them."

"Go ahead. I'm almost full," John said.

Ray took the last of the egg rolls, covered it with another packet of duck sauce and took a bite.

"All the children were pale and not one of them made a single sound?" John asked. "That's highly unusual. Perhaps I'll pay them a visit myself. Are the children and babies allowed out in the sunshine?"

"Say, what are those cookies over there? Pass them here, please," Beth said. She pulled out a piece of white paper from one of the cookies. She chuckled then said, "Listen to this. 'Great spirits will guide your decisions.'"

"I've heard of those. I think they're called fortune cookies. Standard in Chinese restaurants," Ray said.

"I'll pass on the cookie," John said. "Feel free if you want mine."

No one took another fortune cookie. They were a bit absorbed in their conversation about the children.

"Ray," Lynda Lee said. "I do know that those children should have rosy cheeks and some form of interaction. Something just isn't right."

"John, how about the two of us pay a visit to that orphanage? We can do what Lynda Lee and Beth did. Have a look around. We'll go early around breakfast time and see for ourselves how the children behave."

"Sure, I'm game," John said, "if we can arrange the time off. They have me curious now about the state of the children."

"Good, I'll talk to Patterson and tell him we're planning on an impromptu visit, just to see for ourselves how the children are. I'm sure he'll give us an hour or so for a tour."

Lynda Lee put her hand on Ray's and smiled.

"Thank you so very much, my love. I appreciate it more than I can say."

"My curiosity is in high gear," Ray said. "If those children are sick, then I'll personally pay a visit to the Broadhursts. Those little ones are their responsibility, and I intend to make sure they're doing a good job with them. Even knowing that those babies are cold makes my skin crawl."

Lynda Lee smiled and blotted her mouth.

"The dinner was wonderful. But knowing you believe me about the children warms my heart. I know, I just know, that something is wrong there."

"If there is, we'll find it and make sure it gets fixed. I have some authority and so does John. If it takes multiple visits and a few, uh, threats along the way, then so be it. I want those children taken care of."

"Indeed," John said. "No worries, Lynda Lee. We're on mission now to keep those children healthy and to make sure their lives are as pleasant and comfortable as possible."

Lynda Lee wiped a tear from her eye.

Chapter 28

The dream came almost as soon as Lynda Lee's head hit the pillow.

She traveled up the same road, dust kicking at the hem of her ball gown, but this time, there were no large bushes or brambles to impede her. The dusty road was clean of debris.

"Maman?" she called.

"Ah, I see ye have come back," Maman said from behind her. "Ye've gone too far on this road."

Lynda Lee turned and smiled at the old weaver at her loom.

"I wanted to see you," she said. "I've missed you, Maman. What has happened to all the bushes and brambles?"

"It's the years, Child, just the years. Everything changes in time."

"You don't change, Maman. You look the very same as you did the first time I saw you."

"Now, Child, you know that looks can be deceiving. You can't always trust your eyes to see the truth."

"And what of Scaylee? Has he changed?"

"No, not much. He's down the road a piece telling his stories. The crowds get bigger each time. He's happy about that."

"Hello," Scaylee called from far down the road. "Hello, Lynda Lee. Come and join us. I'm just beginning a new story."

Lynda Lee looked at Maman.

"Should I go?"

"Do what your heart tells you, Child. That's the best way to get along in this world."

Lynda Lee bent and kissed the old weaver on the cheek.

"Thank you, Maman," she said and hurried down the road. "I'm coming, Scaylee."

When at last she joined Scaylee and the others, he took her hand and led her to a chair.

"Sit," he said. "I'm glad you're here. I think you'll like this story."

Scaylee sat on a large boulder that Lynda Lee hadn't noticed before. His feet touched the ground as he made himself comfortable. She noticed that he was clean shaven, that his teeth almost gleamed, and that he wore that beret at all times, even though he appeared to have a full head of hair. He had an olive complexion, big brown eyes with thick brows, and all in all, was quite handsome.

"Today, lads and lassies, I'm going to tell you about the bean sidhe, banshee as most of you say, but it's really pronounced as bawn sheeda."

A collective gasp came from within the crowd.

"I don't know that word," Lynda Lee said. "What is a banshee?"

Another gasp came from the crowd.

Scaylee chuckled.

"In Ireland, the banshee is a fairy woman who wails when someone is going to die. People fear her because she is believed to summon death."

Lynda Lee's eyes widened.

"She predicts death?"

"That's the tale, yes, but here is how it started. When a beloved member of a family dies, the women of the household would cry, of course." He leaned forward, "But they had a special high-pitched cry called keening to indicate their extreme grief. Sometimes, for an especially loved family member, they would hire mourners who were very good at keening. Their cries could be heard from many miles away so that everyone knew the depth of their grief."

"That was important?"

"Yes, very important," he said, his large hands emphasizing his words. "But keening was also a sort of status symbol. It meant that the person's grief was more important than the grief of someone else."

"But what does the banshee have to do with this?"

"The wail or keening of the banshee outdid the normal human cries. It was much louder, higher pitched, and the cry would last fifteen minutes or so. In about the twelfth century, though, the cry of the banshee became something different. It became a wail that meant death was approaching. The banshee was thought to be a spirit that could never be seen. So that wail coming from everywhere and nowhere became a symbol of fear and death."

"So, if someone heard the wail of the banshee, they knew that someone was going to die?"

"Exactly. The wail of the banshee meant death to someone. You can imagine how frightening it was to hear the wail all across the land. Not knowing who would be the one to die next, the people became terrified. Was the wail meant for them, for someone in their family, for their friends and neighbors?"

"Oh, I see," Lynda Lee said. "Is the banshee still around? Do people still hear her?"

"The banshee is heard even today by people all over Ireland."

"So, she's still here after all these years?"

Scaylee nodded.

"Many people have claimed to hear her. Those people believe that the wail is meant for someone in their immediate family or a close friend or relative."

Lynda Lee shifted in place.

"Scaylee, would she still be heard in my time?"

"I don't think you'd hear her, Lynda Lee. There's no evidence that the banshee appears anywhere but in Ireland and possibly some parts of Britain."

"But what about those of us who have Irish ancestry? Does the banshee come to us?"

"I'm not at all sure," Scaylee said and stood. "But I'd be interested to find out. So you let me know when you come back if you hear anything."

"I hope I don't," Lynda Lee said. "If her cry means death for someone I care about, then no, I don't want to hear it."

Chapter 29

"Lynda Lee!" the voice called. "Lynda Lee! I need help!"

She sat straight up.

Was it the banshee who called her?

"Lynda Lee!" the voice came louder. "Help me, please."

She stood, straightened herself, wiped her eyes, and went to the front door.

"Lynda Lee!" came the voice again.

As she opened the door, she heard Beth, and when she looked down she could see that Beth was sprawled on the front steps, crying in agony.

"I'm here, Beth. "What's happened to you?"

"My leg. I think I've broken my leg. I tripped going up the stairs and fell. I heard the bones crunch when I fell. Please call an ambulance. It hurts, Lynda Lee. It really hurts."

Lynda Lee ran back to the kitchen and called for an ambulance.

"My friend has fallen and she thinks her leg is broken. We're on Weaver Street, 625 Weaver Street. Please hurry."

She hung up and dialed Ray's office.

He picked up immediately.

"Lynda Lee, is something wrong?" he asked as he shuffled through the papers on his desk.

"Ray, Beth has fallen on the front steps. I've called an ambulance, but you might want to warn John. Beth thinks she's broken her leg."

"Stay with her. I'll find John and tell him. Are you okay?"

Lynda Lee's hands shook as she spoke.

"I'm fine, but Beth is in terrible pain."

"I'll double check that call for an ambulance and then find John. He'll meet you both in the ER."

Lynda Lee felt tears rolling down her cheeks. She grabbed a dish towel and blotted them away. Beth didn't need to see her so upset. She needed to be strong now.

"The ambulance is on its way, Beth. It won't be long."

"I'm in such pain, Lynda Lee."

Lynda Lee squatted next to her friend and patted her on the shoulder.

"Hang on, Beth. Just hang on for a few minutes. I talked to Ray. He's going to find John so that he can meet you in the ER. Everything will be fine."

When Lynda Lee heard the siren, she ran to the edge of the road and flagged down the ambulance.

"She's here!" she called and pointed to the front steps.

The crew wasted no time getting to Beth, checking her vitals, and gently lifting her to a gurney.

"You're going to be fine," one of them said.

"Lynda Lee, come with me. Please, come with me."

"Is it all right?"

"Are you family?"

"YES!" Beth cried. "YES!"

Lynda Lee climbed into the ambulance and held Beth's hand while the vehicle sped toward the hospital. Suddenly, her mind was filled with images of the tale Scaylee told about the wail of the banshee. But then she realized that the banshee's call meant that someone would die. Beth was in pain, but she wouldn't die from a broken leg.

"Beth, I'm here. Don't worry," Lynda Lee said. "John will meet us in the ER and the doctors will take good care of you."

"It doesn't hurt anymore," Beth said as her eyes fluttered and closed.

"Beth? Beth?"

"We gave her something for the pain. It will make her sleepy," one of the crew said. "We're only three minutes away now."

Several hours later, Ray and Lynda Lee sat with John in the hospital's cafeteria. They each ordered the Special of the Day, a roast beef sandwich with lettuce and tomato, a bag of potato chips, a slice of apple pie topped with ice cream, and a glass of iced tea. They took their trays to a table nearby.

"How are you feeling, John?" Ray asked as he spread mustard on his sandwich. "Did you see the x-rays?"

"The break is pretty bad, but thank goodness it was just her ankle," John said as he took a bite of his sandwich.

"Why would that have caused her such pain?" Lynda Lee asked. "She was convinced that her leg was broken."

John wiped his mouth with the napkin.

"The ankle bone is shattered. I'm not sure how it happened, but pain always radiates in a situation like this. So, I'm sure she felt pain throughout her entire leg. It's going to be a long haul for her. Did you see the x-rays, Ray?"

Ray nodded and took a sip of tea.

"Surgery is her only option, in my opinion. Without it, that ankle might never heal."

"I agree," John said. "Who's the best orthopedic surgeon we know?"

"I'd say Larry Johnson has the best reputation. Anyone else you can think of?" Ray asked as he took a bite of the apple pie. "This is delicious. Lynda Lee, you've barely touched your food. You need to eat something. Beth's going to need your help, so you have to keep yourself fit as a fiddle for her."

Lynda Lee took the first bite of her sandwich.

"It's not very good," she said. "I'll just have my pie."

"Pie's just a dessert," Ray said. "You need food, Lynda Lee. Please, finish at least half of your sandwich. Try it with some mustard and mayo," he said as he passed them toward her. "And a little salt and pepper."

Lynda Lee did as she was told and finally took another bite of the sandwich.

"That's much better," she said as she chewed.

Ray smiled and patted her hand.

"That's my girl," he said.

"Do you know Dr. Johnson well?" John asked Ray.

"Pretty well," Ray said. "He's on the floor a good bit, and I see his interns regularly. I know he's capable because he has such a fine reputation among the nurses and staff. It's the nurses, you know, who spread the word about doctors!"

John smiled.

"I'm well aware of their skill and their influence. You know the one on the sixth floor they call the Admiral?"

Ray chuckled.

"I think everyone knows her. She's a real stickler for written orders. Isn't she the one who called one of the doctors when she thought his orders were incomplete?"

"That's right! I'd forgotten about that. But it was a good lesson for all of us. And we surely can't complain when she takes her job so seriously. The patients brag about her all the time. The doctors, not so much," John said and chuckled.

"Did you know that she's enrolled in med school to become a doctor?"

"I don't see how she finds the time to go to school and work as many hours as she does," John said as he took the last bite of his sandwich and dug into the apple pie.

"I don't either, but I did a letter of recommendation for her. Occasionally, she drops by my office to ask a question or to brag about making good marks. I'm happy for her."

"That was good," Lynda Lee said as she took the last bite of her sandwich. "Now, let's try the apple pie. I'm so glad you're helping one of the nurses, Ray. That's very kind of you."

"By the time she finishes her medical training, she'll be both a certified RN and a medical doctor, as well. She is determined to get that medical license, so I'll help all I can."

"What field of medicine is she interested in?" John asked.

"Cardiology," Ray said, "which is why she asked me for a letter. Apparently, her husband suffers from heart disease. He's a young man, too. They don't have children, so I think her goal is to be able to help him as well as her patients."

"Goodness," John said. "She's in it for the long haul. That's what, about six more years of her life?"

"About that, yes, but she is a determined woman who is already an RN. That degree and training will knock off some time, I'm sure.

I'd say she can finish in five years if she keeps going the way she is now," Ray said as he took the last bite of his apple pie and leaned back in his chair. He patted his stomach. "I'm full, can't eat another bite. Not bad for cafeteria food."

"What is her name?" Lynda Lee asked as she sipped her tea.

"I think her name is Ellen Daniels, but we all refer to her as the nurses do: The Admiral."

"But surely they don't call her that to her face. That's quite rude."

"No, I'm sure they call her Nurse Daniels."

"Well, I wish her the best of luck," Lynda Lee said.

After a moment, Lynda Lee said, "Ray, do you think Nurse Daniels might want a handmade jacket for her or for her husband? I'm working at the loom and the sewing machine every day, and I'm already making jackets. It wouldn't be any trouble to make an extra."

"She wears some colorful sweaters over her scrubs, so she might enjoy a light sweater."

Lynda Lee smiled.

"We'd better go check on Beth," she said.

"I thought I might just let her rest. She was asleep when we left, and right now, she needs all the rest she can get."

"Is it all right if I just peek in on her very quietly?"

"Sure," John said. "We'll all go and see how she's doing."

Chapter 30

Two weeks later, in June of 1964, Weaver Street was abuzz with the news that Beth was home and recovering from surgery on her ankle. Janine and Sarah checked in on her every day, and with Lynda Lee's help, they made sure that someone was available all the time. They took turns cooking delicious casseroles and making fresh salads for Beth and John. Their refrigerator was filled with all sorts of goodies, including pitchers of sweet iced tea and occasionally, lemonade.

Beth was fond of lemonade and her friends made sure she didn't run out of it. Lynda Lee used her baking skills to provide blueberry muffins, Beth's favorites, and chocolate cake for John. And while she was in the kitchen, she'd whip up a spaghetti casserole or one of their favorites: scalloped potato and ham casserole topped with melted cheese. Then, she'd make a side dish of a healthy vegetable: green beans, baked asparagus, or a fresh salad with lettuce, tomatoes, radishes, and carrots.

In his wisdom, John, against Beth's wishes, had hired a temporary live-in nurse to both see to Beth's needs and to help her with physical therapy. Beth's foot and ankle were in a cast up to her knee, but with physical therapy every day, Beth had managed to steady herself on a walker so that she could stand. She was not allowed to put any weight at all on her ankle, so the cast had to stay up off the ground.

The ladies of Weaver Street worked like a well-oiled machine. With Beth as their primary focus, they worked extra duty to keep both their own homes clean and their husbands happy and to do the same with Beth and John. When Ray had to work overnight shifts, Lynda

Lee often went to Beth's house and played a game of Canasta with her until John came home since John, too, had been bitten by the Cardiology Specialty bug.

Lynda Lee surprised herself when she realized that she had become a harsh taskmaster. She found herself saying no to many of Beth's requests to get up and about and made sure that she followed a strict schedule for meals, snacks, and most of all, physical therapy. Since the nurse was always there, Lynda Lee assisted when it was time for therapy every day. And when she was there in the evenings, she continued following a strict schedule.

The therapy was especially difficult for Beth. She almost always cried with pain and frustration afterwards. Lynda Lee thought of offering her one of her pain pills but John had insisted that she stick to the pills the doctor prescribed. Even though they didn't work very well to ease the pain, Lynda Lee could only watch and hold back tears as Beth cried in pain. But she knew enough about medicine that she stopped herself every time she thought of giving Beth one of her stronger pain pills.

Lynda Lee's doctor had given her a new prescription weeks earlier. After the examination, he found nothing that would cause such headaches. But since she obviously suffered, he prescribed a milder pain pill. He told her to take two if the pain was severe.

"I'd say that you're suffering from headaches caused from stress. Anxiety and stress can certainly affect our systems, and a headache can be the result of that stress. There isn't another physical reason that I can find to explain the headaches."

That evening when Ray came home, he asked about her doctor's visit.

"Did he figure out what's causing the headaches?"

Lynda Lee shook her head.

"No, he couldn't find a physical cause. He said that the headaches were most likely caused from stress."

"Stress?"

Lynda Lee nodded.

"Stress?" he asked again. "What do you have to be stressed about? You have everything you could want or need. You have a lovely bunch of friends. You spend your time doing what you love, weaving and sewing for the children at the orphanage. You're only thirty-one,

Lynda Lee. You're young and healthy and you have practically everything you could want. What is it about your life that causes you such stress?"

Lynda Lee didn't answer. Instead, she turned and walked into the kitchen. She stood at the stove stirring a pot of spaghetti sauce.

Ray followed her and sat at the kitchen table.

"Tell me, Lynda Lee. What is causing you stress?"

"Nothing, Ray. It's just that sometimes, I'm not happy. It's as if I'm searching for something that I just can't find."

Ray stood beside her and took her hand. He kissed it gently.

"I wish I could understand, sweetheart, but I don't. We have everything a couple could want. We're living what people call the American Dream," he said and hugged her. "We don't need anything more."

Lynda Lee hugged him tightly then turned back to her cooking.

"Go change clothes and get out of that suit. I'll just make a fresh salad to go with the spaghetti," she said and opened the refrigerator to get lettuce, carrots, green onions, and radishes.

"See?" he said. "I knew you couldn't be suffering too much about your life. You're the Goddess of Weaver Street, still as beautiful as the first day we met. Your friends adore you, and you've been a Godsend for those children you're helping. Your husband loves you so much he can't even put it into words. You have everything, Lynda Lee, the perfect life. That's what I've worked so hard to give you, what I've wanted the most for you."

Lynda Lee didn't smile.

"Dinner will be ready soon."

Ray stood up straight and saluted her.

"Yes, Ma'am," he said as he walked from the room.

When she was sure he'd gone, she took one of her pills from the bottle and swallowed it. Then she took a deep breath.

"Everything will be fine," she whispered to herself. "Just hang in there. Everything will work out."

Chapter 31

For the next two weeks, the ladies of Weaver Street busied themselves with the task of making sure Beth and John had everything they needed: food, drinks, and entertainment.

Lynda Lee had told Beth about the new doctor and the lack of a proper diagnosis to explain the headaches.

"Did he say it might be migraines?" Beth asked from the sofa. "My mother had those. They were terrible."

"No, he said they might be but eventually, he changed his mind and said they were probably just stress headaches."

"Oh, well stress can do that to you," Beth said. "If I get really nervous about something, I always suffer with a headache afterwards. I know from experience that stress causes a lot of different ailments, including headaches."

Lynda Lee sat on a chair beside the sofa.

"Really?"

"Oh, of course," Beth said. "I'm a living example of it. The thing is that you have to attack the attacker. In other words, you need to try to find out what is stressing you so much and then get rid of it. It's not easy, but it works."

"But how do you find out what the stressor is? I wasn't even aware that I'm stressed."

"Well," Beth said and scooted back on her pillows. "I was working when John and I were first married. I didn't mind the work at all, and we needed it to make ends meet."

Lynda Lee chuckled.

"I remember those days perfectly," she said. "It was a struggle to get by. We did it, but it took a great deal of time and effort."

"Yes, it did. When I started getting headaches, I passed it off to just being tired. I worked a full-time shift at a retail store, and sometimes, if I could get them, overtime hours were available. So, I ended up working my eight-hour shift plus an extra four hours in the evening. You wouldn't think four extra hours would hurt anyone, but after a year of doing this, I began to get severe headaches."

"All those hours," Lynda Lee said. "You were probably working more than John was!"

"But the pay was really good. My paycheck kept us in groceries and kept the bills paid. John's salary went into savings, so we were making headway with our plans."

"Plans?" Lynda Lee asked and took a sip of iced tea.

"Yes, our plans for a home and a family. We eventually found a nice little house, paid cash for it, and we were happy there. Our own home, our own yard, our own garden. It was the perfect place for us."

"And," Lynda Lee said, "what happened?"

Beth chuckled.

"Hearts," she said. "Cardiac surgery. When John decided that he wanted to learn from the best, we moved here to Alabama. At that time, it had the leading cardiac team in the nation. And that's how we ended up here in Tuscaloosa."

"And here on Weaver Street," Lynda Lee said.

Beth nodded.

"Yep," she said. "I occasionally miss my little house, but the place here has become my home. I love the apartment, my friends, all of it. I'm happy here. Are you happy here, Lynda Lee?"

Lynda Lee didn't answer immediately. She stared out the window for a moment.

"Ray says we have the perfect life," she said. "He says I have everything a woman could ask for and then some."

Beth fussed with her blankets.

"But what do *you* say, Lynda Lee? Do you have a perfect life?"

"More tea?" she asked. "I need a refill."

"No, I'm fine," Beth said.

When Lynda Lee returned with her refill, she sat in the chair opposite the sofa.

"I'll answer your question now," she said.

"Oh, good," Beth said. "I thought you were ignoring me."

"No," she said and took a sip of sweet tea. "I wasn't ignoring you. We've been friends now for a long time, almost thirteen years, isn't it? We moved in at the same time in 1950, and now, it's 1963, so we have quite a history together. Beth, I just didn't quite know what to say to your question, but if you want to listen, I'll tell you about my perfect life"

Beth rubbed her hands together.

"Oh, this should be exciting! Tell me."

"First of all, do you promise and swear that you will never tell another living soul? Not even John, especially not John, and none of our friends. Will you promise to keep my secret?"

"So, this is a special *secret* secret?"

Lynda Lee leaned forward.

"Yes, a very special one that absolutely cannot be shared, not with anyone."

"Oh my, are you a serial killer in disguise?" Beth asked and chuckled.

Lynda Lee laughed.

"I wish it were that simple," she said.

"So, come on, tell me. I've got goosebumps in anticipation."

"First, you have to promise."

Beth grabbed Lynda Lee's hands.

"I give you my solemn promise that I will never tell anyone what you're going to share with me. Whatever it is, it's a secret between us, a bond that only we will share for the rest of our lives. Hand me that bag of chips, if you don't mind."

Lynda Lee gave Beth the chips and sat back in the chair to find her comfy spot.

"I do have a perfect place, yes, but it's not here, Beth. As far as I know, it exists only in my dreams. But there is a part of me that believes that the dream place is my true home. It's where I'm meant to be."

"Well, where is it?"

"Galway, Ireland, with a group of people I love as if they are my true family."

"Have you ever been to Ireland?"

Lynda Lee shook her head.

"Go on," Beth said and wiped her nose with a tissue. "Tell me all about it."

Chapter 32

"Mercy, Lynda Lee, that is quite a dream," Beth said when she'd finished listening. "And you are certain that you've never been there before?"

"I've never been, but I hope to go very soon," she said and took a sip of water.

"It won't be the same, I fear," Beth said. "Do you know the exact year it is in the dream?"

"I'm not sure. Maman talks about war and soldiers, then about weaving clothes for them. One strange thing about it is that Maman's tiny little cottage has changed. When I first saw it, it was nothing more than a hovel. But the last time I saw it, it had been entirely renovated, almost as if it were brand new. When I asked her about it, Maman said, 'It's the years, Child. Just the years.'"

Beth cocked her head.

"Apparently, time passes quickly between one dream and the other. What does Ray say about the dreams?"

"Mostly, he dismisses them, so I've stopped telling him about what happens in the dreams. He scoffs and tells me it's just a dream and it means nothing."

Beth scooted back on her pillows and covered her legs with a thick blanket then took a sip of her iced tea.

Lynda Lee dug in her purse to find her bottle of pills. She went into the kitchen, took out two pills and swallowed them with water. Then she walked back into the living room. She was prepared for the headaches now, so she just kept going, doing her normal routine, visiting and helping her friends. When the threat of a headache reared its ugly head, she simply took a pill or two to stop it.

And not a single one of the ladies of Weaver Street noticed.

"But what if it isn't nothing," Beth said, interrupting her reverie. "What if there is a reason that you keep having these same dreams over and over? Is there a message in them, something you haven't quite figured out? Some warning or direction?"

"I keep thinking the very same thing," Lynda Lee said. "Otherwise, why would I keep having these dreams? I've bought several books about dreams and recurring dreams. But they're not really helpful. A recurring dream is the mind's attempt at a solution for an unresolved and persistent conflict in a person's life."

"So," Beth said, "do you have something like that in your life? Something that just won't go away? Perhaps something you want that you can't have. Or something you're hiding from Ray?"

Lynda Lee took off her shoes and propped her feet on the coffee table.

"There's only one thing I want that I haven't been able to get. I want very much to go to Galway, Ireland. We have plenty of money for a trip, but Ray's work schedule, like John's, is grueling. He hardly ever has a day off, and when he does, we go out to dinner at the Relay House. Then we come home. That's it."

"So, why do you have to go with Ray? You asked us all earlier if we would get passports and take a trip to Ireland together. So, we could do this as a group, couldn't we?"

"Janine's been to France, hasn't she?" Lynda Lee asked.

Lynda Lee glanced at her watch.

"Oh, mercy," she said. "I have work to do, Beth. I'm still making some sweaters and coats for the children at Broadhurst. Winter will be here soon, and I don't want those children to be cold. Did I mention that scuttlebutt is that Mrs. Mitchell might lose her job?

"Really? That terrible Mrs. Mitchell?"

Lynda Lee nodded.

Beth moved around on the sofa.

"Didn't you think that something was terribly wrong when all those precious children were eating and not a single sound came from them?" Lynda Lee said. "They were like little robots. It frightened me, but I can't explain why."

Lynda Lee grabbed her purse.

"I've not been around too many small children, but there was definitely something terribly wrong with their behavior. You're right, Beth. They were like little robots, even the smallest ones. Babies and toddlers are famous for the noises they make, but these babies didn't make a sound."

"Maybe we should plan another visit. You can donate some jackets and sweaters. And as soon as I'm able to put some weight on this foot, we'll get the girls and pay another unannounced visit to the orphanage. How's that?"

"A perfect plan," Lynda Lee said. "See you tomorrow, and be sure to call me if you need my help. May I get you anything before I leave?"

"I'm perfectly content," Beth said. "Janine will be here shortly."

Chapter 33

By the end of the next week, Lynda Lee had finished ten heavy sweaters and five warm jackets. She'd also made Julie a special sweater embroidered with her name on it. She had spent every waking moment at her loom and her sewing machine. Ray understood her mission to help the children and didn't complain about a week's worth of warming over the pan of lasagna, along with a casserole of potatoes in cream of chicken soup topped with multiple cheeses, or simple fresh salads with crunchy lettuce, ripe tomatoes, little green onions, slices of chicken or beef, and warm, homemade bread. With his erratic work schedule, he ate whenever he came in and never said a harsh word about having to warm his own dinner.

He didn't even complain about cleaning up after himself, though Lynda Lee had told him that she'd clean when she was through for the night. But he ignored her and washed his dishes, put them in the drainer, then left the kitchen. When he returned wearing his shorts and tee shirt, he got a cup of coffee, and sat in his recliner to read the newspaper.

On this particular night, Lynda Lee said, "I think I've finished for now. I've done ten sweaters and five jackets. I'm exhausted, Ray."

"That's quite an accomplishment," he said. "I do hope the children will be grateful for the work you've put into this. Honestly, though, sweetheart, you're looking a bit haggard. I think sleep would be good for you. Have you been eating properly, taking care of yourself?"

"I eat when I get hungry," she said. "So, yes, I'm taking care of myself, but I'm tired, and this headache just won't go away."

"Speaking of those headaches, do you think we need to find another specialist? Maybe a neurologist who might be able to find a cause for them?"

"My doctor is a headache specialist, mostly for migraines, but he says my headaches are not typical migraines. They're likely caused by some unknown stress. But they're no better or worse than they were, so I don't see a need for another doctor."

Ray got up out of his recliner and walked over to her.

"It's time for you to go to bed and get some rest," he said. "Rest will help you. You're exhausted and you're probably on the verge of being dehydrated. So, do what I've been telling you, please. Drink a full glass of water when you take your night meds. Then drift away into some easy, peaceful sleep."

He stroked the side of her face.

"Will you do that for me?"

Lynda Lee smiled.

"A full glass of water, right before bed?"

Ray nodded.

"I'll be up all night running to the bathroom," she said.

"Okay, well, tonight, take your meds as usual," Ray said. "Then, in the morning when you take your vitamins, drink the full glass of water. Do it for me?"

"You honestly think water is going to help this headache?

"No, it won't help the headache, but it will keep you from getting dehydrated and ending up in the hospital. So, take your pick. Drink a glass of water twice during the day, or end up in the hospital with dehydration."

"You're so demanding," she said and smiled. "How have I put up with these demands all these years?"

Ray chuckled.

"I'm leaving you a note. Two full glasses of water per day."

"Well, I have to have my coffee, Ray."

"You can have your coffee as long as you have your water, as well."

Lynda Lee got out of her chair.

"I know how I'll be spending my time," she said. "It's a good thing I've finished those sweaters and jackets."

"Would you like for me to deliver those for you on my way in tomorrow? The orphanage is only a block from the hospital."

Lynda Lee walked toward the bedroom and grabbed a towel from the cabinet. Then she turned on the shower.

"Not necessary, dearest husband. Beth and Janine and I will deliver the goods ourselves. Three of us against that nasty Mrs. Miller. Surely she won't turn us away."

"Why would she?"

"She says that the Broadhursts take care of all the clothing for winter."

Ray chuckled.

"How often do they visit during cold weather?"

"I doubt they even leave their own home," Lynda Lee said as she stepped into the shower. "I'll be through in a few minutes. Then we can talk some more. Go to bed, Ray. You're as tired as I am."

When Lynda Lee finished her shower and dried her hair, she put on her pajamas and walked into the bedroom, where she found Ray with the covers scrunched around him. She slipped quietly into bed beside him. Once she had taken her pills, she drifted into sleep.

Her nap dream took over her night sleep.

Chapter 34

Lynda Lee found herself on a dirt road, this one with tiny rocks that dug into her bare feet. Her long gown made a dust trail behind her, and when she bent to look at it, she found that the bottom of her gown had holes in it where the rocks had torn it.

She stood confused in the middle of the rocky road. No one answered when she called, "Maman." No sound, no movement, nothing she recognized.

The land around her looked barren.

Where were the trees? Where was the cottage? Had she mistakenly climbed onto the wrong road?

"Maman," she called again. "Where are you, Maman?"

Only silence met her call, so she started walking, the rocks stinging her feet. Several times she called out to Maman but got no answer, but she kept walking, desperately searching for anyone who could tell her what had happened.

And when she thought she couldn't take another step, she saw the old weaver at her loom directly ahead of her.

"Maman!" she called and ran toward her. She dropped to her knees beside the old woman.

"Oh, Maman," she said. "I was lost. I couldn't find you anywhere. My heart nearly burst wide open to think I wouldn't be able to find you."

"Whatever is the matter, Child? I've been right here all along at my loom, right outside the cottage."

"No, no," Lynda Lee said. "You were not there when I came up to the road. The trees were gone. The cottage was gone, and you … you were not there at your loom, Maman. I searched and couldn't find you."

"Child, I have been right here all along. I have not moved. There is so much work to do with the uprisings. The North is always against the Republic, picking fights over nothing. And now, the Republic itself has its own civil wars, so our soldiers need my help. They need warm clothes. I've been at this loom for days."

"But how is that possible? I looked everywhere for you."

"Stand up, Child. Look around you."

"Everything is in place, Maman, just as it should be."

"Exactly. You took a wrong road, Child."

Lynda Lee shook her head.

"No," she said, "there has only ever been one road, Maman."

"Roads are like choices, Child. There is always more than one."

"So, for all these years, I've taken the right road, but today, I took the wrong one?"

Maman nodded.

Lynda Lee sat on the stool beside Maman.

"I never knew," she said. "I've always let the dream lead me and for me, there was always only one road. Now, I must worry that I will take the wrong road again, and I might lose you and Scaylee and the cottage forever. I might never find you again, Maman, and if you are not in my life, I don't want my life."

"Oh, but you must make the most of your life while you can, Child. You must do everything in your power to make your life one of meaning and purpose, a life meant to help those in need."

Lynda Lee shook her head.

"No, no, I cannot go on if I know that I will lose you. I simply can't. I love the life here so much more than I love my life on Weaver Street."

Maman stopped her weaving and took Lynda Lee's hands in hers.

"Child," she said, "you must listen. Your life on Weaver Street is important. It is the place chosen for you to do good works. Didn't you just make sweaters and jackets for those poor children in the orphanage?"

"How did you know about that?" Lynda Lee asked, cherishing the feel of the old woman's warm, ancient hands in hers.

Maman smiled.

"There is more work to be done, Child. There is always more work to be done. Remember that and do what you can to help those around you."

Lynda Lee lowered her head.

"It's so hard, Maman, to do the work with these headaches. My husband thinks I'm a drug addict because I take pills for the pain. But my doctor found no cause for them. No one listens when I tell them I'm suffering."

Maman squeezed her hands tighter.

"Then say nothing about your suffering. Just take your medicine and go on about your business."

"Is that the key, Maman? Keep my suffering to myself and just take my pills?"

Maman let go of her hands and went back to her weaving.

"Lynda Lee," Ray said as he shook her gently. "I'm leaving for work. Don't forget about dinner tonight. I thought we'd go to the Relay House with the new doctor and his wife. Remember?"

Lynda Lee blinked her eyes.

"I'm gone," Ray called as he left. Then he opened the door again. "Please don't forget about dinner."

Chapter 35

Lynda Lee showered and washed her long dark hair. Since Ray had purchased a new hand-held dryer for her, the task of drying her newly-washed hair was much easier, though the dryer was heavy and she couldn't hold it for too long.

For almost an hour, she stood in front of the mirror and dried her thick hair. She stopped occasionally and checked for any signs of gray that might be growing, but happily, she found none. Graying at the temples was handsome on Ray, but Lynda Lee and her years of experience with beauty pageants convinced her that gray was fine for men but not for women. For once, she thought her mother might agree with her.

She glanced at the clock and found she had at least another hour before Ray came home, so with the drying complete, she waited for only a few minutes before she removed the large rollers from her hair. She didn't brush it right away. She simply let the rolls set and cool, a trick she learned from her mother during her days as a beauty queen.

She and Ray had seen her mother and father only a few times since they'd been married. Every visit turned out the same. Her mother still criticized her furniture choices, her manner of dress, her cooking, and anything else she could think of, but Lynda Lee had learned that, to her, the criticism didn't sting anymore. She had accepted that she could never please her mother and so her caustic words didn't faze her anymore.

Lynda Lee knew that her design skills, her dress, and her cooking were completely acceptable to all of her friends and most of all, to Ray. In fact, Ray still complimented her on all of them. He rarely criticized her at all, except for the use of pain pills, which she had learned to hide from him. She had learned how to be a good wife, a good friend, and someone who was admired by those who knew her.

A year ago, when she'd received word that her father had passed away, she and Ray went to New York City for the funeral. They'd stayed three days with her mother, and in those three days, her mother had seemed smaller, weaker, and less critical. Her father had left a hefty insurance policy so that her mother would never have to work. And, he'd also left Lynda Lee not only money, but one of their three homes in New York City.

It took days for her and Ray to decide what to do about the home, finally choosing to keep it and let the renters continue to live there. The house was in a wealthy gated community populated by New York's elite. Lynda Lee knew many of them, and even though a part of her dreamed of going back to New York City, she knew that Ray's work would keep them on Weaver Street for a very long time. She just couldn't bring herself to let go of the property, so she and Ray visited the tenants and spent an afternoon going over the details of the rental agreement.

She explained carefully that she would maintain ownership of the home, but that the tenants, who'd lived there for almost five years, would agree to pay their rent on time, and keep up the home in its current pristine condition. Should any emergency repairs be needed, the tenants would send her an invoice and that amount would be subtracted from the rent payment. It was the way her father conducted the original transaction, so Lynda Lee followed his plan. The tenants agreed and signed a new five-year contract, this time with Ray's name added to hers as owner.

"Are you interested at all in selling us the house?" the wife asked.

"No," Lynda Lee said. "My father left his house to me, and I want to keep it, to honor him. If you are unhappy here, I can find other renters."

"We love the house," the wife said. "But will you promise to let us know if you decide to change your mind? We'd hoped to buy it one day."

Lynda Lee smiled.

"Of course. The house looks beautiful. I can see how well you've maintained it, and if we change our minds and want to sell, you'll be the first to know. I think we would even be willing to take what you've paid in rent so far as a down payment. But, for now, I want to keep my father's house."

Lynda Lee took a deep breath. Today marked the one-year anniversary of her father's death. Did Ray remember? She took a chance, and while she was choosing the perfect outfit for dinner, she dialed her mother's phone number.

"Mother, it's me, Lynda Lee. I just wondered how you're doing."

"Well, of course, I'm doing just fine," her mother said. "I miss your father, but an old friend has moved in with me, and we get along just fine. Do you remember Melba Roosevelt?"

"Oh yes, I think so. She sponsored several of the scholarship programs at beauty school, didn't she?"

"Yes, she did. Her husband died a few years back, so I called just to talk to her, old times revisited and all."

"And she's moved into the house with you?"

"She has, and we are doing fine. Neither of us has to worry about money, so we spend our time shopping, going to lunch with friends, and of course, working with the charities."

"I'm so glad to hear it. Is there anything I can do for you, Mother?"

"You? Nothing I can think of."

"Will you let me know if I can help you in any way?" Lynda Lee asked as she grabbed a new bright pink beaded sheath dress from the closet.

"I will, but honestly, I saw you just a year ago, and since Melba is here, we are both doing fine. Have you heard from the tenants at your house? Are they paying their rent on time? You father would be livid if … never mind. It's your house now."

"The tenants are lovely people, and yes, they pay their rent like clockwork every month."

"I really need to get ready. Melba and I are going out for dinner tonight."

"Okay, Mother. I'm glad to hear that you're doing so well. If you need …."

Without a goodbye, her mother hung up.

Lynda Lee stared at the phone for a few seconds. Then, she hung it up.

"She'll never love you," she whispered to herself and sighed.

Her mind went to dinner tonight and the beaded pink sheath dress she'd chosen. It fell just below her knees and had a matching beaded waist-length jacket.

She'd had shoes dyed to match the exact shade of pink. She carefully laid the dress and jacket on the bed as she removed the tags. Then, she brushed out her hair, used a pink headband to hold it off her face, and did her makeup. A dab of foundation, a light dusting of powder, a hint of rouge, and her brand-new Max Factor lipstick called Pink Yum Yum. She stood back and turned her head this way and that to make sure her makeup was smooth and perfect. She blotted her lips, smiled and added just a touch of shine to her lipstick, the little brush perfectly centered on her bottom lip. As she touched her lips together, the shine did exactly what she wanted. It gave her a hint of pearly shine, just a hint.

As she slipped on her pantyhose, then into her half-slip, the phone rang.

"Are you ready?" Ray asked.

"Only a few more minutes. I'm dressing now."

"Good girl. I'll see you in about twenty minutes. Okay?"

"I'll be ready," she said.

She unzipped her new sheath, stepped into it, and somehow managed to zip it by herself. Then she slipped on the matching jacket and stepped into her new pink shoes. She turned this way and that, checking to make sure that she looked her very best with no slip showing, nothing out of place, and her hair and makeup perfect. She removed the pink beaded headband, saw the tiny tag on it and quickly cut it off. Then she brushed one last time through her hair and put on the sparkly headband.

An image came to her immediately. She saw herself on a runway in the swimsuit competition. Instead of letting her long hair flow, her mother had insisted that she wear a sparkly headband to keep her hair off her face. The headband, though, was tight and uncomfortable and gave her a terrible headache. She could remember vividly jerking it off her head after the swimsuit portion of the pageant.

She shook her head and adjusted her new headband. It was comfortable, not too tight and the perfect complement to her outfit. But again, the headache began to throb at her temples. She grabbed her pill bottle, took two of the pills and went to the door just as Ray pulled up.

Chapter 36

"Oh, look," Lynda Lee said. "Look at this sign! Is there a fashion show here tonight? Ray, look, the sign says, September 24th, 1964. There's a fashion show tonight. Can we stay for it?"

Ray looked at the sign and furrowed his brow.

"A fashion show? Here? That can't be right. Let me find Mr. Bugg."

Ray returned shortly.

"The sign is right. It's a special benefit to raise money for a group called Women's Progressive Coalition. It's headed by the governor's wife and run by other political women. Any money they make goes to strengthening their cause."

"I didn't even know about that group."

"Well, maybe they'll have a pretty dress for you to buy. Don't worry. It's only for an hour. Let's go to the dining room. Beth, you and John use the elevator. Linda and I will take the stairs."

"Lynda is strictly a stairs person, which probably explains one of the reasons she's stayed so slim all these years while the rest of us have put on weight. John, let's take this one. It's close."

"Well, I do love my evening walks around the community on Weaver Street, and now that we have a beautiful paved pathway, the walks are even better. And, we have some new, very powerful, street lights now. I feel as if I'm taking a morning stroll, except for the heat of course. Summers here in Alabama are so hot!"

"What about in New York City? Aren't the summers hot there, too?" Beth asked and pushed the button to hold the elevator as the others piled in.

"Well, sure they are, but it's different. I spent most of my time indoors or in a car getting back and forth. Our driver always made sure we were comfortable no matter what the weather."

"Your driver? You had a driver?"

"Yes, his name was Max. Very kind man."

Ray held out his arm.

"Now, allow me to escort the Goddess of Weaver Street to the dining room. By the way, you look stunning this evening. I like the way you have your hair. That sparkly headband is quite the show-stopper."

Lynda Lee smiled, took Ray's arm, and headed up the flight of stairs.

"Thank you," she said. "I hoped you'd like it."

"Well, as I've said before, you could wear anything or nothing and you'd be the most beautiful woman in the room, no matter where we went."

Lynda Lee giggled.

"You're such a charmer, Ray. Besides, I'm older now, 34, and I doubt if I could still hold my title of the Goddess of Weaver Street. I've seen Dr. Grant's wife. She is a beauty."

Ray chuckled.

"You've never understood just how lovely you are, Lynda Lee. I'm a very fortunate man to be married to such a stunning woman," he said as he led her into the dining room. "There's our table. Ready to join the others?"

Just then, Mr. Bugg appeared.

"Good evening," he said in his strange accent. "Are you dining with the others?"

"Yes, there will be a group of us," Lynda Lee said, "and Mr. Bugg, I'd love a platter of those French cheeses if you have them."

He smiled as he led them to their table. John and Beth were already seated, as were Dr. Grant and his wife, Elizabeth. Sarah, Laura, and Janine seemed to be running a bit late. But then, just as they were taking their seats, they heard Janine's voice.

"We're here," she called and waved as she and Sarah walked in with their husbands. When they seated themselves, Janine said, "Laura can't make it. Luke is not feeling well tonight, so she's taking care of him."

Ray said, "Do all of you know Dr. Grant and his wife, Elizabeth?"

"Yes," Janine said. "I think we've all met at least once before. Elizabeth, you look beautiful tonight. I love the French twist in your hair."

Elizabeth smiled.

"Thank you," she said softly.

Mr. Bugg appeared at the table with a rolling tray of ice water, sweet tea, and coffee.

He placed a glass of ice water beside each plate.

"We have both sweet tea and coffee," he said. "May I have your drink orders?"

"I'll have some sweet tea, Mr. Bugg," Lynda Lee said.

The announcement was followed by three more orders for tea.

"Nothing for me," Ray said, "but I'll end my meal with a cup of coffee later. What is the house specialty tonight?"

"We have two to choose from," Mr. Bugg said. "Our first is seared scallops with baby spinach and roasted potatoes. The second is Scandinavian steak with steamed broccoli and a baked potato. Both are served with a house salad."

Ray spoke up.

"My wife will have the scallops, along with a plate of those French cheeses if you have them. I think I'll try the Scandinavian steak."

Mr. Bugg smiled.

"Excellent choices," Mr. Bugg said.

The others at the table whispered to their partners while Mr. Bugg moved closer to them to take their orders.

After another moment, he said, "Four steaks, four scallops. Someone will return with your orders in just a few moments. I'll see that you have your salads right away."

He turned then and went toward the kitchen.

"Isn't he the nicest person?" Lynda Lee said. "I love to listen to his accent, and he knows a great deal about food. He's never steered us wrong, and just wait until you sample those French cheeses. They're delicious."

"But he won't be here much longer, will he?" John Martin asked. "I heard he'd accepted a new job in New York City."

"What?" Lynda Lee asked, her voice raised slightly. "Mr. Bugg is leaving? I can't believe that. He is what makes this place so special. Without him, it's just another restaurant."

She clutched her chest.

"Is this true, Ray?"

"I'm not sure, sweetheart, but if he is leaving, I'm sure it's for a promotion. Please don't say anything to him just yet. That's not something that makes for good table conversation."

"Then, I shall ask him as we leave," Lynda Lee said.

After a wonderful dinner, a special dessert of Cherries Jubilee, and a finishing cup of coffee, the lights dimmed and music played while the governor's wife took the stage and went to the microphone.

"Good evening," she said. "My name is Sally Betterman. I belong to a group called Women's Progressive Coalition, and tonight is our first fundraiser. The goal of our group is to raise awareness of women who are widowed or divorced and who have become the main breadwinners for their families. We have six beautiful, unique gowns and dresses shipped here from Paris from the House of Dior. So, please, enjoy."

"The dresses are from Paris?" Beth asked Lynda Lee. "From Christian Dior?"

Lynda Lee smiled.

"We must have one, Beth. We must."

Ray leaned over and whispered in Lynda Lee's ear.

"Choose the most beautiful one, and it's yours."

Lynda Lee patted his hand and smiled at him.

Soon, a woman walked across the stage. She wore a shirt-waist dress with a full skirt, a large bow at the waist, and a stunning black hat. White gloves and black heels completed the look.

"Oh, that's classy looking, isn't it? It would look good with your svelte figure," Beth said.

Just then, a hand went up from the audience. Lynda Lee heard the sound of a gavel but couldn't see where it was coming from.

"I'm thinking that was Dr. Grant," Ray said. "He told me he was going to buy Elizabeth the first gown they showed."

"I'm waiting for something special," Lynda Lee said. "Something unusual."

The next model wore a white strapless gown whose full skirt, in a bell shape, fell to just below the knee. The tight-fitting bodice was embroidered with tiny red roses. As she stood in the center of the stage, she donned a smooth white sweater with roses around the cuffs of the sleeve. She, too, wore a large hat that matched the dress perfectly.

Lynda Lee gasped when she saw it.

"It's just lovely," she said.

"Do you want it?" Ray asked.

Lynda Lee shook her head.

Then the gavel sounded again. Someone had bought the dress.

Beth leaned forward. "I wonder how much that one set them back?"

"Don't be crude, Beth. What does it matter if it makes the lady happy!"

The third model came to the stage wearing a black shirt waist dress with a fairly straight skirt, elbow sleeves, and an enormous collar studded around its edge with sparkly jewels of some kind. They glittered in the light. She wore a rather small black hat that curved around the top of her head and ended in a matching bow.

Lynda Lee watched as the model did a turn and when the turned to face them, the broad black collar to the dress had disappeared. Without it, the dress took on a more formal look.

"A removable collar?" Beth asked. "I love it. I just love it."

Ray spoke up,

"John, your wife wants this dress."

Beth's face turned bright red.

"It's too much, John," Beth said in her humiliation. "Just forget about it."

"The price of each dress is on the wall beside the stage. Haven't you been watching?" Ray asked.

"My wife loves it, too. Beth, may I steal this one from you and buy it for my wife?" Dr. Grant asked.

"Of course," Beth said.

Once again, the gavel sounded.

When the next model came out, she wore a stunning white and purple satin knee-length gown and topped by a purple coat jacket with white and purple trim along the hemline.

"It's just exquisite," Lynda Lee said and brought her hand to her chest.

"Is that the one?" Ray asked.

Lynda Lee shook her head.

The gavel sounded.

When the woman stepped to the microphone, she said, "I want to thank you so very much for your participation tonight. Your purchases will ensure that our cause is carried forth. We have two more gowns to present. These two are very special as Mr. Dior kindly made them especially for us. They are both one-of-a-kind treasures. So, ladies, when you wear these dresses, you'll know that no one else has one like it and that it was designed and created by Dior himself."

When the model came out, Beth heard herself gasp.

"Oh, my," she said. "Would you look at that."

The model wore a black and white polka dot full blouse that fell to her upper thigh with a straight black skirt. When the model turned, the blouse ballooned out in a delightful cascade of pleats. From the sheen of it, Lynda Lee was sure it was silk. Atop her head was a small black hat with a single feather sticking out of it.

The gavel sounded quickly.

Beth sighed.

"It is a beauty, isn't it?

"It is," Lynda Lee said and smiled at Ray. Something told her that John had just bought that dress for Beth.

When the next model came out, Lynda Lee's eyes fixed on her and the gorgeous gown she wore. It was white satin embroidered all over with tiny purple dragonflies. The model put on the purple satin coat that matched, and Lynda Lee's heart skipped a beat. The model wore a large white hat that almost hid her face and with one tiny dragonfly embroidered onto it. When she did a turn, both the skirt and the coat ballooned in a beautiful wave of colors.

The gavel sounded.

Lynda Lee put her face in her hands.

"Oh, Ray," she said. "I wanted that one. It's the one I've been waiting for, so elegant, so unusual, and I missed my chance."

"Just wait right here, sweetheart. I'll be back shortly. John, please join me."

As the crowd began to disperse, Lynda Lee waited for Ray. Beth waited for John.

Lynda Lee tried to contain her grief, but every now and then, a tear slid down her cheek.

After waiting long enough, she said, "Let's go find Ray and John and see what they're up to."

They had to go backstage to find them, but there they both were talking to the woman who narrated the fashion show.

Lynda Lee walked directly to Ray.

"Oh, Mrs. Betterman," Ray said. "I'd like for you to meet my wife, Lynda Lee."

"Oh my word," she said. "You are every bit as beautiful as everyone says you are. I can see why they call you the Goddess of Weaver Street. You are simply stunning, my dear."

Lynda Lee smiled.

"Thank you," she said. "You're very kind to say that. This is my friend Beth Martin. Beth, this is Mrs. Betterman."

"My pleasure," Beth said. "Your fashions were magnificent. Thank you so much for allowing us to see them. I never thought I'd get to see original Christian Dior fashions. So, you sold all of them?"

"Yes, thank goodness. I was right to come to the Weaver Street crowd. It was so very generous of all of you to purchase the gowns. Now, if you'll follow me, I'll get your outfits."

"No, we don't have any outfits," Lynda Lee said. "We were out-bid."

"Really?" Mrs. Betterman said. "Come with me while I check my sales slips. Ah, I thought I was right. Follow me, ladies."

They walked toward two rows of hanging racks and watched as Mrs. Betterman looked at each garment, carefully wrapped in plastic, before choosing one of them. On the outside was a label that said, 'Beth Martin.'

"This is yours, my dear. You'll have to see your personal tailor so that it fits properly, but you'll look wonderful in it. Oh, and there's a note attached to it."

Beth read the note and frowned.

"Your Ireland money paid for this dress. Enjoy."

Beth's mouth was still open.

"How marvelous for you, Beth," Lynda Lee said. "John came through for you. How very kind of him."

Mrs. Betterman pulled out another gown labeled, "Lynda Lee."

"This is yours, Lynda Lee, a fitting gown for a magnificently beautiful woman."

Lynda Lee held the satin treasure close to her and turned her head to find Ray.

He was looking right at her and nodded. A big smile crossed his face.

Lynda Lee walked over to him.

"Thank you, Ray. Thank you so much."

"Are you happy?"

"Yes, very. I just have to figure out where I'm going to wear it."

Ray hugged her.

"I just want to make you happy, that's all."

As they were leaving, Mrs. Betterman called to them. "Wait up, if you can," she said as she walked over to them. "In two months, we're having a benefit for a large orphanage that we support. It's outside of Tuscaloosa, a more rural setting, but the children are well cared for. Our group is the primary patron for it. It will be a semi-formal event here at The Relay House with food, live entertainment, and of course, a bit of fundraising. We'd love to have all of you," she said as she handed Ray her business card. "May I send you an invitation?"

"Of course," Ray said. "If Dr. Martin and I can arrange our schedules, we'd all love to come," he said and handed her a business card.

"Wonderful," Mrs. Betterman said as she left.

As their group filed out, Lynda Lee found Mr. Bugg and quietly asked him if he was leaving The Relay House. He motioned her to the side and told her that he would still be working for The Relay House but in a different capacity as concierge at their headquarters. He explained that the wages were much higher and the responsibilities almost the same, except for being a waiter.

"I will miss you and Dr. Rogers, but I have a family to think of. The extra money in these times will help me put my son through college and give my wife a better home."

"It won't be the same without you, Mr. Bugg, but I understand that you must do your best for yourself and your family."

Then she hugged him and wished him well.

Chapter 37

"Well, what did you think of the gala event?" Ray asked. "You seemed to enjoy yourself, and that made me happy."

Lynda Lee smiled despite her throbbing headache.

"It was lovely," she said. "I enjoyed it but I keep thinking about Mr. Bugg. I regret that I won't see him again."

"Mr. Bugg?"

"Yes, I like him. He's kind and considerate and he makes every experience at The Relay House something special. He' really the heart of that dining area, and I will miss him."

"Maybe they'll find someone as wonderful as Mr. Bugg to replace him as Concierge. Is your head hurting, Lynda Lee? You seem to be in pain."

Lynda Lee fluffed her pillow and remembered what Maman had said about keeping her suffering to herself.

"It's nothing," she said and snuggled her head into her pillow. "Just another headache."

Ray leaned over and kissed her on the forehead.

"You'd tell me, wouldn't you, if it were something worse? I've talked to your doctor, but he says there's nothing amiss as far as he can tell. Perhaps we should consult another doctor. Those constant headaches worry me."

Lynda Lee pulled the covers over her.

"I've had them forever. No need to worry about them now. Besides, I've taken my pain pills. Maybe a good night's sleep will help."

She didn't mention the sleeping tablet she took.

Ray removed his reading glasses, folded the newspaper and took it over to the bureau so he could catch up tomorrow night. Then he climbed back in bed and savored the feel of stretching out and relaxing.

"I love you, Lynda Lee. Sleep well, my dear."

But Lynda Lee had already fallen asleep and was lost in a dream.

In the dream, Lynda Lee wore her same blue, sequined gown. This time, she didn't have to climb up to find the right road. Instead, when she looked down, she stood in the middle of the road, the rocks and pebbles gone, the road smooth and easy on her bare feet. Just ahead of her sat the old Irish weaver at her loom.

Lynda Lee smiled with relief.

"There you are, Maman," she said. "I didn't have to climb, and look how smooth the road is. It feels wonderful on my feet. How are you, Maman?"

"Still hard at work with these uniforms," she said. "Hand me a large spool of that dark blue wool, will you?"

Lynda Lee bent to get the spool and when she straightened, she noticed something different about Maman. She still wore the same tight-fitting cap over her head. It covered her hair and ears. But her apron and long dress seemed to look new, even though they were the very same clothes she'd always worn. Her work boots seemed a bit shinier than before.

"Maman, do you have a new dress?"

"Not new, Child, just polished, that's all. It was time, so I made use of the fabric you brought years ago."

"Really? You used my fabric? I'm so glad. Do you know where Scaylee is? I'd hoped he'd be here."

"He's where he always is, Child, amongst the listeners, telling his stories. There's an enormous crowd this time just down the road apiece. Go, see for yourself."

Lynda Lee walked down the dirt road until she came upon a crowd of people. They were all looking in one direction, toward a tall, handsome man standing dressed in a long black coat and wearing a beret. He stood atop an old tree stump so that all could see him as he mesmerized them with a tale of ancient Ireland and, at the end, managed to tie the ancient tale into a present-day lesson on kindness.

"Come and eat with us, Scaylee," some of them said. "You must be tired and thirsty. A good meal will make you feel better."

Before he answered, Scaylee looked around and saw Lynda Lee at the edge of the crowd. He smiled and made his way to her.

"Lynda Lee," he said. "You've come back."

Lynda Lee smiled.

"I think it is all a dream, Scaylee, but I'm pulled here as soon as I close my eyes. My dream won't let me stay away."

Scaylee laughed.

"Is that funny?" Lynda Lee asked.

"No, it's not funny. It simply amuses me that your dreams always bring you here. It is as if they have a lesson to teach you. Wouldn't you agree?"

"Must everything be a lesson?"

"No, not everything," Scaylee said and brushed at his long coat. "But there are lessons all around us, Lynda Lee. Are you still working with the orphanage? That is a lesson for sure, many lessons on sharing, on kindness, on generosity, on opening your heart to what the children need."

"Well," Lynda Lee said, "they needed coats, so I made coats."

"That was kind of you. Perhaps you could delve deeper into the subject of what some of them really need."

"How would I do that?"

"You fancy yourself an investigator. Look into it a little more and give those children something that will last. Would you like a story today?"

"Oh, I'd love one," Lynda Lee said. "Yes, I'd love another tale of ancient Ireland."

Suddenly, Scaylee stopped. He put his hand atop her head.

"How are your headaches today, Lynda Lee?"

"Oh, Scaylee, when I am here, my headaches disappear and I feel wonderful."

"Lynda Lee," Ray called. "Wake up. It's time to get up. You have an appointment at the orphanage."

He shook again.

"Lynda Lee, wake up. You've had a good sleep, right? Now, it's morning and time for me to leave and you to get up and get ready for your meeting."

She could barely open her eyes.

"Go away, Ray. Let me sleep."

"It's time to wake up. Your appointment is in an hour."

"My appointment?"

"Yes, Lynda Lee, your appointment with Mrs. Mitchell from the Broadhurst Orphanage. You have donations, don't you?"

Lynda Lee nodded gently to keep the headache at bay.

"Then, you'd better get up and get ready. You don't want to be late."

Chapter 38

Lynda Lee stood in the shower and gave herself a last rinse before stepping out onto the mat and drying off. Then she spritzed her newest perfume, Diorissimo by Christian Dior, in several places on her body. The last two spritzes were behind her ears. Then she inhaled the heady floral scent of the perfume.

"Umm," she muttered and glanced at the clock. "I'd better hurry." She pulled her long hair into a high ponytail, took care to apply just the right amount of foundation, blush, and powder and topped it off with her Pink Yum Yum lipstick. She turned her head this way and that to make sure the foundation and powder were smooth and the hint of blush just right.

Next, she rolled her long hair up into a wide curl at the nape of her neck, pinned it with bobby pins and checked to make sure they were hidden.

"Perfectly smooth," she muttered as she used her smaller mirror to see the back clearly. She put the mirror away.

Satisfied, she walked to the closet and chose her newest day dress, a black and white polka dot shirt-waist with a slim patent belt. Black patent heels complimented the dress, but it was the black pillbox hat with the black and white dotted bow in front that completed the look. For jewelry, she wore only her wedding rings, and the slim gold Rolex watch Ray had given her a few years ago. Anything more would be too gauche.

"I'm ready," she whispered and glanced at her watch. "I'll be right on time."

As she was preparing to leave, the phone rang.

"Hi, Lynda Lee. It's me, Beth."

"Beth, is everything okay? I adore that dress you bought. You'll look beautiful in it."

"Thanks," Beth said, "but that's why I'm calling. Remember our plans to go to Ireland?"

"Of course, I remember, but none of the girls have even bought passports. Apparently, they're just not interested. But you bought a passport, didn't you?"

"Yes, I have my passport, but John put a note on the back of the card of my new dress. The note said that my saved money for Ireland paid for the dress."

"John used your savings to pay for that dress? How could he! Why would he do such a thing, Beth?"

"He never wanted me to go. It's as simple as that. He wants me home so that I will be a good housewife and tend to all his needs. He was never going to let me leave, Lynda Lee. And he chose the meanest way possible to tell me that."

"Did you confront him?"

"I tried, but he just laughed. Then, this morning he left for another of those business symposiums. Did Ray go?"

"Ray? No, he hasn't mentioned any business symposium, and I'm sure he would have because he's usually a speaker or a panel participant."

"I see," Beth said. "I'm so sorry, Lynda Lee. I'd made so many plans for that trip, and I was looking forward to it, but it just isn't going to happen, not for me, anyway. Perhaps you and Ray can go one of these days."

"Maybe, but I'm mostly sorry for you, Beth. You seem to be in a bit of a spot. If there's anything I can do, please come over for a chat, and we'll talk. Or better yet, bring your swimsuit and we'll take a dip in the lake. Right now, I have to meet with Mrs Mitchell. I'll call you when I get back."

Lynda Lee walked briskly down the street toward the Broadhurst Orphanage, her thoughts no longer on the children, but on Beth. That husband of hers might not be not a good man. It made Lynda Lee a bit nauseous to think about what Beth had gone through, but she walked on carrying a single shopping bag. Up the steps she went and knocked on the door. Almost immediately, Mrs. Miller opened the door.

"Mrs. Rogers," she said but did not smile. "If you'll follow me, we can talk in the conference room. Does that suit you?

"Yes," Lynda Lee said.

"It's quiet today because the children are either in school or being tutored. We place a high value on education here," she said as if Lynda Lee had never been there before. "Now, how may I help you today?"

Lynda Lee pulled the shopping bag into her lap and withdrew a black wool coat with pearlized buttons down the front. Lynda Lee stood to show off the coat.

"I made this for you," she said to Mrs. Miller. "It's high quality and should be a good fit."

"This is for me?" Mrs. Miller asked. "I appreciate your efforts, but I already have several black coats."

Lynda Lee smiled.

"A lady of fashion can never have too many black coats," she said. "I'll put it in the bag and you can use it or do what you want with it."

"It was a kind gesture," Mrs. Miller said shuffling papers as the talked. "Is there anything else?"

Lynda Lee sat down again and leaned forward.

"There is," she said. "I wondered if you would allow Julie Kramer to help me do some light work around the house. I have these blinding headaches and I could use some help. Also, her brother Mark might be useful, as well."

"Julie Kramer?" Mrs. Miller said.

"Yes, she and her brother Mark. I could really use the help."

"Julie is thirteen now. And Mark is eleven. I'm afraid it's against our policy to let our children work outside the orphanage."

Lynda Lee reached into her purse, pulled out an envelope, and handed it to Mrs. Miller.

"Perhaps this will help," she said.

Mrs. Miller's eyes widened when she read the letter.

"I see you've taken the liberty to go over my head to get what you want."

"The Broadhursts and I are very good friends. He agreed that working outside the orphanage might be good for Julie and Mark."

"But of course you're not planning to adopt either of them are you? To give them a true home?"

Lynda Lee looked at her and opened her mouth to speak, but no words would come.

Chapter 39

"What did you say, Lynda Lee? Did I misunderstand? You want us to do what?"

His raised voice, so unlike him, frightened her just a bit. Then he flopped back down onto his recliner and picked up the newspaper.

"Calm down, Ray. I'd like for us to have a polite conversation about this. Are you not even willing to discuss it?"

"No, Lynda Lee," he said as he continued to read. "We're not bringing two orphans into our beautiful home to wreak havoc with what we've created. No, it's too big a risk. And these are teenagers, no less."

"Julie is thirteen now, and Mark is eleven, I think."

"See, exactly my point. They're both just fine where they are."

Lynda Lee got up and sat at the foot of the recliner.

"Ray, it's what I want. I haven't asked you for much, have I?"

Ray put down his newspaper.

"No, my dearest, you've never asked for much. You've never really asked for anything, but Lynda Lee, I don't think you understand how difficult this might be. We might be unfit as parents. Neither of us knows anything at all about parenting. And you want to adopt two children? It's absurd."

Lynda Lee put her hand on Ray's.

"You're gone most of the time. Nights, overnights, long days that last until night. You're hardly ever here, Ray."

"That's my point, Lynda Lee. I'm gone most of the time, so you'll be left to deal with these kids by yourself. And don't forget about your headaches. How can you care for children when your head is hurting so badly that you have to take pain pills?"

"Well, how about this, Ray? We talk to the Broadhursts and arrange for Julie and Mark to stay with us for a month."

"So, we give them a home for a month and then pull the rug out from under them and send them back to the orphanage? That's a terrible plan."

Lynda Lee got up and went into the kitchen. Ray got out of his recliner and followed her.

"Please be reasonable, Lynda Lee. We don't know anything about kids. We're clueless. Why would you want to bring two kids into this house to live when we know nothing about them?"

Lynda Lee put away the dishes in the drainer.

"You and Mr. Broadhurst could work this out, Ray. We could foster them for a month, just to see how it goes. People do it all the time."

Ray sat at the kitchen table with his head in his hands.

"Ray?" Lynda Lee said and sat next to him. "Can't we try?"

"You mean try to ruin the lives of two children who are healthy and happy where they are?"

Lynda Lee stood up.

"If you bothered to talk to your doctor friends, you would know that they are neither healthy nor happy. They are grossly underweight. They're pale and get no outside play time. Their daily routine is work, just work. Whatever Mrs. Miller decides to demand of them, they do without question because they have no choice, and she is a cold-hearted woman whose only interest is her paycheck. So, you think what you want, Ray, but these children need a good home, and even though we don't know much, we know enough to feed and care for them. I can cook and you can get them the medical care they need!"

Lynda Lee stomped out of the room then.

Ray walked to the phone and picked up the receiver. Then he dialed a number and waited for an answer.

"Mr. Broadhurst," he said. "This is Dr. Ray Rogers."

Right before they were to hang up, Ray said, "Oh yes, we're Presbyterians."

The two men talked on for almost an hour, and when they were finished, Ray thanked him and hung up.

"What have I done?" he mumbled. "What in God's name have I done?"

Chapter 40

After three months, many visits to the orphanage, and endless meetings with Mr. Broadhurst and his committee members, a miracle happened. The committee did not vote for fostering, but instead gave clearance for Ray and Lynda Lee to adopt Julie and Mark.

"You're a stable, respected couple in this community. Your ages are fine, though a bit older than we normally see. But there is one condition," Mr. Broadhurst said. "The only condition is that first, we need to see and approve your home.

"Our home?" Lynda Lee asked.

"Of course, we need to approve the home in which the children will be living. How about tomorrow? If your home is approved, we can sign the papers."

"Tomorrow will be fine," Ray said. "Let's just get this done."

At nine the next morning, Ray, already late for work, opened the door for the committee. They surveyed every inch of the house and yards, both front and back.

"You'll need a fence in the back yard, Ray, just for safety, of course."

Ray glanced at Lynda Lee and rolled his eyes.

"A fence. Okay."

"We're done here. Everything is fine, except for the fence. Please see to that, will you? Otherwise, you're cleared to take in these children. I think they'll be happy here."

As soon as they'd left, Ray kissed Lynda Lee goodbye and headed out to work.

"I'll call the fence company, so be expecting someone to come out and measure the yard. Tell him just to leave the estimate on the table."

"I will Ray. Have a good day."

Lynda Lee sat at the kitchen table and looked out over the yard, all the way down to the lake. She thought she would be happier, that somehow, the idea of having the children would be the thing that kept her depression at bay.

She longed to be in the water, to go back to being a mermaid, so on a whim, she left the kitchen and went down to the lake. She shrugged off her clothes and dove into the water. She swam and said to the water, "I used to be a mermaid." A few fish swam by, but they didn't bother her at all. She swam for almost an hour, noting that as she swam, her headache vanished.

"I have to do this more often," she said. "I'm a mermaid after all."

As she dried off and dressed, she toweled her long dark hair and remembered what Scaylee had said to her. "Find out what they need and provide it for them. Give them something that will last."

Dressed and with her wet hair smoothed as much as possible, she went back inside.

When the knock sounded at the door, she smoothed her hair once again, checked herself in the hall mirror and opened the door.

"Beth," she said when she opened the door. "Oh, Beth, it is so good to see you. I adore those casual slacks and that floral blouse. You look adorable."

"Oh, you must get some of these slacks, Lynda Lee. If you once started wearing them, you'd find them so handy for yard work or for casual visits, running errands. No more dressing up to go out the front door."

They hugged each other and then sat at the kitchen table.

"What can I get you?"

"Not a thing," Beth said. "I've had my allotted share of coffee this morning and I've had breakfast, so I'm good. So, tell me all about the Board. What did they say?"

Lynda Lee chuckled.

"They said we need a fence."

"A fence? Oh, none of us has a fence. Your hair is wet. Did I get you out of the shower?"

"No, I've been using my mermaid powers and taking a swim."

Beth chuckled.

"Whatever works," she said. "About this fence business. We didn't want fences to ruin the look of the houses. But it's a requirement for you to have the children?"

"Yes, I'm afraid so. The children aren't familiar with the neighborhood and could possibly wander off, I guess. I know everyone will be angry with us, so I'm going to put it off as long as possible."

A tear rolled down her cheek.

"Whatever is the matter, Lynda Lee? Tell me."

Lynda Lee wiped her face with a tissue.

"You know, it was my idea to adopt the children. I thought it was the right thing to do. Ray opposed it vehemently, but he went along with it, went through all the court dates, the endless meetings and paperwork–there's a ton of paperwork involved. And gradually, it all became so complicated. And there were many times that I completely forgot about the children. We were so bogged down in paperwork that it's just been so much harder than I thought," she said as the tears began to flow.

Beth put her hand over Lynda Lee's.

"But the hard part's over. You've done it. You've been approved. So, now, you can step back, refresh your thinking and begin to think about building a family, something you've always wanted, Lynda Lee."

Lynda Lee chuckled.

"What are you laughing about?

"A friend used that same phrase not long ago. Refresh. Yes, now I understand. It is time to refresh and think differently."

"Now, you forget about that ugly fence for a while. Think, instead of what you can do to make the children feel welcome. Julie is thirteen, and Mark is eleven, right? So, we need to go shopping and find a few personal items for each of them, something that will make their rooms decidedly theirs. Agreed?"

"Agreed," Lynda Lee said.

"What color are their rooms?"

"Mark's is deep green and Julie's is a deep lavender. They each have double beds with new mattresses and furniture of course."

"Does Julie have a vanity dresser?"

"No, but she does have a small dresser with a large mirror

mounted above it. When she begins to wear makeup, I think it will be perfect. Ray agreed to hang a full-length mirror on the back of the door of the bathroom."

"Don't you worry, Lynda Lee. Those children will think they're living in a palace. They'll love it here."

"I thought about getting some paint and painting their names on their doors, but I don't know."

"How about a throw cushion for their beds with their names embroidered on them?" Beth said as she dug into her purse. "My friend at the outlet shop could do them in just a day or two. I have her name right here."

"That's perfect."

"So, let's go talk to her. She might have more ideas to personalize the space. And, you need to make sure that you have a painting or two in their rooms, nice paintings, copies from the Old Masters."

"Really? Not stuff for kids?"

"No, these are strictly for exposure to beauty and hopefully, as they get older, they'll want to know more about the artists. They won't always be kids, Lynda Lee, and you'll have to start teaching them about artists and what's out there in the world."

"What about Gainsborough's Blue Boy and Lady Pink? I think they would be perfect. Blue Boy in Mark's room and Lady Pink in Julie's."

"Yes," Beth said. "It's a perfect pair for a start. If they seem to like art, then you can buy them other paintings as they grow. But wasn't Lady Pink done by Sir Thomas Arthur? I believe the art shop downtown carries copies of the large size of both. Oh, I'm so excited! Let's go find them!"

They returned a few hours later with two rather large paintings, one for each of the children's rooms. When they were hung and balanced, Lynda Lee stood back.

"What do you think, Beth? Will they like them?"

"I hope so," Beth said. "If nothing else, perhaps these paintings will give them a love for art, or perhaps you just wasted your money!"

Beth laughed out loud.

Lynda Lee chuckled.

"Did you remember to get the books about Gainsborough and Thomas Lawrence? Not many people know that the paintings were done by two different artists. You'll have to teach them about them, you know, so that one day, they'll be able to recognize the works," Beth asked.

"I did. Now, I'm worn out and my head is throbbing."

"Why haven't you been able to get any help for those headaches, Lynda Lee?"

"I've been to two specialists, but all they do is take an x-ray and prescribe pain pills. Neither of them was able to tell me anything about why I have them. Both of them said it was just stress and the pills would help. I'm not going to another doctor, no offense to either of our husbands, but the two doctors I saw acted as if a headache was nothing, just some woman thing. They both brushed me off."

Beth hugged her.

"Listen," she said. "If you need anything at all, anything, I'm right next door. I can help with the children. I can cook, clean. I'll never forget how kind and helpful you were when I broke my leg. So, if you need any little thing, just call me. Okay? Besides, I want to get to know the children, Lynda Lee."

"Okay, I'll call you. On the other hand, you feel free to come by any time to meet them."

"Aren't you going to have a party to introduce them to all of us? Surely you're not going to bypass that opportunity."

"Where should I have it?"

"Let's have it at Janine's house. They have that brand new Weber grill, and you know that she loves to entertain. I'll call her and see what she has on her schedule. We could have hot dogs and hamburgers, food for the kids and the adults and anything else we can think of."

"Let's give the kids a chance to settle in. Then, we'll see about having a 'coming out' party for them. How's that?"

"Great. I'll call Janine and arrange the whole thing."

"When are the children coming?"

"Next week," Lynda Lee said. "Next week, we will be a family of four!"

"We're all so excited for you. They're thirteen and eleven, right?"

Lynda Lee nodded.

Beth clapped her hands.

"It will be so nice to hear the laughter of children in our neighborhood."

Chapter 41

When Lynda Lee opened the door, her head still throbbing, she was surprised to see Julie and Mark with a social worker standing behind them. The social worker wore a plain brown dress and shoes, no makeup, no accessories. Julie and Mark wore clean but unmatched clothes with no shoes.

"You don't have shoes, Julie?" Lynda Lee asked.

"We have shoes," Julie said and parked her hair behind her ears, "but they belong to the orphanage, so we had to leave them behind. Is it all right that we came barefoot? Do you want us to go back?"

"Come in," Lynda Lee said to them. "Have a seat in the living room. Anywhere is fine."

The social worker introduced herself as Helen.

"My job is to see that the children safely arrive at their new home."

"I appreciate it, Helen. I would say that you've done your job. May I get you some coffee or tea?" Lynda Lee said as she closed the door.

"No, thank you. I'm sorry about the shoes," Helen said, "but I couldn't convince Mrs. Miller to let them wear their shoes here. I've never run into anyone like her before, and I've been doing this for a long time. I've never in my life seen newly adopted children delivered to their new parents without a stich of decent clothes or, Heaven forbid, barefoot. Usually, the children are wearing their best clothes and their nicest shoes. But not this time. I think someone needs to call whoever owns this orphanage and lodge a complaint."

"Yes, Mrs. Miller is quite difficult," Lynda Lee said. "But don't worry. I've heard that the Broadhursts have several complaints against her, one that might even lead to court proceedings. So, perhaps she won't be there much longer."

"Julie, Mark, do you like your new home so far?"

"It looks like a palace," Julie said. "It's so fine and elegant."

"Very well, then, I'll see you in a month or so, just to check in on the children."

She waved goodbye and then told Lynda Lee, "A monthly visit will be required for three months, just to ensure that the children are happy here. I'm sure they will be. It is a beautiful home."

"I don't mind the visits," Lynda Lee said. "Come whenever you wish."

At that, Lynda Lee closed the door and turned to the children.

She held out her hand.

"Come with me. I want to show you the rest of the house and then we'll go into the backyard. It's a place where you can play."

Lynda Lee led them through the house, showing them each room. Finally, toward the back of the house, they came to the children's bedrooms and bath.

"Mark, this is your room. "Do you like it?"

Mark nodded, but he did not smile, nor did he speak.

"You have plenty of room in here to do whatever you want. You have a toy box right here filled with toys. And if you think of something you want or need, just tell us and we'll get it for you. Okay?"

Mark nodded.

"Julie," she said as they walked down the hallway, "this is your room."

Julie gasped.

"All of it? All of this is mine?"

Lynda Lee smiled.

"Yes, dear, all of it is yours. Everything you see belongs only to you. For now, you and Mark share a bathroom, but it's large and very pretty and you can take a bath or a shower. There are cabinets where you can store your things."

"Everything in here is mine? The clothes and everything? The dolls and the puzzles? The bed? This pretty piece?"

"It's a sort of vanity mirror where you can sit and brush your hair. Everything belongs to you now, Julie. This is your room and these are your things."

Julie stood in the middle of the room and slowly turned around taking in as much as she could.

"It's so big, Lynda Lee. And all of it is mine?"

"How about you and Mark calling me Mama Lynda. Is that all right with you?"

Julie ran to her and hugged her.

"I'm so happy, Mama Lynda. It's so beautiful here. Thank you."

Lynda Lee hugged her back.

"Now, let's go see the backyard."

On the way to the backyard, they passed through the kitchen.

Julie stopped and looked at everything.

"It's so beautiful," she said. "This is where we cook and eat?"

"Yes, it is, and here is our family table over here. I like to keep it clean and tidy with the white lace tablecloth on it."

Julie rubbed the edge of the tablecloth between her fingers and smiled.

"This is the way rich people eat," she said.

"Julie, this is the way we will eat every day. Now, come. Let's go to the back. You've plenty of time to look at each room in the house."

When Lynda Lee opened the door and stepped out onto the grass, the children stayed put at the threshold.

"Come on," Lynda Lee said. "It's nice out here with the thick grass and the beautiful flowers. And see, we have two gardens. I'll teach you both how to garden and grow flowers and vegetables."

"We're not allowed on the grass," Julie said.

"Why aren't you allowed on the grass?"

"Mrs. Miller said it had fleas and nasty bugs in it. They would bite us and it would hurt."

"Julie," Lynda Lee said, "Mrs. Miller doesn't live here. Now that you live here, you will listen to Papa Ray and Mama Lynda. Ray and I are your new parents. You'll have nothing to do with her ever again. Do you understand?"

"Never?" Julie asked. "She won't be watching us and coming to get us again?"

Julie smiled.

Lynda Lee said, "Now, I am standing out here in our lovely backyard. There are no fleas or nasty bugs. So, please, come and join me, both of you."

The children took their first steps onto the grass.

"Oh, it's soft and cool on my feet," Julie said as she tugged at Mark to walk beside her. "Does it feel good to you, Mark?"

Mark nodded and smiled.

The three of them walked all around the backyard, stopping to smell the flowers and to see the variety of plants in the gardens.

Mark was especially taken with the gardens. He bent down and ran his fingers through the soil, sniffed at each of the plants. He whispered to Julie that he wanted to know their names.

"Mama Lynda, Mark wants to know the name of each plant. He loves the gardens and the plants, but he wants to know what they are called."

"I think we can arrange to have tags on each plant. It won't be too much trouble, and if it makes Mark happy, then we'll do it. We can do it together."

As they walked back to the house, Mark spotted a plant that looked different than the others. He walked over to it and ran his hand down the leaves. Then, he looked at Lynda Lee.

"That one is called a hydrangea." she said. "They're usually easy to grow, but this one is dying. The brown on its leaves tell me that it isn't going to live. I water it and give it fertilizer, but it just doesn't seem to respond. I'm not sure it's going to make it, Mark, and I don't know what to do about it."

Suddenly, Mark used his hands to scoop the dying plant out of its spot. He walked to the area with the most morning sun and setting it carefully aside, he dug a hole deep and big enough to hold the small plant. He planted it carefully and packed the soil tightly around it.

Then he summoned Julie and whispered something to her.

"He needs a big glass of water," she said to Lynda Lee.

"Take this," Lynda Lee said. "It's a watering can. Come, we have a hose out here so that we can fill it with water."

When the watering can was about half full, Lynda Lee handed it to Julie.

"Take this to him."

Mark took the can, stood and watered the hydrangea next to the bottom of the plant underneath the leaves. He let the first watering soak in then watered a second time. As the second watering went into the soil, Mark stripped away all of the brown leaves. What remained were a few green leaves, small but healthy looking.

Mark washed off his hands with the water, dried them on his shorts, and smiled.

"I'll check on you tomorrow," he whispered.

Just then, Lynda Lee walked to the spot where he had replanted, and put a sticker on one of the wooden beams that bordered the gardens.

"There you go. It's called a hydrangea. We'll make the other stickers in the morning."

As they walked back into the house, Lynda Lee asked, "Mark, where did you learn about gardening?"

Mark whispered to Julie.

"He learned by watching Maria. She tended the garden in the back of the orphanage. She would let him help her when Mrs. Miller wasn't around."

"How brave Maria was to get out in the grass with all those fleas and nasty bugs!" Lynda Lee said and chuckled. "Now, let's get cleaned up. I'll show you how to work the showers, and I'll put clean clothes on your beds. Papa Ray should be here in an hour or so. Now, do both of you know how to turn on the shower?"

"We're not used to that," Julie said. "A lot of us shower together once a week. We have to use the soap carefully so that we have enough for everybody."

"You shower together?" Lynda Lee asked. "Boys and girls alike?"

"Yes, that's what we've always done. Those are the rules so that we won't waste water or soap."

"Those are not the rules in this house, Julie. I'll show you how to use the shower , and be sure to wash your hair. Use as much soap as you want. There's a big bottle of shampoo in there. You'll see it."

"Wash our hair, too?" Julie asked.

"Of course," Lynda Lee said. "Now, Julie, here is how the shower works."

Lynda Lee pointed to the handle on the faucet portion of the shower.

"Just turn this handle to the left for hot water and to the right for cold water. But, the best place to keep it is right in the middle." She turned the handle to the middle and a stream of water flowed from the shower head. "You have to wait just a minute for the water to warm. Then, you're ready. Mark, did you see how the shower works?"

Mark nodded.

"Okay, Julie, yours is ready."

"Mark, here is your towel. When Julie finishes, you can take a shower. I've put your clean clothes on the bed. When Papa Ray gets here, we'll have our dinner. Are you getting hungry?"

The boy nodded.

"Good. I'll get dinner started then. I'll check on you in a few minutes."

Lynda Lee left the boy in his room. She hoped she'd explained about the shower well enough that he understood how to use it properly. She had to remember that these children were not accustomed to living in a home and doing things on their own.

She rubbed her temples and moaned. Then she walked to the kitchen, got her bottle of pills out of the small cabinet drawer and took two of them with a glass of water. Then she walked back to check on Julie, making sure she called and knocked first.

She opened the door and saw that Julie was still in the shower, so she left and went to check on Mark. When she opened the door, she found him sitting on the bed, still in his dirty clothes.

"What's wrong, Mark?" she asked and sat beside him.

Mark shook his head.

"If you're worried about the shower, Julie will show you. It's easy to use and you'll be spic and span when you finish. I need to get dinner ready. Just wait for Julie. She'll show you what to do, okay?"

Lynda Lee walked into her bedroom, grabbed two boxes off the floor, and slipped into their rooms leaving one box for Julie and one for Mark while both of them were gathered in Julie's room for a shower.

"Time to get out of the shower, Children. You have a surprise waiting for you."

Immediately, she heard the shower water stop. She heard bustling in both rooms and smiled. After a few moments, she opened Julie's door and found her dressed, her wet hair combed straight.

"In your dresser drawer is a hair dryer. See," she said as pulled open a drawer. "It's just right here and you can plug it into the wall socket right down here."

"But what about the box? Is it mine? Can I open it?"

Lynda Lee smiled.

"As soon as we get Mark dressed, you can open your box. Okay?"

"Mark," Julie yelled. "Hurry up in there."

"You didn't have to yell. We'll just go check on him."

When they knocked on the bathroom door and went in, Mark was dressed and ready.

Julie walked over to him, looked in the cabinet for the hair dryer and plugged it in.

"Come here," she said and used the dryer to dry his long, thick hair. "Now, you're all done. You look quite handsome for a boy."

Lynda Lee laughed.

"A boy who will very soon need a haircut," she said.

Mark pointed to the box.

"It's yours," Lynda Lee said. "Open it if you want to."

Mark tore into the box and pulled out a very large smiling teddy bear brown with a red scarf tied around his neck. It was plush and soft.

"You'll have to give him a name because he doesn't have one yet, and if you're going to be sleeping buddies, he'll need a name," Lynda Lee said. "You choose whatever name you wish. Let's go see what's in Julie's box, shall we?"

Carrying his teddy bear hugged tightly against him, which was almost as big as he was, Mark followed them to Julie's room where she opened her box carefully and found another very large teddy bear, this one a soft brown with a bright floral scarf tied around the neck.

"Your sleeping buddy," Lynda Lee said. "She's soft and squishy and will make good company. You can tell her all your secrets and whisper to her at night. She'll keep all your secrets safe. But first, like Mark, you must give her a name."

"She's almost as big as I am," Julie said. "And Mark's is huge, too. Thank you. They're both great."

Lynda Lee smiled.

"It will take some time to get used to separate bedrooms, and I wanted each of you to have a sleeping buddy so that you wouldn't get lonely in the night. I do understand how difficult this new phase of your life will be. But please, just give it some time, and before you know it, you'll become comfortable here."

Julie hugged Lynda Lee.

"You're so good to us, Mama Lynda. We love it here already."

"I want you both to remember to say your prayers before bed. Will you do that for me?"

"Can I say my prayers in the shower?" Julie asked.

"I don't think it matters one bit where you say your prayers as long as you say them, so yes, say them wherever you want."

"Do we go to church?" Julie asked.

"Yes, we try to make it every Sunday. Sometimes, Papa Ray has to work. When he works, I usually stay home, but we're regular members, so we go pretty often to the Presbyterian church. It's only a few blocks away, so we can walk there and back."

"I'm home, Lynda Lee, with nobody to greet me at the door," Ray called.

Lynda Lee had Mark and Julie by the hand. She stood on tiptoe to give Ray a kiss.

"You're home so early," she said. "I haven't even started making dinner yet."

Ray smiled.

"And who are these two ragamuffins?"

"Papa Ray, my name is Julie and this is my little brother Mark. I'm thirteen and he is eleven. Thank you for bringing us into your lovely home."

"Julie and Mark," he said. "It's very nice to have you with us, at last. You both look nice. I see you're wearing some of your new clothes."

"We showered and changed after being outside," Julie said.

Ray knelt down.

"Mark, come here, boy," he said. "What is that enormous creature you're holding?"

Mark walked forward carrying his teddy bear and almost stumbling over it.

"And who might this be?" Ray asked.

Mark whispered in his ear, "Theodore."

"Theodore, well, that's a perfect name for such a big bear," he said.

Mark whispered to him again, "My sleeping buddy."

"Ah, I see. Your sleeping buddy. Well, everybody needs one of those. He'll make a fine buddy because he won't talk too much."

Ray stood up and smiled.

"So, how would everyone like to go out to dinner tonight?"

"Oh, Ray, that would be wonderful. Where did you have in mind?" Lynda Lee asked.

Ray sat in his recliner and took off his tie.

"I thought we might try that new restaurant called Britling's. I hear the food is very good and it's a new cafeteria-style place. Not another one like it in Tuscaloosa. And best of all, it's casual dress, so we can go just the way we are."

Within a couple of hours, they arrived at the new restaurant and walked in to stand in line.

"Watch me," Lynda Lee said as she grabbed the next tray off the stack. Then she reached up and got her silverware wrapped in a napkin. She put one on her tray and watched as the children did the same.

"You can have one dessert," she said, "and whatever else you want. You simply tell the servers what you want and they will fix your plates for you."

"I've never seen this much food," Julie said. "And we can eat all we want?"

Ray said, "Get whatever you want, but be sure to eat what you get if you can. No need to waste food."

A wide-eyed Julie chose a pear salad, chicken and dumplings, green beans, and a cornbread muffin, while Mark decided on a pear salad, a bowl of vegetable soup, two servings of creamed potatoes, and some fried okra, along with a corn muffin and a dinner roll.

Seated and eating, Lynda Lee watched Mark cover one of his rolls with a napkin and stuff it into his pants pocket. Julie did the same, both of them being quiet and very careful.

"How is your food, children?" she asked.

"It's wonderful," Julie said, "and there's plenty of it, so we'll have full tummies when we go to bed tonight."

"Whatever you can't eat, we'll get a bag and take it home with us so that you can have it later if you wish."

"We can do that? It's allowed?"

Ray chuckled.

"We've paid for the food, so it is ours to do with as we please. Lynda Lee and I often take home at least a dessert. It's quite common."

Julie looked at Mark and smiled.

"But what if it's almost bedtime and we're hungry? Do we still have to go to bed hungry?"

"Don't be silly, boy," Ray said. "No one goes to bed hungry in our house. You can eat whatever you want to. There's no need to go to bed hungry. Our fridge is always stocked with goodies. But check with Mama Lynda and see that she approves of your choice."

Lynda Lee wiped her mouth with her napkin.

"Do you often go to bed hungry?"

"All of us do, Mama Lynda. We're not allowed to have food after 5:00. And there are no snacks before bed."

Lynda Lee felt a tiny piece of her heart break. These children, oh, these children. What terrible lives they'd had.

"Those rules from the orphanage do not apply at our house," she said and sniffed. "If you want something to eat, ask permission, then go and get what you want. If you need help, just tell me. I'll help you, as long as what you want isn't too sugary. Too much sugar is not healthy for you."

Ray cleared his throat.

"I think you'll find that my wife is a little picky about food. She wants us all to eat healthy food."

"As long as it's food, we'll eat it," Mark said.

As it turned out, Mark was exactly right about what he said. The two of them never scoffed at vegetables or fruits. They ate whatever Lynda Lee prepared and always cleaned their plates. Several times, Lynda Lee caught them peering around as they ate, almost like little wolves protecting their food. As a treat, once a week, Lynda Lee made a sumptuous cake of some sort, chocolate, vanilla, strawberry. Whatever she made, they treated it like a piece of gold. Between Ray and the children, the cake would last two days at most. But that made her happy. And though she smiled a lot more these days, her headaches just kept getting worse.

Chapter 42

After a few months, when the newness of their situation began to wear off, Julie and Mark acted more like themselves, like the brother and sister they had been at the orphanage. Occasionally, especially if they were outside, they had arguments, but nothing serious. Julie ruled the roost whether inside or out ... except in one place: the four gardens. Those were Mark's territories and his alone.

Each day, Lynda Lee was astonished at how well the plants were growing. Mark had created four separate gardens, two for vegetables, one for perennials, and one for annuals. Ray hired a woodcrafter to create raised beds surrounded by wooden borders. Mark replanted with the utmost care. Their backyard looked as if a master gardener had created it. In the middle of the yard, Mark had put their hardly-seen two white wrought-iron benches so that they faced each other and in the middle of them a round table. He'd added a birdbath in one corner next to the birdfeeder. On pleasant evenings, the four of them would sit on the benches and admire Mark's handiwork.

"You know, Mark," Ray said one evening as he gazed around their beautiful yard, "you have such skill as a gardener that one of these days, you could have your own company."

"But what would I do?"

"You'd do what you've done here. Restore people's gardens. In Alabama, people are proud of their gardens, but many of them work and don't have the time to take care of a garden properly. It's something to think about. Of course, it would take some studying on your part. You'd have to read about plants, all types of plants."

"But if I did, I could become a Master Gardener with papers and everything?"

"I'm sure of it," Ray said. "In fact, if you learn enough, people like us would pay you good money to keep their lawns and gardens in good order. You could even call your business The Four Gardens."

Mark smiled.

"Papa Ray, where would I study and learn about plants?"

"First of all, we'd get you some books about gardening. Then perhaps we could find someone who's already in business and let you work for him as an apprentice. Maybe you could get a job part time at the Botanical Gardens. Then later, maybe Auburn University. It offers courses in horticulture. It's far away, but by the time you're old enough, it might be a path to pursue," Dr Ray said and blew a big puff from his cigar.

"So," Lynda Lee said, "Who's ready for some warm apple pie with ice cream?"

"I am," Mark said.

"Good," she said. "It's getting dark, so let's all go inside and have some pie."

"And ice cream," Mark said.

Ray chuckled.

As the children ran ahead of them to wash their hands, Ray looked at Lynda Lee.

"So, what do you think, sweetheart? Does being a mother and having a family suit you? Does it make you happy?"

"It suits me just fine. But what about you? Does fatherhood make you happy?

"It's a lot of responsibility, but I find I'm rather enjoying it. Do you think I did right by encouraging Mark to learn more about gardening?"

"Just remember that Mark has trouble reading. Books are sort of his enemies, but perhaps in time, that will change. He's a natural at it. Maybe all it would take would be to get him to work with someone who's already doing this. I think Mark has the talent, don't you?"

"Yes, he does," Ray said, "so I don't want to overwhelm with books. Let's see how it goes this summer and then look into other companies later. He's only eleven. It's hard to believe that our adoption took less than a year and that now, we have two children. We should let Mark progress at his own pace. We'll let him do what he wants with the gardens, and then toward the end of summer, we'll have a garden party here with all of our friends so that they can see his handiwork. How's that?"

"Now, that sounds like a plan," Lynda Lee said and gave him a kiss on the cheek.

"Ooh, they're smooching," Julie said as they walked in.

"I'm never gonna kiss a girl," Mark said. "Yuck."

Chapter 43

That night, exhausted from the pain of the constant headaches and her responsibilities as a new mother, Lynda Lee fell fast asleep almost as soon as her head hit the pillow.

The dream came quickly.

Again, she found herself making her way through brambles and bushes that ended at a smooth dirt road. She wore her blue sequined gown whose train trailed behind her. Barefoot, she scrunched her toes in the soft dirt. She wasn't lost but some things had changed since she was last here. The cottage to her right was even bigger than last time. It was painted white with a blue door, with multi-colored roses growing wild all around it. The colors were vivid and bright. Pinks, reds, apricots, and even one blue rose bush spread its way across the front of the cottage.

"How beautiful they all are," Lynda Lee mumbled.

"Ah, you've come back, Child," the old Irish weaver said from her loom down the road a bit.

"Maman," Lynda Lee said and walked quickly to her. She wrapped her arms around her and gave her a hug. "I've missed you. I'm so happy to see you."

"It's been a while since we've seen you, Child. How is your life now?"

"Oh, Maman, you wouldn't believe it. Ray and I adopted two children who needed a home. The girl is Julie and her little brother is Mark. They are good children who've come from bad situations. The four of us are happy."

Lynda Lee watched the old Irish weaver as she spun her loom.

"What cloth is that you're using, Maman?"

"Just common cotton, Child. We've known a bit of peace lately, so these are for the women and children who've lost husbands in the wars. So many wars. So much loss. But we Irish never give up, Child. It's who we are as a people. We fight to the very end."

Lynda Lee smiled.

"I've learned that about you with all my visits here. The cottage looks just beautiful, Maman. The roses are stunning."

"It's the years, Child. We have to be prepared because here, things can change rapidly."

"Well, well, just look who's come to visit," the deep voice said.

Lynda Lee turned.

"Scaylee," she cried as he dismounted his horse. "I'm so happy to see you," she said as she ran to him and hugged him.

"And I am glad to see you, Lynda Lee. We've missed you."

"Are you still telling your stories?"

"Of course, I am. I'm just a storyteller at heart. That's what my Irish name means. Scaylee is a pronunciation of an old Gaelic word for storyteller."

"I wish I could bring Julie and Mark to see all of you. Ray and I adopted two children and they have brought much happiness to us."

"I see," Scaylee said and smiled. "So now, you have the family you've always wanted."

"Yes, I do. It warms my heart when I think of the children. They endured some rough times at the orphanage, but now, we've grown accustomed to one another, and we are all happy together."

"And how about those headaches that plague you? Have you found a remedy for them?"

Lynda Lee shook her head.

"I take pills, like always, though these are a bit stronger than the others. My doctor says it's just stress, no medical reason for them. Since the pills are stronger, I'm sure they make me even sleepier than the others did. I looked forward to nap time because I could take one of my pills and then dream of being here. Still, the newer ones don't seem to help much."

"I'm sorry about that, Lynda Lee. Perhaps you keep searching for a doctor who knows what really causes them so that you can get some relief. It must be difficult to absorb this happy family and all of the responsibilities while dealing with these terrible headaches."

"Sometimes, while the children are occupied with playing and coloring in their books, I sneak away, take a few of my pills, then go to bed for a bit. When I wake, I'm better for a little while."

Scaylee put his hand under her chin.

"Find a good doctor, Lynda Lee, and see if he can help relieve you of that pain. Promise?"

"It's no use, Scaylee. The doctors all say the same thing. I'm a woman dealing with stress. The headaches are just part of it. They dismiss me as if I'm not even there."

"Do you feel up to a walk?"

Lynda Lee smiled.

"I do, indeed."

"Good, there's something I'd like to show you, but it's quite a walk."

"Show me," Lynda Lee said.

They walked together until Lynda Lee was no longer aware of the time. And then it appeared and Lynda Lee gasped.

"Oh my," she said. "What is it, Scaylee?"

"It's called Kylemore Abbey and it was once the most beautiful structure in Galway. It was built for Benedictine nuns in the 19th century but was a family home for many years until the wars took over. The lakes are called Castle Lakes. Pretty, aren't they?"

"Beautiful," Lynda Lee said. "And do people live here now?"

"Oh yes, the original family moved away but left the home to the nuns. Many of them live there, still. They tend the gardens and keep up the castle with the help of the locals. I just wanted you to see it, Lynda Lee, to understand that we're not just dusty roads and tiny cottages. Galway has a rich heritage."

Lynda Lee sighed.

"How I'd love to live here and be of service to the nuns," she said.

"I'm sure they'd appreciate your special weaving talents. They're always in need of something. I'm sure you'd be welcomed there."

"That's just a dream, Scaylee, a dream that won't come true."

"How do you know it won't come true?"

"Because I've finally figured out that my dream world and my real world are not the same."

"There is nothing wrong with dreaming, Lynda Lee. Your dreams seem real enough when you're here, so perhaps they exist on another plane. Perhaps your dream of being here is as real as your life with Ray. You must simply believe in those dreams, Lynda Lee. Without faith, there is nothing. Hold fast to what you want, Lynda Lee, and have faith that what you want will come to pass."

"Lynda Lee? Are you all right? It's evening time. Where are the children and why are you in bed?"

Lynda Lee slowly opened her eyes.

"Headache, Ray. Terrible headache."

Ray took off his jacket, his tie, and his white button-down shirt. He dropped them all haphazardly on the nearest chair.

"Lynda Lee, get up, please. You're a mother now. You can't just go to bed and leave the children to fend for themselves."

Ray walked into the kitchen and found Julie at the stove checking on a casserole. He looked up and saw Mark outside in the garden.

"Have you children had a snack since you came home from school?"

"Mama Lynda gave us a piece of cake and some milk. It was really good. She sat with us while we ate. Then she said she had a terrible headache and needed to lie down for a while. She said she set the timer for the casserole and to just turn off the oven when the timer went off."

At that moment, the timer dinged.

"I'll get the casserole," Lynda Lee said from the kitchen doorway. She made her way slowly to the stove, grabbed a couple of pot holders, and took the potato, ham, and cheese casserole out of the oven.

"Would you help me with the salad, Julie?"

Julie hopped up from the table.

"What do you need from the fridge?"

"Lettuce, radishes, green onions, and those green beans in the colander. I'll get a couple of tomatoes from the window ledge."

The two of them worked in silence as they cut and diced the ingredients for the salad.

When they'd finished, Lynda Lee said, "What do you think? Does that look good?"

"Looks yummy," Julie said. "But we forgot the final touch, salt and pepper."

"Why don't you do the honors," Lynda Lee said. "Careful now. Not too much."

When the salad was finished, Lynda Lee asked Julie to help her set the dining table. They worked together and soon the table was set. Lynda Lee grabbed the casserole and set it on top of a trivet to keep the heat off the table. Julie got the salad and put it in the center of the table.

"What about the cake?" Julie asked.

"We'll save that for after dinner," Lynda Lee said. "You can help me serve the dessert, okay?"

"I love working in the kitchen. I want to learn how to cook wonderful dishes like you do, Mama Lynda."

"Then, we'll start working together, after homework."

"I've already finished my homework. It's Friday. I just have a little reading to do.

"What about Mark. Does he have homework?"

"He has a math sheet to do, but he won't do it. He doesn't understand it. Maybe Papa Ray could help him."

"You tell Mark to ask Papa Ray to help him with his math," she said and glanced at Ray. "It will be a good thing for both of them."

Julie nodded.

"I'll tell him right after dinner," Julie said.

"Wonderful, then I'll teach you what I can. And later, we'll get you a cookbook of your own so that you can begin to create dishes by yourself. Would you like that? Oh, and the garden party is next week, so you can help me make the dishes for that."

"I can help you with the garden party?"

"Of course, you can. We'll work together to make it spectacular. Now, go and call your brother and tell him to come in and wash up. Scoot."

As soon as Julie walked out, Lynda Lee turned to Ray.

"I didn't appreciate your tone or your accusations, Ray. How dare you accuse me of neglecting these children. How dare you!"

Ray stood close to her and put his hands on her slim shoulders.

"Forgive me, Lynda Lee. Please, forgive me. I came into the bedroom and saw you sleeping and ... I thought the very worst. I thought you'd taken pills for the headache, and it made me angry, but I didn't mean to accuse you of anything."

"But you did, Ray. That's exactly what you did. You didn't stop to think that I had things under control. Mark was busy outside and Julie was in here listening for the timer. She knew to wake me when the timer went off. I'd given them both specific instructions, and they both knew that I was going to take a short nap. They knew to come get me if anything went wrong."

"All I can do is keep apologizing, Lynda Lee. Please forgive me for my accusations and my harsh tone."

"No, that's not true, Ray. I don't ever want to hear another of your apologies again because they're just not enough. You don't trust me to be a good mother. You get angry about the pain pills, but you can't find a doctor who can help me. I'm sick of your apologies and your lack of trust in me."

"Please, please, Lynda Lee. I promise that it won't happen again. The fact is that I do trust you. It's just that I don't want you to become addicted to those pills."

"I'm still learning how to be a good mother to these precious children, and for you to accuse me of neglecting them is so hurtful that I'm not sure I'm ready to forgive you. But for their sakes, I'll forgive you, Ray, but I won't forget this so easily. You stung me to my core."

"What can I do, Lynda Lee, to make things better? Just tell me what to do, and I'll do it. I'll do anything to make you happy."

Lynda Lee put down her drying rag and turned to him.

"You can, for once, stop treating me like a drug addict. I have horrible headaches. I take pills to ease the pain. The pills sometimes make me sleepy. But my first priority is you and the children. But when I have one of those horrible headaches, my only relief is pain pills, Ray. You can't understand because you don't have them. But I want you to stop treating me like I'm some kind of addict in one of your clinics. Is that clear?" she asked as her voice got louder.

Just then, Julie and Mark burst through the back door.

"I'm starving," Mark said.

Lynda Lee smiled.

"Dinner is on the table. Go ...."

"I know, Mama Lynda. Go wash up. We can't come to the table dirty. That just wouldn't do," Mark called as he raced down the hall to his bathroom. "I'll be back in a jiffy after I wash my face and my hands."

"Is everything okay, Mama Lynda? How's your headache?" Julie asked.

"Better, thank you."

"I'll just go wash up and get ready for dinner. Is there anything you need me to do?"

"Not right now, dear. But after dinner, you can help me serve the cake and ice cream."

Julie smiled and walked down the hall to her bathroom.

Ray kissed Lynda Lee on the forehead.

"You're a terrific mother," he said.

"Before the children come back, I want to tell you what I'd like to do for them. Remember the money my mother gave me?"

"The ten thousand?"

"Yes, I'd like to go to the bank and open an account for Julie and for Mark. If anything happens to me, I want them to each have five thousand dollars in an account for their futures. The accounts would be savings accounts, and I want to make you the primary signer at my death. If they need access to the money for some reason before my death, then I can sign for them."

"That's a lot of money, Lynda Lee. You're sure you want to give it to the children? I thought you wanted to use it for an extended vacation abroad."

"A vacation doesn't really appeal to me now. The girls and I planned a trip to Ireland, a place I've always wanted to see. I got so excited thinking about it. We each ordered passports, and I just knew it would be the trip of a lifetime. But nothing worked out. In the end, we weren't able to go, either because of money or flimsy excuses. So, there will be no trips for me, Ray. I'd rather know that the children will have that money in case they need it for something in the future. It will help them make a good start when they are independent."

"I've left them and you plenty of money, Lynda Lee. I don't think you and the children will want for anything."

"Yes, I know about your life insurance, Ray, but this is just a little extra. I don't want them to face poverty and abuse ever again. Sometimes, the world is unkind. I want Julie and Mark to be able to afford a good life."

"Let's eat," Mark said as he and Julie came into the kitchen. "I'm starving!"

Seated at the table, Ray said the blessing and within twenty minutes there was nothing left of the casserole. It had been wiped clean.

Chapter 44

The sweltering heat, a record-breaker for April, had all but dried up the beautiful lake at the edge of their property on Weaver Street. Ray had insisted on following the guidelines and fulfilling the request from the orphanage that a fence be installed. So, he put a new chain-link fence around the property but with the fence, there was no view of the once-beautiful lake. No one in the house seemed to mind it at all.

"I wish we hadn't had to comply with the adoption regulations and put up that fence. It blocks some of our view."

"We really didn't have a choice, Lynda Lee. The committee demanded that we have a fence to protect the kids. The children are happy and healthy, at last, and I want them to be safe here. You want the same thing, don't you, Lynda Lee?"

"Of course, I do. It's just that all of that construction has ruined the look of the yard for now, and our Garden Party will have to be held at Beth and John's house. I was so looking forward to having it here. I just don't think the ugly fence adds any beauty to the property, so I'm hoping that in addition to the safety factor, it will add value to the home. We're the only ones on Weaver Street who have such a fence."

"This chain link is the latest in fencing materials. It's strong and durable with a fine mesh that looks quite nice when it's installed. The children will be able to play outside and see everyone else, as well. A wooden fence would have obstructed their views of the neighbors. You can understand that, can't you?"

Lynda Lee straightened the dining table and put on a new cloth.

Ray walked up behind her and kissed her neck.

"I didn't mean to upset you. The salesman came by the hospital a few weeks ago and had a special meeting about the new chain-link fences, new and improved and strong enough to protect anyone within its walls. I thought it would be a great thing for the children and for our peace of mind."

Lynda Lee shrugged.

"I guess it's just as well," she said and wiped her hands on a dishcloth, "I can't see the lake anymore since it's just about dried up. I loved looking out the sliding glass doors at that glistening lake."

"Ah, I see," Ray said. "It's the lake you miss, your sort of sanctuary."

"Yes, Ray, I miss that lake. It's one of the things that appealed to me most about living here on Weaver Street. We have a beautiful home, but I can't get up every morning, sit at the table, and watch the sun glinting on the lake. I miss that. It's so much hotter here than in New York City."

"Yes, I know it is, but since it was a man-made lake, we can see about getting it back. I'll talk to the County Commissioner to see if there is anything that can be done about it. There's certainly no lack of water here. So, perhaps there's a chance."

Lynda Lee smiled.

"Do you really think so?"

"Anything's possible," he said and winked. "But shouldn't we be getting ready for the Garden Party at Beth and John's house?"

He glanced at his watch.

"We've only a couple of hours before it starts. John's doing some barbecue, I think, on his new grill."

"Right, I'd almost forgotten. I need to get the children in and let them get ready."

Lynda Lee opened the back door and called to Julie and Mark.

"Time to come in," she said. "We have a Garden Party tonight, and we must be on our very best behavior. We also have to be clean and polished. So, go clean up and change clothes. We don't want Beth and John to think you're little ragamuffins," she said with a chuckle.

"I'm going to change, too," she said to Ray. "My beauty routine needs a boost. Otherwise, I'll lose my title as the Goddess of Weaver

Street. I'd be devastated," she said and grinned.

"Go," Ray said, "and pretty yourself up. I'll change into some shorts before we go."

Lynda Lee left to go change while Ray made a phone call.

"Mr. Broadhurst," he said. "This is Ray Rogers. Oh, the children are doing just fine, thank you. They're growing like weeds. They're a great addition to our household. But I'm calling about a different matter entirely," Ray said as he stepped outside and lit a cigar. "You're familiar with Weaver Street, aren't you? I'd like to ask something of you that might not be possible, but I'm hoping there's a way between the two of us that we can make it happen."

Ray took a puff off his cigar.

"Yes, I agree, we are two prominent members of our respective communities. Here on Weaver Street, we seem to have a problem. I've spoken already to the City Commissioner, but between us, he was no help. I thought, perhaps, that you might be able to persuade him to consider my proposal."

Ray listened as he walked around outside and admired Mark's skill with gardening. His new plants seemed to be shooting out of the ground at a rapid pace.

"Yes," Ray said. "One of the reasons we moved here was the lake, which has now all but dried up. Surely there is enough water here to refill it again. It's man-made, after all, and honestly, without the lake, I fear that people in the community will begin to sell their homes and leave. And that would be a tragedy. It's only gossip now, but you can never tell about such things. Everyone here is extremely disappointed with the lack of that lake."

Ray knelt and smelled the first of the blooming roses. He smiled in wonder at Mark's skill with gardening.

"Oh, I'd appreciate whatever you could do to help bring back our lake, Mr. Broadhurst. If financing is a problem, I'd be glad to help with that. And if it's just a matter of bringing it to someone's attention, then there's no one with more influence in this town than you. I've always said that if you want something done, you contact Mr. Broadhurst."

Ray took another puff from his cigar.

"Thank you so much, Mr. Broadhurst. All of us in the community would be grateful for anything you could do. And you can be sure that you'd have our support in the next election. You'd make a fine mayor, and I for one, will be vocal in my support of you. Thank you. Thank you again. I'll talk to you soon."

"I'm ready," Mark said as he ran into the kitchen.

"We're both ready," Julie said. "How do we look?"

Julie turned in a circle just as Ray came back in.

"Well, well," he said. "You both look great. Clean and tidy, just the way your Mama Lynda likes you to be."

"Aren't you going to change, Papa Ray?"

"I'm on my way," he said and smiled. "Be sure all the doors are locked and everything in the kitchen is in its proper place. And remember to check all the appliances. Make sure the stove is off. Doors are closed. Nothing is on while we are gone."

As he walked out the door, he turned.

"I like the new outfits," he said. "You two make a fine-looking pair. Beth and John will think so, too."

Mark ran outside to check on his garden one more time before nightfall. Julie busied herself in the kitchen making sure everything was in its proper place. She wiped off the counters again until they were shiny. Then she ran a clean rag over the fronts of the cabinets, the refrigerator door, the oven and the table until everything was spotless.

"What a fine job you've done, Julie. The kitchen looks just perfect," Lynda Lee said and hugged her. "And I love you new outfit. The floral print on the pants and top look just lovely."

"Thank you, Mama Lynda. Let me look at you," Julie said. "Your eyes are a little bloodshot, but other than that, you look amazing. I adore that beautiful silk blouse paired with those capri pants. And your hair, pulled up in a ponytail. It looks great. I hope that someday, I'll be as beautiful as you are."

"So," Ray said, "are we ready?"

"Yes, I think we're all ready to go. We don't want to be late for Beth and John's party."

The four of them walked down the block to Beth and John's house. They were met at the door by Beth herself.

"Well, look who it is, the beautiful Goddess of Weaver Street and her adorable family. Welcome to our first party of the summer," Beth said and invited them in.

Chapter 45

Several weeks later, Lynda Lee heard a knock on the door.

"Just a minute," she called and wiped her hands on her apron.

As she walked to the door, she stopped briefly and looked at herself in the mirror.

"Mercy," she mumbled. "I look a fright."

The knock came again, so she walked to the door and opened it.

Several men in work clothes stood outside her house.

"Mrs. Rogers?" one of them said.

"I'm Mrs. Rogers, yes. How may I help you?"

"We're from the city," the first one said. "We just wanted everyone to be aware that we'll be working around here for a few days."

"Working?" she asked.

"Yes, we have been assigned to try to refill the lake behind the houses. It will take some work, but we have our orders."

"You're filling the lake?"

The man nodded.

"Is there a problem?" the man said.

"No, no problem at all. We here on Weaver Street will be delighted to have our lake back. And just who is it we thank for restoring our lake?"

The man shrugged.

"We have our work order from the city, Mrs. Rogers. That's all I know."

"May I see it?"

The man handed her a set of papers. She combed through looking for a name she recognized, and right before she handed back the set of papers, she found the name: Broadhurst.

She smiled and handed the papers back to the worker.

"Thank you," she said. "Can the children still play in the back yard while you're working?"

"Sure, we won't be near any of the houses. The lake will be filled with recycled water from the Black Warrior River. That just means that it will be filtered as it's filled, so the lake should be clean."

Lynda Lee smiled.

"I'm delighted to hear it. Everyone on Weaver Street will be pleased as punch to know that our beautiful lake has been restored. Is there anything I can do to help?"

"We've got it covered, thank you. We'll get to work tomorrow morning. You could tell the others in the neighborhood if you felt like it. We don't have time to go to every house. You're the second person we've contacted, but we really need to get back to work. So, if you don't mind, you could tell the others that we'll be working for a few weeks at the lake."

"I'll be happy to," Lynda Lee said. "I'm so excited to hear it, and the neighbors will be, too."

"Good day to you," the worker said as his crew followed him to the truck.

As soon as they'd pulled out of sight, Lynda Lee called Beth.

"Did you hear the good news?"

"What news?" Beth asked. "If it's good news, tell me. If it's not, then ...."

"Oh, Beth, it's good news. We're getting our lake back. Isn't it exciting?"

"Really, how on earth did that happen?"

Lynda Lee stood in front of the mirror and ran her fingers through her hair. Then, she shook her head to let her hair flow naturally. She smoothed the skirt of her shirt-waist dress and smiled at her reflection.

"I really don't know how it happened," Lynda Lee said. "I was just complaining to Ray about how much I missed the lake, but that was weeks ago. Maybe he made a call or something."

"Well, I for one will be happy to have our lake back. I just hope it doesn't dry up again. It's so hot here that I'm surprised any lake can stay full. This heat is oppressive. We run our air units day and night. John has already complained about the bills, but I just can't survive without that air conditioner."

"The news reporters say that this is the hottest May on record for the last fifty years. As long as we've lived here, I've never felt such stifling heat. We run our units, too. Otherwise, Alabama would just be unbearable, and just think, when our lake is restored, we can go and have a swim."

"Now, that is something I can look forward to," Beth said. "I've missed that lake. Hey, do Julie and Mark know how to swim? Maybe you should enroll them in the YMCA for the summer. They're out of school now, aren't they?"

"Two more weeks," Lynda Lee said. "They get out at the end of May."

"Good, then you've plenty of time to enroll them in swim classes. If we're going to have our lake back, the children need to know how to swim. Don't you think?"

"I hadn't thought of it. I'll call and find out when swim classes start."

"Don't forget about the barbecue tonight at Janine's house. She wants us all to come."

"Is she feeling up to it?" Lynda Lee asked. "I thought she had the flu."

"It was just a bad cold," Beth said. "I'm going over early to help her get things ready. Now that they have one of those new grills, her hubby is ready to show off his skills."

"Mark prefers hot dogs. Do you think they'll have them along with the burgers?"

"Yep," Beth said. "I saw all the meat in the fridge when I went over yesterday. They have a little of everything, including a couple of chickens."

"They'll have cheese, too, right? Julie likes cheese on her hamburgers."

"I take it you like being a mother. Are you adjusting fairly well?"

"I'm adjusting, yes. Why don't you come over for a glass of iced tea? We can talk in person before the children come home."

"Be right there. You call the Y and see about the classes. See you in five."

Lynda Lee got out the phone book and found the number for the YMCA.

When the receptionist answered in a chirpy voice, Lynda Lee said, "I'd like to see about enrolling my children for the swim classes this summer."

"What level class do you need?"

"I don't think they know how to swim at all."

"The Beginners class then. We call it the Minnows. It will begin in two weeks."

"The Minnows," Lynda Lee repeated. "And what time are the classes?"

"We open at 9:00 for swimming. The Minnows are the first class of the day, on Mondays and Wednesdays, so they should be here, in their swim suits, by 9:00. The class is one hour. They'll need a towel. The girl will need a swim cap, as well."

Lynda Lee waved as Beth walked in and motioned her to the kitchen.

"And I pick them up when the class is over?"

"Yes, ma'am. Class will end at 10:00. If you don't want to drive back home, you're welcome to join the Y and enroll in a class for adults or you can use the indoor walking path for exercise."

"That sounds like a good idea," Lynda Lee said. "When do I pay for joining?"

"You can just write a check when you come. The total for the swim classes and for you to join yourself will be ten dollars for the summer."

"I thought everything at the YMCA was free, but I'm happy to pay for the lessons."

"We have to pay our instructors, so classes aren't free but very reasonably priced. If you'll give me your address, I'll send out a card as a reminder."

Lynda Lee gave the girl her address, said a cheery good-bye, and hung up the phone.

"That was easy," she said to Beth. "They'll be in the Minnows class from nine until ten on Mondays and Wednesdays. I signed up to do the walking path while they're swimming. Would you want to go with me?"

"Sure, that sounds like fun. Goodness knows, I could use the exercise. Maybe I'll be able to lose a few pounds while I'm at it. Should I call in advance?"

"Probably. I can't imagine that the indoor walking path would be full, but maybe just call so you'll get a reminder card."

"Oh, look," Beth said. "I think I see some of the workers already down at the lake! How exciting."

Lynda Lee smiled, although inside, something gnawed at her. She'd be oh, so happy to have the lake back, but ... something, something kept making her feel uneasy, and she suddenly wished she hadn't mentioned it to Ray.

Chapter 46

Three weeks into the swimming class, as they were about to leave, Lynda Lee noticed that Mark wasn't in the car.

"Julie, where's Mark?"

Julie shrugged.

"Julie, if you know where Mark is, please tell me," Lynda Lee said. "We're going to be late for our classes."

"All I know is that he didn't want to go to swim class any more. He told me last night."

Lynda Lee got out of the Beth's car, walked through the house and out the back door. She found Mark outside tending his garden.

"You have some fine plants, Mark. I'm very proud of you," she said and knelt beside him.

Mark said nothing. He didn't even acknowledge that she was there.

"Is there something bothering you, Mark? If there is, you can tell me. I won't be mad or angry, but right now, it's time for our swim class. We don't want to be late."

Mark stood up and removed his gardening gloves.

"I don't like them," he said. "I don't like being in the water. It's too scary."

"That's exactly why we need to go, Mark. The lake in the back of us will soon be filled. If an accident happened and you fell in, you might drown. So, you need to learn to swim to protect yourself. And even though it's scary, learning to swim might save your life one of these days."

She ran a hand through his shaggy hair, which he refused to have cut.

"Please, be a brave boy and let's go to the swimming lesson. I'll go in swimming with you if you want."

"Would Papa Ray be able to go?"

"No, I'm afraid not, Mark. Papa Ray is at work."

Mark sighed.

"Then can't you just leave me here? I won't get into anything. I promise."

Lynda Lee put her arm around Mark.

"It's my job, brave boy, to teach you the things you need to know to get along in this world. One day you will need to know how to swim, and I want you to be prepared. So, if you'll go with us one more time, just today, and do your very best, I promise that we'll do something fun this afternoon. Okay?"

"Will you make some of my favorite chocolate cookies?"

Lynda Lee smiled.

"I will if you promise me that you will try your best in class today. Be brave. Try to have fun in the water, okay?"

When the two of them finally climbed into the car, Julie said, "You've made us late already. Where have you been?"

"I hate swimming lessons. I told you that. Leave me alone."

Lynda Lee looked over at Beth and shook her head.

Within a few minutes, they were parked in the lot at the YMCA.

Mark grumbled all the way inside while Julie skipped along beside him. Every now and then, she put her hand on his shoulder and smiled.

They heard the whistle that meant swim class had begun.

Lynda Lee knelt down in front of Mark.

"Chocolate cookies this afternoon if you do a good job in there. Just swim like you love it and do what Papa Ray always says: 'Walk in like you own the place.'"

Mark giggled.

"I'll do my best," he said.

Beth and Lynda Lee signed in and headed toward the walking path.

"How's your headache this morning?" Beth asked.

"Not great but a little less painful than it is most of the time. I have only a few brief periods of no pain, but I've tried to quit complaining about it. I do try to get a nap each day, though. That seems to help if I take my pain pills."

"Doesn't Ray think you need to see a specialist?"

"Sure," she said, "but my doctor is a specialist. He's a neurologist, but I've only seen him once. He did some sort of x-ray, found nothing, and recommended another doctor who treats migraines. He gave me a more powerful pain killer. Ray wasn't happy about that."

"Doesn't Ray want you to get relief from the headaches? Of all people, I thought he'd be the one who'd insist you kept going to doctors to get relief."

"Oh yes," Lynda Lee said. "He wants me to get relief, just not from pills. His take on it is that I'm already addicted to the pills and that my head hurts only when my body craves the effects of the pills."

"Walk slower," Beth said. "I can hardly keep up with you, Miss Beauty Pageant Queen!"

Lynda Lee chuckled.

"I have had a lot of experience training for runways, but that was long ago."

"But it's evident whenever anyone sees you. You still have that beautiful runway posture. After all these years, Lynda Lee, you are still as beautiful as you were the first time I saw you. I don't think you've gained a single ounce in all these years."

"I have, but don't tell Ray. In fact, I'm five pounds over my ideal weight. Maybe walking will help shake off those pounds."

"Oh, look," Beth said. "There are the benches. Let's sit for a bit while the children swim."

Lynda Lee put her bag and towels on the bench.

"I have my swimsuit on beneath my clothes," she said.

"Oh, I don't want to get into that water," Beth said. "I'm not a good swimmer."

"I'm going to peek in on Mark to see if he's in the water. Be right back."

Lynda Lee peeked into the swimming pool area. Mark was at least in the water, but he was sitting on the third step that led into the pool. She saw Julie in line with the others in the shallow end practicing kicking her legs and then moving her arms. But Mark sat stone still on the steps.

After a moment, Julie waded over to him and held out her hand, but Mark refused to take it.

Finally, Lynda Lee heard the instructor's whistle.

"Line up on the side of the pool," the instructor said. "And that includes you, Mark. Come and join the others."

Mark looked angry, but he got up and joined the others in a line across the outside of the pool.

"Now," the instructor said, "One at a time, I want you to jump in and see if you can swim to the other side of the pool. Take your time. I'll be right in the water beside you."

Just then, Mark looked up and saw Lynda Lee standing at the door. She smiled and gave him a thumbs up. In turn, he dropped his head.

Some of the children had trouble making it to the other side of the pool, but the instructor was right there beside them to help. And then it was Mark's turn.

"Come on, Mark. You're the last. So, just jump in and I'll be right beside you. Go!"

Mark glanced up at Lynda Lee then jumped feet first into the water, but he sank like a stone. He flailed his arms and legs but made no headway. The instructor pulled him up and put him on the first of the pool steps.

"It's okay, Mark. You jumped in like a pro," she said. "With a little more practice, you'll be a good swimmer."

She wrapped him in a towel.

"Come on. Let's get you dried off," Lynda Lee said as she knelt beside him.

"They're all going to make fun of me, Mama Lynda. I'm not coming back. They'll call me all sorts of ugly names."

"Mark, it doesn't matter what other children say. It's hurtful, yes, but what's important is how you feel about yourself. You have to believe in yourself, then their ugly words won't bother you so much because you'll know that they're not true."

Mark shrugged.

"So, how about if I get in the water and you jump to me? Then, we'll swim together across the pool. Are you brave enough to try again? I'll tell you a secret if you do."

Mark looked up at her.

"A secret?"

Lynda Lee nodded.

"If you'll swim with me, I'll tell you my secret."

"You're getting in the water? Where's your swim suit?"

"I have it on underneath my robe, silly boy. Want to give it a try?"

"You'll be right there with me? Promise?"

Lynda Lee ran a hand through his wet hair.

"I promise. The others have gone. Let's give it a go, shall we?"

Lynda Lee removed her robe. Underneath, she wore a fashionable Jantzen purple polka dot halter top suit that fit at the waist then flared into a swim skirt that fell just to the tops of her legs. She donned her purple and white swim cap, pushing her long hair in and out to make it fit.

Then, she took Mark's hand and positioned him toward the shallow end. She walked down the pool steps and into the water. She reached up and took Mark's hand again and moved further toward the deeper end.

"Now, Mark, you can see that I am right here with you. So, just jump and I'll catch you. You can do this, Mark. Treat this pool as if you own it and you can tell it what to do!" she said and smiled.

All of a sudden, Mark jumped in.

Lynda Lee caught him.

"Now, we're going to swim," she said and put her arms under his.

"Kick your feet," she said as she guided him toward the other side of the pool, her arms still under his.

"That's it," she yelled. "You're swimming, Mark! Now, you're only two feet from the other side. I'm right here beside you."

She removed her hands from under his arms and watched his hands stretch toward the side, his feet kicking like crazy. Finally, he grabbed the side of the pool and looked at her.

"I made it all by myself, didn't I?"

"You most certainly did, Mark. What a brave boy you are!" she said and kissed the top of his head.

"Can we do it again?" he asked. "One more time?"

"I'm ready if you are," she said. "Let's move to the shallow end."

He jumped off one more time with Lynda Lee standing ready to catch him.

After he jumped in, she guided him for a few steps then let him go on his own. He did a basic dog paddle, but he made it to the other side all on his own. He was swimming!

"So, what is the big secret, Mama Lynda? You promised to tell me a secret."

"That's right," she said and whispered the secret in Mark's ear.

"What?" he said. "You used to be a what?"

"A mermaid," Lynda Lee said and took off in the water, swimming laps back and forth, doing some somersaults under the water and the front and back strokes to impress Mark. Then for her final move, she ducked under the water, swam around under the waves and stayed. Little by little she let out the breath she'd been holding.

"Mama Lynda, come up," Mark yelled. "You'll drown under there. Please come up."

But Lynda Lee stayed another minute and then shot to the surface, arms perfectly straight by her sides.

Mark ran to the side of the pool.

"I was worried," he said. "You stayed under so long. You scared me."

As she climbed out of the pool, she said to him.

"No need to be afraid, Mark. I used to be a mermaid. Mermaids don't drown," she smiled and winked at him.

"Can we go home now? You made a pretty mermaid with all those tricks, but I'm ready to go home."

Both of them were unaware that the instructor had been watching them the whole time. And that is how Lynda Lee ended up being the swim team coach for the rest of the summer.

Chapter 47

By the end of the summer, Lynda Lee had lost the five pounds she complained about and Beth, who, as it turned out, loved to swim, had dropped fifteen pounds. Their weekly routine at the YMCA, and Lynda Lee's job as swim coach kept them both trim and fit. They enjoyed the routine and became even closer friends than before.

So, when Beth announced that she and John were leaving Weaver Street, Lynda Lee broke down into sobs.

"Oh, Beth, what will I do without you?"

Beth wiped away tears.

"I don't want to go," she said and sniffed. "I don't want to leave the best friend I've ever had in the world, but it's not up to me, Lynda Lee. John's been offered a position in Huntsville. It's a great promotion for him, more money, more authority. He'll move up to Chief of Surgery for the cardiac intensive care unit. It's his dream job. How can I say no?"

Lynda Lee wiped her face and stammered,

"Y-You can't."

Lynda Lee broke down again.

"I'll miss you so much," she muttered. "I'm losing my only friend in this world."

They hugged each other tightly.

"When do you go?"

"Three weeks," Beth said.

"What about the house? What will you do with it?"

"I'm not sure. I just learned of this yesterday, and I don't know what we'll do about anything," she said and sniffed again. "I just don't know, Lynda Lee."

The two of them sat at the kitchen table.

"I'll make some coffee," Lynda Lee said as she wiped her eyes again. "Ray bought another new coffeemaker. The one we had was almost new, but he insisted that we got the top of the line for our coffee. This one is called a Braun Coffee Master. How silly."

Beth stared out the large window.

"Your yard looks beautiful, and I can see all the way to the top of the lake. I wish I had this view from my kitchen window. I might never leave it."

Lynda Lee poured each of them a cup of coffee, cream and sugar a must. Then she put the pot on the burner again.

"Ray bought this new coffee called Jamaican Blue Mountain coffee. It's really good. I use it every day now. Try it. You'll like it, I think."

Beth took a sip.

"Wow," she said. "It's deep and rich, just the way I like it. Congratulations to Ray and his fine taste in coffees."

"The back yard I owe to Mark," Lynda Lee said. "He's a magnificent gardener and working in the yard with the dirt on his hands and the plants all around, well, he's worked something akin to magic in the yard."

"I agree. It's really beautiful."

"I'm grateful to Mark and his gardening skills and to Ray because he's so good about complimenting Mark and making him feel special. The two of them have become just like a real father and son team," she said as she took her seat at the table. She blew on the cup of hot coffee.

"Do you think we'll ever see each other again, Lynda Lee? I can hardly stand the thought of it," Beth said and wiped at her nose.

"I'm not sure, Beth," Lynda Lee said and took a sip of her cooled coffee. "Huntsville is a four- to five-hour journey from here. Ray doesn't get much time off these days, but I guess you just never know. There's that gathering once a year for everyone in all the cardiac units in Alabama. So, I guess it's possible."

"Yes," Beth said. "We all went together to last year's statewide conference. I remember how we both worried about what we'd wear that night. You chose that pink sheath dress with the crystals embroidered on it and a pink headband. At that banquet, you were the most beautiful woman there. The men could hardly keep their eyes off you. Ray hardly left your side."

Lynda Lee took another sip of coffee.

"I didn't notice," she said. "But we had a good time."

"We did," Beth said and teared up again. "And every time I looked your way, I felt so fortunate to have the Goddess of Weaver Street as my closest friend."

Lynda Lee smiled.

"Do you remember when we first met? It seems so long ago now."

"I remember," Beth said. "How well I remember those days. You haven't changed one bit."

"Don't be silly," Lynda Lee said as she rubbed her temples. "I'm not the same person I was all those years ago. I've grown up a little more. And, I have two children whom I adore."

"By the way, where are the children?"

"They're with Mrs. Baker, one of the school moms. She took a group of them to a place called Moundville today. They won't be back until dark."

"That's good," Beth said. "Another headache? I thought they might be better since you don't say much about them anymore."

"They never left, Beth, but over time, they just got worse and now, they're worse than ever."

"Do you still have some pain pills to take?" Beth asked as she took her cup to the sink.

"Yes, I have a whole bottle and even a spare one that the specialist gave me."

"Want me to get them for you while I'm up?" Beth asked as she wiped her hands on the dishcloth.

"No, not now. I'll take a couple and then get a nap before Ray gets home."

After they had both cried again and said their good-byes, Lynda Lee closed the door and went back to the kitchen. She sat at the table, looked out at the yard, and cried.

Beth was leaving. She hadn't taken the time to get to know the other wives. She knew them, of course, but she hadn't formed a bond with them. With Beth gone, she would be friendless.

She opened her bottle of pills and took two for her throbbing headache. Then she got up and walked to the daybed in the den. She wiped her face, took off her shoes, let her hair down, and settled herself comfortably on the soft cushions.

Within a few minutes, she relaxed, dug herself deeper into the cushions, and feel fast asleep. The dream came almost immediately.

Chapter 48

Lynda Lee struggled up the rocky cliffside to reach the roadway, but it was rough going. Her feet seemed unable to find the right outcroppings to get a good balance.

"I've come the wrong way again," she mumbled to herself.

Slowly and painfully, she inched herself up the rocky cliff, scraping her hands and legs on the sharp places that jutted from the rocks. By the time she reached the top, she was almost in tears when suddenly a large hand took hold of hers and pulled her effortlessly onto the dusty road.

"Scaylee! It's so good to see you. Thank you for helping me up the path. I'd almost decided to try to get back home."

"Sometimes, that path can be a rocky one," he said. "It's good that I came along at just the right time, eh?"

"Your timing is impeccable."

"We haven't seen you in a while, Lynda Lee. How are things at home? Come, let's go inside and sit."

"Where is Maman? Why isn't she at her loom?"

Scaylee opened the cottage door for her and shooed her inside.

"Take a seat. Maman will be here shortly. She had others to see about, and it's been quiet here, so she doesn't have much weaving to do."

Lynda Lee sat in the chair and relaxed.

"Tea?" Scaylee asked. "Coffee?"

"Tea would be perfect," she said as she looked around the cottage. "It all looks so different now. But I see Maman's blue roses climbing all over the outside. And all the furniture is the same. It just, somehow, seems different. I can clearly see that it's not different, but the feel of it seems more welcoming somehow."

"It's just the years, Lynda Lee. As they pass, changes come. It will always be so. But just remember that even though it might look different on the outside, the cottage serves the very same purpose. It's a haven for those who seek it, those like you who dream of a different life, a life here."

Scaylee poured her tea and added a bit of cream and sugar. Then he placed it on the small table, removed his hat, and took the chair opposite her.

"So, Lynda Lee, tell me what's been going on in your life."

Lynda Lee smiled.

"Our children have enriched our lives, Scaylee. We are a happier family now that they've been with us a while."

"And how does Ray feel about them?"

"You wouldn't believe it, Scaylee. He and Mark, the boy, have become a bonded pair. They do things together when Ray finds time off. They even read the newspaper together at night. It's quite sweet to watch them. They speak a language of their own. I've seen Ray do some hand signals and Mark responds each time. It's just precious."

"So, you're pleased with your life, then?"

"Yes, most of the time, I feel content, grateful for what we have together. If I could just get rid of these blinding headaches, I'd be much better."

"Have you had any news from the doctors about what might be causing the headaches?"

Lynda Lee shook her head.

"I've been to specialists, had x-rays done, all sorts of tests, but each one resorts to the same old diagnosis, stress. It's so very hard for me to understand, Scaylee. The pain is debilitating. The only way I can get through it is with pain pills and sleep."

"Do your pills still help?"

"Yes, this newest doctor prescribed a stronger medicine, and it works well," she said as she sipped the last of her tea. "But of course, it makes me sleepy, and I have no choice except to go to bed. It's hard on the children to see me in pain, but they've grown accustomed to my nap sessions throughout the day."

"How old is the older?"

"Julie is fifteen now. She's great in the kitchen. She loves to cook and bake, so when I have one of my headaches, she takes over the household. She cooks, serves everyone, then cleans up the kitchen to her high standards. She is such a blessing to me. If she had to, she could take charge and run the house by herself."

"And the other one?"

"Mark, he's thirteen," she said and crossed her arms over her. "His passion is gardening. Our back yard is the most beautiful yard on the block. He's planted blooming flowers that add so much color to our yard. And he's planted an entire vegetable garden, as well, so that we have fresh vegetables all the time. Even at his age, he is a master gardener."

"It certainly sounds like a very happy and healthy home, Lynda Lee. I'm delighted that things have gone so well for you."

Lynda Lee lowered her eyes.

"What's wrong?" Scaylee asked. "Is something bothering you? You shouldn't be bothered with the headaches here."

Lynda Lee shook her head.

"I have a fine life now, Scaylee. It's just that I thought I had everything to make me happy, but most of the time, I'm very sad. I just don't show it."

"Why are you sad, Lynda Lee?"

"Because no matter how successful I am or how many friends I have or how many functions I attend, I never feel at peace. It's as if ... as if something is missing, something I need. And each time I get this way, all I can think of is being here with you and Maman."

When the door opened, Maman stepped gently across the threshold.

"Well, well, Child. It's lovely to see you again. We've missed you."

Lynda Lee jumped up from her chair and hugged the old Irish weaver.

"Oh, Maman, I've missed you so," she said. "There's hardly a moment that goes by when I'm not thinking of you or Scaylee or this wonderful place."

"Take your seat now, Child. No need to go on so. I'll sit with you while Scaylee fixes me some of his miracle tea."

"Miracle tea?"

"Oh yes," Maman said. "I can be worn out, just worn to a nub, and a cup of Scaylee's tea invigorates me so that I can finish my work. That boy has always had magic with tea."

"You knew Scaylee when he was a boy?"

"I did, indeed. He was born in Galway, too."

"Scaylee, you never mentioned you'd been born in Galway."

Scaylee smiled.

"You haven't changed at all, Maman. You even have the same blue dress and apron, but they both look sparkling clean. Even your white cap looks brighter. How I've missed seeing you."

"We've missed you, Child. It's been a while since we've seen you."

"I've longed to be here with you and Scaylee, Maman. I'm taking new pills for my headaches and they put me to sleep. And in that sleep, I can dream. I can come here again and be in the place I love most."

"Ah, but this isn't the place it used to be, Lynda Lee," Scaylee said. "It isn't Galway any longer. We moved far north of Galway. Is that still all right with you?"

"I'll follow you wherever you and Maman go, Scaylee. I don't care where it is, as long as I can get to it, and I hope the next time won't be as difficult as this time. It was so hard to reach you."

"You were away for a long time, Lynda Lee. You just took the hardest path. Next time, you'll know exactly how to get here, and it will be easy for you."

"I'm so glad you were there to help me, Scaylee. If it hadn't been for you, I might not have made it."

"As you said, my timing is impeccable," Scaylee said and laughed out loud.

"Lynda Lee? Lynda Lee. Wake up. Come on now. It's time to get up," said the harsh voice. "Come on, Lynda Lee."

"Leave me alone, Ray. I'm happy where I am. Go away. Just go away."

But by then, she was back in the living room on the day bed.

"Why do you do that, Ray? Why do you insist on waking me up when you know I've been in pain and I need my sleep?"

"We have somewhere to go," Ray said. "So, you and the children need to get dressed. We have someplace to be in an hour or so."

"What place, Ray? There's nothing on the calendar. So, you're wrong. Now, let me go back to sleep."

"Mama Lynda?"

"Yes, Julie, what is it dear?" she asked as she wiped her eyes.

"We have a surprise for you. We're going someplace special."

Lynda Lee smiled.

"And where would that be?"

"I can't tell or it wouldn't be a surprise," Julie said and giggled; then she helped Lynda Lee get up off the day bed. "I think you'll love it."

"Wear your best," Ray said to her. "This is a very special occasion. Even Beth and John are going, so be quick about it and put on your finest."

Chapter 49

When they pulled up in front of The Relay House, Lynda Lee looked over at Ray.

"What are we doing here?"

"We're having dinner with Beth and John."

"That's the special surprise?" she asked. "They're our best friends. We have dinner with Beth and John every week. So, what's so special about tonight?"

"You'll see. Just be patient," Ray said as the valet ushered them to the elevators and then took their cars to valet parking.

As they rode the elevator to the second floor, Lynda Lee sighed.

"I just don't see why this is so special," she said.

Ray took her hand.

"Be patient, my love. Just be patient."

When the elevator stopped and the four of them got out, Lynda Lee immediately saw Beth and John sitting at one of the front tables. Beth motioned for them.

"Just look at the Rogers' family. Julie, you look beautiful, honey, and look at Mark in his suit. How handsome you look, Mark."

"Thank you, Beth," Mark and Julie said in unison.

"And here she is. Lynda Lee, you look absolutely stunning in that pink sheath dress. I think it's my favorite on you. Sit," she said. "I hope for once your headache is bearable. Is it?"

"It is, thankfully. Is that a new dress?"

Beth smiled.

"John bought this for me as a surprise gift, so yes, it's new."

Beth stood up and twirled around.

What do you think about it?"

"It's a great color on you. I don't think I've ever seen you wear red before, but it suits you. It's bright and bold, and brings out the gold flecks in your brown eyes. It's very flattering."

"The full skirt doesn't make me look too, uh, pudgy?"

Lynda Lee laughed.

"You're not pudgy, Beth. You're healthy and in fine form," Lynda Lee said.

Beth sat back down and waited with the others.

Then, all of a sudden, a familiar brown face appeared, a familiar deep voice with a slight British accent welcomed them.

Lynda Lee could hardly contain herself. She was out of her chair within seconds.

"Mr. Bugg," she said and put her hand on his. "You're back. Oh, how we've missed you."

Mr. Bugg smiled.

"Oh, Mrs. Rogers, you cannot imagine how much I have missed working here at The Relay House."

"So, your other job didn't work out?"

"What job could compare to the one I have here? I was offered a promotion, so I left the other job and came back as quickly as I could. Now, how may I serve you? Would you like the four-cheese plate for a starter?"

"Yes," Lynda Lee said, "but first, I'd like for you to meet Julie and Mark, our children."

Julie and Mark smiled up at him.

"It's very nice to meet you, Mr. Bugg," Julie said.

"The pleasure is all mine," he said. "I must say that the two of you are welcome here any time. I'm delighted to meet you both. Is there anything on the menu that you fancy?"

"We don't want steak," Mark said. "Isn't that right, Julie?"

"Right," she said. "I think Mark and I will have vegetable plates. Whatever you have will be fine. And may we try the cheese plate, too, and plenty of those rolls Papa Ray is always talking about?"

"Of course," Mr. Bugg said. "Are both of you vegetarians?"

Julie surveyed the menu again.

"We both like fish," she said. "But we just don't like red meat. Is it all right for me to say that, Mama Lynda?"

"It's perfectly fine, but I haven't heard you mention that before. When did you become vegetarians?"

"It was Mark's idea. He sees all these little bugs and insects in the garden, and there's a stray dog that wanders by each day. Mark always gives him a few scraps. So, he just decided that he didn't want to eat any animals. He asked me if you'd be mad, but I said no."

"I don't see that there's anything wrong with that, Julie," Lynda Lee said. "Mr. Bugg, you should see what a fine gardener Mark is. Our back yard is full of vegetables and beautiful blooming flowers. He's turned it into a thing of beauty."

"Then, perhaps he's found his calling in life, and at such a young age."

When the orders were taken, Mr. Bugg excused himself.

Another waiter stood at the ready to bring iced tea, water, and a large basket of rolls and different sorts of breads, and within only a few moments, they were served two cheese plates with a variety of crackers and more rolls.

Lynda Lee picked up the small cheese knife and showed it to Julie and Mark.

"This is the knife you use especially for cheese," she said and placed it back on the plate. "You'll have different utensils for each dish."

Another waiter appeared with an enormous bowl of salad that he placed in the center of the table. Two tongs on either side made serving easy.

"May I serve anyone a house salad?"

Lynda Lee touched her salad plate so that Mark and Julie could see which one to use. Then, she showed them the salad fork.

"Your plate and your fork for salad," she said.

In turn, they each raised their plates for the salad.

"Julie, will you pass around the rolls, please?" Lynda Lee asked.

Julie took one, gave one to Mark, and passed them to Lynda Lee, who took one and handed the basket to Ray.

Every now and then as they ate, Lynda looked at Julie and Mark and smiled. They smiled in return knowing that they were using their best manners and not making mistakes with the utensils.

Ray got up to go in the other room and make a phone call.

"Can't it wait until after we eat?" Lynda Lee asked.

Ray leaned down and kissed the top of her head.

"I'm afraid it can't. It's something I must attend to right now."

"Don't tell me you have to leave and go back to work. No, please don't tell me that, Ray."

Ray shook his head.

"It's not that. It's something much more important than that," he said and winked at her.

"It's a mystery," Julie said and smiled. "Mark and I love mysteries."

In a few moments, Ray returned to the table with a smile on his face. He looked over to Julie and Mark and winked at them.

"It's all taken care of," he said.

"What is taken care of?" Lynda Lee asked. "We shouldn't get into the habit of keeping secrets from Mama."

"I'll explain when we get home," Ray said. "I think you'll be happy about it."

Julie and Mark giggled, then went back to their food.

"So, John," Ray said. "When are you and Beth leaving for the new job?"

"Two weeks," John said. "Beth is not at all happy about it, but I've assured her that she will make friends quickly there, and we'll be living in a community similar to Weaver Street. Sometimes, you just have to turn your life upside down and take a leap of faith. That's what I'm doing."

Beth dabbed at her eyes with a handkerchief.

"Don't worry, honey," John said. "Once we've settled in, I know that you'll love it there. You'll have good people around you, plenty of doctors' wives, a beautiful home to live in, and lots of activities with the wives to keep you interested. And, you'll have a whole new set of folks to use your genealogy degree on. I truly think you'll love it there."

"And for all that," Beth said, "I'll be losing the best friend I've ever had. Why do you think for one minute that it's a good thing to lose your best friend?"

"I didn't mean it that way, but sometimes, you just have to take that leap of faith and go where your heart leads you. Mine is telling me that passing up this promotion would be folly, sheer folly. I might never get another opportunity like this one, Beth. Can't you understand that?"

"Beth, dear, John is right," Ray said. "He's been offered a chance that might not come around again. It's a job with so much potential for him. He'll be head of the cardiac unit in less than a month, I'd imagine."

"I know," Beth said, "but it doesn't make my heart feel any better. I'm settled here. I'm home and happy to be so."

Lynda Lee dabbed at her eyes with a napkin.

"Sometimes, Beth, life throws us a curve ball, and when it does, all we can do is make the best of it. I'll miss you like crazy, and my heart is very sad that you're going, but I also recognize what a chance this is for John. And knowing you the way I do, I know that you will make friends easily. You'll have them clamoring to be your friend because you are the perfect hostess with the most beautiful smile."

Beth smiled a thin smile.

"Thank you, my dear friend. I'll miss you, but perhaps you're right. Maybe it is time to move on, to take that leap of faith and see where it leads."

"So," Ray said, "have you decided what you're going to do about the house?"

"I think we're just going to try to find renters for a few months until we get settled and see what Huntsville is like. I want to keep my options open in case things don't work out. The house in Huntsville is already furnished. We can change whatever we want, but for now, we'll just live there without making too many changes."

"Sounds like a sensible plan to me," Ray said. "That's a good idea."

After the meal, they left The Relay House.

"I'll talk to you tomorrow, Beth," Lynda Lee said. "If this was to be our last dinner together, I'm glad that we decided on The Relay House. You just can't get a finer meal anywhere else."

"Let's have coffee in the morning," Beth said. "I'll come over around nine, if that's okay."

"Fine, see you in the morning."

On their way home, Ray talked about the wonderful opportunity for John. He talked about Huntsville, conventions, and various conferences, but Lynda Lee had tuned him out. Her headache kept nothing but pain on her mind.

When they drove up to the house and went in, Julie and Mark said, "Close your eyes, Mama Lynda. Papa Ray has a surprise for you."

So, Lynda Lee closed her eyes.

Julie and Mark guided her into the house, stood for a moment, and then said, "Okay, you can open your eyes now."

"Happy Early Twentieth Anniversary, my love," Ray said and hugged her.

When Lynda Lee looked up above the mantle, she gasped and took another step forward. She beheld a portrait of herself dressed in one of her beauty pageant dresses, a long blue sequined formal gown that fit at the waist while the long full skirt pooled on the floor at her feet. Her hair was done up in a French twist. She wore a simple diamond choker necklace and matching earrings. Her make up was flawless. A diamond tiara fit neatly into her hair.

Instantly, she remembered that very pageant day. She remembered her confidence, her posture, her certainty that she would be the new Miss Long Island.

Immediately, she straightened herself, put her shoulders back and assumed the stance she'd practiced year upon year in the childhood.

She turned to Ray.

"How did you do this?"

Ray smiled.

"From an old photo of you that I've kept all these years. You gave it to me when we married, and I've kept it safe and secure all these years. Look closer at that gold tag and see what it says."

Lynda Lee walked a bit closer until she could see the words on the small golden tag attached to the ornate frame.

"Lynda Lee Brennan, Miss Long Island."

Underneath that line was another.

"The Goddess of Weaver Street."

Chapter 50

"Mama Lynda," Julie said. "What are we wearing to the party tonight?"

"The party?" Lynda Lee asked as she lifted her head off the table-top. The pain had been almost unbearable for the last few hours.

"Beth and John's party before they leave for Huntsville tomorrow. Remember?"

"What time is the party?"

"At six, I think," Julie said and poured the white cake batter into the two pans.

After she'd put them in the oven, she washed her hands then went to sit next to Lynda Lee.

"Can I get you a pain pill, Mama Lynda?"

"What time is it now, Julie?"

"A little after three. I'll have plenty of time to finish the cakes. I decided on a chocolate center and white icing, but I can't think of what to put on top as decoration."

Lynda Lee lifted her head and tried to sit straight in her chair. Then she took a deep breath.

"What about making a border of Hershey's kisses? Everyone likes them, and it would be very easy to do. You could spray them on the top with some of our gold decorative food coloring. If you want a design in the middle, you can put one of our plastic lacy coasters and spray it with gold, too. You'd have a gold center and chocolate kisses topped with gold."

Julie smiled.

"You are amazing, Mama Lynda. You always have such creative ideas. I think it would be beautiful."

"Just make sure we have enough kisses. Mark and Papa Ray love them, so we might be running low on them."

Julie walked to the pantry and found two full bags of Hershey's Kisses. Then she found the gold spray food coloring. She walked past Lynda Lee and opened one of the drawers of the china cabinet. She saw the stack of plastic coasters and took one out.

"Thank you so much, Mama Lynda, for this idea. I'd never have thought of it by myself."

Lynda Lee got up from the table and hugged Julie.

"You'd have thought of it, dear. You're very creative, but for some reason, you hold yourself back. Just imagine that this kitchen is your very own bakery, and everything you turn out should be a treasure."

Julie smiled.

"I'd love to have my very own bakery, but first, I need to learn more about baking. I couldn't find many cookbooks on baking, but I'm sure they're around here somewhere. If not, could we get a book about cake baking, one with pictures and instructions so that I can get some ideas?"

"Oh, I have several cookbooks in that chest over there. I just don't use them very much, but of course," Lynda Lee said, "we can get all you'll need. Janine works at the book store in town. I'll call her and see what she has before she leaves work."

While Lynda Lee talked to Janine, she glanced at the back yard and saw Mark watering the wealth of plants in the garden.

"Thank you so much, Janine. Julie will be so excited about the books tonight."

When she hung up, she opened the back door and called to Mark.

"Why don't you gather some of the prettiest blooms together and we'll make an arrangement for Beth and John. I have plenty of vases stacked in the corner of the shed. Just pick one that you like and see what you can do, okay?"

Mark gave her a salute and a smile.

"So, you didn't tell me what you're going to wear," Julie said as she sat at the table.

"What would you like for me to wear?" Lynda Lee asked. "It's not a formal party, more of a casual barbecue and cocktail party."

"Hmm," Julie said. "I think I might wear my blue short sleeve dress. It's not too dressy and it fits me well. It's comfortable."

"The new one with the floral designs on the skirt?"

"Yes, Ma'am," she said. "It's one of my favorites."

"Then, shall I wear my matching one or would you like the spotlight all to yourself?" Lynda Lee said and chuckled.

"Oh, yes, wear your matching one. Then, everyone will know we're mother and daughter. Oh, my cakes are ready," she said and carefully took each pan out of the oven and put them upside down on the cooling rack.

"Darling," Lynda Lee said and searched through her purse for her bottle of pills. "I think everyone there already knows that we're mother and daughter."

As Julie fussed with her cake decorations putting them in order, Mark came in the back door with a handful of beautiful roses: red ones, pink ones, white ones. In the very center of the roses was his pride and joy: the blue and white striped Blue Dragon Rose, a rare and fragile rose that only a few could grow successfully.

Papa Ray had heard of the Blue Dragon Rose from one of his colleagues and had gone to great lengths to procure a handful of seeds from a Botanical Nursery in France. Mark had planted them in a special section of the rose garden using special soil, a specific rose food, and a hearty wooden stake for them to attach themselves to as they grew taller. He talked to his blue roses every day, as he did to all of his plants. Sometimes, he even sang to them. He was a quiet child, but he'd grown into a masterful vocal gardener.

"Oh, my goodness, Mark," Lynda Lee said. "Those will make the loveliest bouquet. What an amazing gardener you are. Beth will love these," Lynda Lee said and set about creating a bouquet with the blue dragon rose in the very center. She added some baby's breath, a few large hydrangea leaves, and made sure that they all fit into the foam rubber circle that would hold them in place.

"Well, what do you think, my boy?" Lynda Lee asked.

Mark didn't say anything. Instead, he took the vase and rearranged Lynda Lee's design so that the colored roses sat lower in the vase and the blue dragon became noticeably higher so that the eye went first to it.

Then he turned to Lynda Lee.

"Is it okay?" he asked.

"It's stunning," she said. "Absolutely stunning. I had no idea you could work such wonders with arrangements. You'll be doing ours from now on!"

Lynda Lee wrapped a wide red ribbon around the vase then stood back and looked at it.

"Julie, this red ribbon doesn't suit this beautiful arrangement. See if you can find the wide cobalt one. It's in the dresser with the others."

Julie came back in a jiffy with the wide blue ribbon.

Lynda Lee wrapped it around the vase and tied it into a lovely wide bow. She used a solid gold tie tack right through the center to keep it all in place then straightened each part of the bow and brought it to its fullest.

"There," she said, "how's that?"

Mark smiled.

"It's the best one yet. I've never even seen a bow that wide. It's perfect for the vase. You did a good job, Mama Lynda," he said and gave her a thumbs up.

"Thank you, dear boy. Now, I think it's time for us to get ready. Papa Ray will be here shortly, and you know how he is. He wants everyone else ready when he comes in."

"So he can have the bathroom all to himself," Julie said.

All of them giggled.

"Mama Lynda, is it all right if I wear my new Coach tennis shoes? I promise to keep them clean. And if they get dirty, I'll clean them as soon as we get back home."

"Yes, dear, you may wear your new shoes. They'll look nice with your dress. And Mark, if you want to wear yours, you can."

Mark smiled and said, "I never ever thought I would have five pairs of shoes to choose from, my own shoes that I don't have to share with anyone. Thank you, Mama Lynda."

"I have eight pairs," Julie said. "Eight of my own pairs of shoes."

Lynda Lee slipped an arm around the boy's shoulder.

"Your Broadhurst days are over, Mark. You and Julie won't ever have to live like that again. This is your home now, and it will be your home for as long as you want it."

"I will always want to live here," Mark said. "No matter what I'm doing, I'll always want to come right back here to my home."

"Will it always be my home, too?" Julie asked. "No matter what happens, may I always live here?"

Lynda Lee chuckled.

"Of course you can, Julie. This home will always belong to you and to Mark. Always. Now, let's all go and get ready. It won't be long until Papa Ray comes home. Julie, did you finish your cake?"

"See for yourself," she said and smiled.

Lynda Lee walked to the counter and looked at the beautifully-designed cake with the golden center and the gold-topped chocolates.

"It's perfect," she said. "By the way, Janine is bringing your baking books tonight, so you'll have plenty of material to learn from."

"Yippee," Julie said. "I'll learn and have my own bakery someday."

Then the three of them disappeared to make themselves presentable for Beth and John's party, and as soon as Lynda Lee was by herself, she reached for the bottle of pain pills and popped two into her mouth.

She sat on the bed, a tear rolling down each cheek. She looked around at her beautiful bedroom, considered all that she had, a gorgeous home, two lovely and talented children, a now-famous husband because of the advancements he'd helped create in cardiac care. She had everything a woman could dream of. So, she told herself that one day soon, she wouldn't feel like crying every day.

Chapter 51

Lynda Lee stood at the stove frying bacon and sausage patties on low heat to avoid the scorching splatters. She broke eight eggs and stirred them together in a blue Pyrex bowl. She needed to make toast, so she lifted the lid of the butter dish and buttered eight pieces of bread, put them onto a baking pan, and slid them into the oven. The bacon had begun to curl, so she turned each piece then lowered the heat. She flipped the sausage patties and put the lid back on the pan.

She brushed at her apron then opened the refrigerator and took out a large cantaloupe and a honey dew melon. She carefully peeled and cut both melons and put the small pieces into a bowl. Then she grabbed the box of strawberries out of the fridge and sprinkled them across the top of the melon mixture.

Lynda Lee finished the bacon and laid the strips perfectly straight on a paper towel. She lifted the lid of the sausage patties, decided they were done and forked them out one by one, also onto the paper towel. The toast in the oven was browning, so it was time to put on the eggs. Scrambled eggs were Ray's favorites, so she made plenty and topped them with some melty cheese and poured them into a bowl.

The plates were stacked in front of her, so she fixed everyone a plate with the food she knew they loved.

"Something smells delicious," Ray said and hugged her from the back.

Lynda Lee smiled and told him to put his plate on the table.

"Silverware is already there, along with napkins."

Julie walked groggily into the kitchen and said, "Good morning,

Mama Lynda. Why didn't you wake me so that I could help with all this cooking?"

"Nonsense," Lynda Lee said. "It's Saturday, your day to sleep in."

"But you've made so much!"

"Get the toast out of the oven, quickly, before it burns."

Julie grabbed a couple of potholders and removed the toast.

"It's perfect," she said.

"Just slide the pan right here," Lynda Lee said. "Will you get the milk out of the fridge? You know how much Mark loves his milk. Now, what would you like?"

"Everything," Julie said. "I'm starving."

Lynda Lee chuckled.

"Well, you're a growing girl," she said. "Where is your brother?"

"He's been up. I think he's in the back yard."

"Is he? I had no idea. Please call him in."

Lynda Lee put the large bowl of fruit in the center of the table with a large spoon in the center and put a small fruit bowl beside each place setting.

Mark came inside and sniffed.

"Yummy," he said. "I'm starving. I washed my hands outside, so they're clean. See?"

He held up his hands.

Lynda Lee inspected them.

"They're fine," she said. "I've made you a plate. Just bring it to the table."

"No meat, please," he said, "but plenty of eggs. Oh, they have cheese in them. Great."

"Take your seats, everyone," Lynda Lee said. "Ray, you say the blessing, please."

They all bowed their heads while Ray said a few quick words and ended it with his usual, "Good Lord, good meat, good Lord, let's eat."

Lynda Lee rolled her eyes.

"I'm afraid we're going to have a lot of leftovers," Julie said. "What will we do with them?"

"No worries, Julie. I'm taking Beth and John their breakfasts. I talked to her when I got up and told her I was bringing breakfast for them."

"You don't have much on your plate, sweetheart. Aren't you hungry?" Ray asked. "You can't let this fine meal go to waste, especially since you've worked so hard to prepare it."

"Weren't you listening, Ray? I'm taking breakfast to Beth and John today. So, eat up and eat all you want. We'll have plenty for Beth and John. They're leaving today, you know."

"Ah, yes," he said and helped himself to a bowl of fruit. "Are you all right about it?"

Lynda Lee shook her head.

"No, but it's not my decision to make. If John wants this promotion, he'd be crazy not to take it. But, I'm very sad about Beth. She's my best friend, and I will miss her terribly."

"Did they sell their home?"

"No, they've rented it to a newlywed couple. The man is enrolled in med school here."

"Ah, what division?"

"Pediatrics, I think," Lynda Lee said.

"Good, that department can use all the help it can get. They're always short staffed, but I don't know why. I've met all the doctors there, and they seem friendly and competent, yet none of them stays very long. There's a huge turnover in Pediatrics. Maybe this new guy will like it here and stay for a while."

"I think they're scheduled to be here on Friday of next week. I told Beth that I'd keep watch on the house for her until the new people arrive, so she left the keys with me," Lynda Lee said and took a bite of melon.

"We'll help," Julie said while Mark was busy eating everything he could stuff into his mouth.

"Mark, slow down, son. No one's going to take your food away," Ray said. "If you keep eating so fast, you might get an upset stomach. Give your food time to digest."

Mark looked at Ray and smiled.

"It's just so good," he said. "I love this melon."

"That's called a honey dew melon," Lynda Lee said. "Do you like the cantaloupe and strawberries?"

"It's all delicious," he said, "but my favorite is this honey dew melon. I'm going to plant some in our garden. And cantaloupe, too. Is that all right?"

"It is," Lynda Lee said. "I believe that if you use the seeds from these we're eating, you can use them to start your own melons. You'll probably need some special soil, some seed starter, but I've heard that they're very easy to grow. Of course, you have to dry out the seeds first. You might want to check your gardening book to make sure I'm right."

"I'd rather go to the Botanical Gardens and ask my friend Billy how to plant them," Mark said. "He's a Master Gardener certified by the Botanical Gardens, so he knows everything about planting."

"Okay," Lynda Lee said. "We'll dry out these seeds then take them with us when we go see Billy."

"Then, by next year," Mark said, "we'll have melons and cantaloupe in our garden. Won't that be great? I've already started some strawberries and blueberries. They're pretty easy to grow."

"Goodness, we can have a fruit feast by next year," Ray said. "Good for you, Mark. One of these days, I'm sure you'll be a certified Master Gardener, as well. Just keep learning, reading, and planting and you'll get there."

"When I'm old enough, I hope that the Botanical Gardens will hire me, too, like they did Billy. That's what I want as my career. I want to be a Master Gardener, a certified one."

"Then you must study, Mark. Read all you can about planting. You have plenty of books on the subject, and you must study them carefully. Then, you have to be willing to experiment and find easier and better ways to plant things. If you want to devote your time to gardening, then you must learn all phases of it," Ray said.

"One of these days, Papa Ray," Mark said and wiped his mouth. "One of these days, I'll come home and show you a certificate that says, Mark Rogers, Certified Master Gardener."

"I'm going to hold you to that promise, Mark. I'd be thrilled to see such a thing," Ray said and patted his stomach. "Such a delicious breakfast feast. Thank you, Lynda Lee, for working so hard to give us a wonderful breakfast. I might not be able to move for the rest of the day."

"Mama Lynda," Julie said, "please eat a little more. You've only taken a few bites. Mark and I will clean up the kitchen when we're all done."

"I've had my fill," Lynda Lee said. "I need to get Beth and John's food ready and take it to them."

Lynda Lee rose from her chair, picked up the empty plates with the silverware piled on top, and turned to take them to the kitchen, but as she did a sharp pain shot through her head. She dropped the plates and watched as they crashed to the floor.

Ray was up and holding her by the shoulders.

"Lynda Lee, what's wrong? Are you sick? Here, you sit back down."

"It's gone now, Ray. I had a sharp pain in my head, but it's gone now. No worries."

Julie and Mark stood frozen in place with their hands over their mouths. They'd never seen Mama Lynda drop anything.

"Leave the dishes," Ray said. "I'm getting you into bed so that you can have a rest. Julie and Mark can take care of the kitchen. Julie can fix plates for Beth and John. Mark can help with the dishes. They can all just go in the dishwasher. We'll clean up the broken dishes and get right to it. Right, kids?"

"We've got this, Papa Ray," Julie said. "You take care of Mama Lynda. We'll handle everything else."

"But it's only morning, Ray, and I want to say goodbye to Beth. I can't go to bed. There's so much to do."

"You are going to go to bed, Lynda Lee," Ray said. "Whatever is left to do, the children and I can take care of it."

"But it's Saturday, Ray, your only off day for the next two weeks. I can't just go to bed and leave everything to you and the children. I can't. You need your rest, too."

"Where are you pain pills?" Ray asked.

"In my purse," Lynda Lee said. "There aren't many left. I need to get them refilled."

"I can take care of that. But you, my dear, need to rest. Doctor's orders. The children and I will do whatever needs to be done."

Julie got the bottle of pain pills and took two pills from it then handed them to Ray.

"Now, you take these and then it's off for a nap. Don't fight with me about this, Lynda Lee. You need some rest."

Lynda Lee took the pills and nodded her head.

"Just a short nap," she said and took off her apron.

She shuffled her feet as Ray helped her to the bedroom.

Ray watched her carefully until they got to the bed.

"Now, let's take off your shoes. Do you want to undress and put on your robe? You'd be more comfortable."

"I don't care, Ray."

Ray helped her unzip her dress and strip down. Then he got her silk robe and helped her put it on and button it.

"Now, how does that feel?"

Lynda Lee smiled at him.

"This is all for naught, Ray. The pain is gone and I'm not at all sleepy. I have work to do."

"It's Saturday," he said. "Maybe you can take a short nap and then you'll feel better. Do it for me?"

Lynda Lee patted the side of his cheek then slipped under the covers.

"For you, then," she said. "Don't let me sleep long, Ray. I don't want to miss out on today."

"If you'll sleep for an hour, you'll feel much better. And losing an hour won't be too bad, will it?"

Lynda Lee smiled and nuzzled into her pillow.

When Ray went back into the kitchen, Julie and Mark had everything under control. The broken dishes had been swept up. The floor had been cleaned, the table cleared, and two large plates fixed for Beth and John.

"What a great job you've done," Ray said. "I'll just take these plates over to Beth and John, and that's another chore done."

"Don't worry, Papa Ray, we'll handle things in the kitchen," Julie said.

"I don't know what I'd do without you two," Ray said. "You both make me so proud."

"Papa Ray, is Mama Lynda going to be okay? I've never seen her drop anything before. That pain must have been awful," Julie said.

"She's sleeping now. On Monday, I'm going to make sure she sees another specialist for those headaches. But for now, the pain is gone and she's resting. I'm thankful for that. I promised I'd wake her in an hour, though, but let's wait and see if she can sleep a little longer."

"It's only ten o'clock now, so at 11 o'clock, we'll check in on her," Julie said. "If she's sleeping, we won't wake her."

Ray grabbed the basket that held the two filled plates, both covered with Saran Wrap. There was also a bowl of berries wrapped and stuck between the plates.

"I'll be back shortly, you two," he said. "Listen for Mama Lynda, okay?"

Chapter 52

The dream took her as soon as she closed her eyes, but this time, there were no rocky surfaces to try to climb. She didn't have to dig her hands into the sides of the cliffs, didn't scuff her knees. She simply walked in a straight path right to Maman's cottage.

The old weaver sat at her loom, as usual.

"Maman," she said, "I'm so happy to see you. Is there anything I can do to help?"

"Sit, Child," the weaver said. "Rest those aching bones of yours."

"I'll sit, but I'm not aching anywhere. All of my aches and pains vanish as soon as I come here. Isn't that odd?"

"Perhaps, but that's the way pain is. It comes and goes."

"I did something unusual today, Maman. I cooked a big breakfast for Ray and the children and as I was gathering the dishes, I dropped them. The plates all broke and splintered on the floor. I don't think I've ever dropped a plate before. Maybe I'm getting older and clumsier."

The old Irish weaver burst into laughter.

"Child," she said. "Dropping a few dishes is nothing to worry about. We are all clumsy at times."

"I think it's the headaches, Maman. The pain from them is almost unbearable now. I dropped the dishes because a sharp pain ran through my head. It nearly knocked me off my feet."

"Well, well, look who's come to see us again!" his loud voice called. "Welcome back, Lynda Lee."

Scaylee climbed down from his horse and gave her a hug.

"How have you been, Lynda Lee? Did you have any trouble getting here this time?"

"No, actually, it was quite easy. I didn't come across any rocky cliffs or sharp rocks, and I didn't even need help. I just walked right here with no trouble at all."

Scaylee smiled.

"You're learning the right path to take, then. From now on, you shouldn't have any trouble at all finding us. I'm glad to hear it."

"But what if I do have trouble, Scaylee? Will you promise to be here to help me?"

Scaylee put his hands on her shoulders.

"I'll be here, Lynda Lee, but you won't need my help. You've learned the right path and you'll remember it next time. Come, would you like to hear a story? I can see the crowds already gathering."

"What story will it be this time?"

"You'll like it," Scaylee said. "It's a little story about a very strong woman named Brigit."

"Brigit?"

"Lynda Lee, wake up. You've been sleeping for two hours. It's time to get up. We're taking Mark to the Botanical Gardens."

Lynda Lee mumbled.

"Go away, Ray. Just leave me alone."

"How is your headache? Better, I hope?"

"Go away, Ray. I was just about to hear a story. Please let me sleep."

"Come on, now. Julie and Mark are waiting for us. We promised them a trip to the Gardens. Mark is eager to talk to his friend Billy about the different types of melons. You impressed him with the honey dew melons and now, he's an eager beaver to get started."

Lynda Lee turned over and looked up at her husband. She desperately wanted to stay in her dream, but she shook herself awake.

"Get my pink capris and the matching top from the closet, please."

Ray did as he was asked and brought the clothes over to the bed.

"How's your headache?" he asked. "Do you feel up to going to the Gardens this afternoon? It's a little hot outside, but not too hot to enjoy a stroll."

Lynda Lee got up, took her clothes into the bathroom and closed the door.

"Don't be too long," Ray called as he changed into his casual wear, some khaki pants and a white short-sleeved shirt. "The children are waiting."

Lynda Lee wiped tears from her eyes as she ran a brush through her long hair and changed into her pink capri set, leaving her other clothes in a pile on the floor. She paid no attention to her makeup and didn't even put on lipstick. She felt as if she were walking in a heavy fog. She had no excitement about being with Ray and the children and absolutely none for walking around the Botanical Gardens. She felt only one thing: yearning.

But as she walked out of the bathroom, she put a smile on her face.

"I'm ready," she said. "Today, this is as good as it gets."

"You look a little tired, sweetheart. Are you sure you're up to this?"

"The children are counting on us, so let's go."

Mark and Julie were sitting in the living room, clean, dressed, and obviously ready to go to the Gardens. They smiled when they saw her. Julie ran to give her a hug.

"Mama Lynda, you look beautiful in your new capri set. Maybe pink will be your new signature color for the summer."

Lynda Lee smiled.

"Thank you, dearest," she said. "Now, let me look at you. Your capri set looks quite nice. Do you like it?"

"I do. I love the bright colors. And I have to admit that I'm partial to the matching sets. I love them."

Lynda Lee kissed the top of her head.

"You look amazing," she said, "and I like that matching headband. Very nice."

Mark stood up.

"Mama Lynda, do I pass muster today?"

Lynda Lee smiled.

"By all means, you do. Do you like your new cargo shorts?

Mark nodded.

"And thank you for this neat camo tee shirt. The pockets are great. I can fill them with my tools when I work in the garden."

"You might soon need a tool box of your very own," Ray said. "Every man needs a tool box."

"Do you have one, Papa Ray?" Mark asked.

"Well, no, but I do have a medical bag. I guess that's my kind of tool box. Let's get on the road. The Gardens close early today, so we want to have plenty of time to look around."

"And to buy seeds if we can," Mark said.

"That's right. We can't forget about the seeds. We might need to check on bird seed, too, while we're there."

Lynda Lee watched as Ray and the children climbed into the car. Mark had kindly opened her door. She had what she'd always dreamed of. A beautiful home, a husband, children. She had it all now.

She brushed a tear from her eye, forced a smile, and climbed into the car.

Chapter 53

It was on the following Monday that Lynda Lee learned that the headaches she'd had all these years were of her own doing. Her heart sank when the doctor told her that the x-rays and the complete physical exam showed that she was in tip-top shape. Not a thing was wrong with her.

"You're just stressed, Lynda Lee. You're in perfect health. It's common in women to have stress headaches. I see it more and more often now, but there's no need to worry. You are probably in early menopause, and that will certainly cause changes in the body and headaches along with it. Keep taking your pain pills when you need them and you should be fine."

He added as she left, "When you see an end to your menstrual cycle and enter into full menopause, we'll change the prescription. You might need a heavier dose."

She grabbed her handbag and left without saying anything.

Ray was waiting for her when she came out.

"Well, do we have any news?" he asked as he opened the car door for her.

"No, Ray, just take me home, please."

Ray climbed in the driver's side and started the car.

"He couldn't find anything?" he asked.

"Stress," Lynda Lee said. "Twenty-five years of stress. That's all it is."

"I see," he said. "And what do you think about his diagnosis?"

Lynda Lee opened her handbag and took out a handkerchief. She dabbed at her eyes.

"He's a specialist, so I guess he knows what he's talking about," she said. "Just take me home, Ray. No more talking about these headaches," she said in a sarcastic tone. "It doesn't do any good at all. All the specialists have said the same thing. I'm just a woman under stress. He sees it more and more. Women who are stressed out by their lives. There couldn't possibly be any other explanation."

She dabbed at her eyes again.

"I don't know what else to do, Lynda Lee. You've seen two specialists and two neurologists. None of them could find anything to cause the headaches, but I am on your side. I know that you wouldn't complain of pain if you weren't going through it."

"Thank you, Ray."

They rode home in silence until they pulled into the driveway where Julie was waving and waiting for them. She ran over and opened the car door for Lynda Lee.

"I'm so glad to see you, Mama Lynda. What did the doctor say? Are you going to be all right?"

Lynda Lee managed a smile.

"Of course, I'll be all right," she said. "In fact, I'm better than all right. There is nothing wrong with me at all."

Julie wrapped her arms around Lynda Lee.

"I'm so glad, Mama Lynda. I've been so worried about you. Let's go inside. I've made you a glass of iced tea. I have dinner cooking. I didn't want you to have to worry about cooking when you came home. Where is Papa Ray going?"

"Back to work, as usual. He still has patients to see. And what is Mark up to?"

"Oh, he's been planting and working this afternoon in the garden. He has a whole notebook filled with the notes he took while Billy was teaching him about the plants at the Botanical Gardens. I've never seen Mark so happy, Mama Lynda. You've made his dreams come true. We'll always love you for that."

Lynda Lee headed to the bedroom.

"I'll change," she said, "and I'll meet you back here in just a few minutes ready for some tea."

"How about a slice of freshly baked peach pie? Remember, we got the fresh peaches at the market Saturday?"

Julie picked up the pie and showed it to Lynda Lee.

"What a marvelous looking pie, Julie. Of course, I'll have just a tiny bit."

Julie smiled and put the pie back on the stovetop.

When Lynda Lee returned dressed in her capris and a flowery blouse, she sat at the table and took a sip of the sweet iced tea.

Julie came over with a tiny saucer that held a spoonful of pie.

"Just taste it, please," she said.

Lynda Lee scooped a bit of the pie onto her spoon and tasted the warm, sweet concoction.

After a moment, with Julie still standing next to her, she said, "It's delicious, Julie. You've outdone yourself."

Julie put her hand over her heart.

"Oh, I'm so glad you like it, Mama Lynda. You're the best cook in the world and your opinion means everything to me."

"I think I'm teaching you well because this is absolutely wonderful," she said and scooped another small bite onto her spoon. "I don't think I've ever made a peach pie before, so you did this all on your own. I'm so proud of you."

Julie sat down beside her.

"If I'm honest, I have to say that I cheated. I used a recipe that I found in one of the cookbooks."

"That is not cheating, dear girl," and put her hand on Julie's. "That is learning, discovering, trying something new. I'm proud of you for it."

Julie got up and went back to the stove.

"I didn't want you to be disappointed in me," she said, "for using someone else's recipe."

Lynda Lee got up and stood beside Julie.

"Those cookbooks are here for both of us to use. We have to keep learning new dishes, experimenting with the foods we cook. That's how we learn, Julie, and in the kitchen, there's always something new to learn."

Julie smiled at her.

"Thank you for all that you do for me and for Mark. You've done so much for us. You're the best mother in the world. Almost every day, Mark and I learn something new. Living with you and Papa Ray has been the best time of our lives, and I thank you for that."

Lynda Lee, suddenly tired, sat down in her chair.

"Julie," she said. "You are my daughter, and I love you. Part of my job as a mother is to teach you what you need to know to survive in this world. But, I do it not because I have to but because I want to. I want you to live your life exactly the way you want to so that you'll be happy and content."

"But are you?" Julie asked. "Are you happy and content?"

Lynda Lee sighed.

"I have everything a woman could want, Julie. Everything."

Chapter 54

When Lynda Lee heard the knock on the door, she wiped her hands on her apron, stopped in front of the mirror to check her hair and makeup, and went to the door.

Janine from down the way stood on her porch with a basket.

"I thought you might like these, you and the children."

"Whatever have you brought me, Janine? Come in. Come in."

"I've been obsessed with breadmaking for the last few weeks, ever since Beth and John left," she said as she followed Lynda Lee to the kitchen and took a seat at the table. "And now that the new people have moved into Beth's house, things just don't seem right anymore. I needed something to take my mind off missing them, so I took up breadmaking."

"I know exactly how you feel," Lynda Lee said. "I miss them more than I can say. Weaver Street is changing right before our eyes, and there's nothing to be done."

Lynda Lee poured a cup of coffee, placed it on a saucer, and put it on the table in front of Janine.

"It's fresh," she said. "It just finished brewing. Ray bought it for me. It's some exotic blend of coffee beans, and it's pretty good."

Janine pushed a stray hair from her face.

"There's nothing better than a good cup of coffee," she said as she spooned in some sugar and added a dash of cream.

"I can't get over how good your backyard looks, Lynda Lee. You've put the rest of us to shame."

"That's all Mark's doing," she said. "He wants to be a Master Gardener."

"Did he do the birdbath and the bird feeders?"

"He did, and I love to watch the little chickadees and the other tiny birds when they come to feed. I've seen them go to the birdbath and just jump in and bathe. They dunk themselves and then ruffle their feathers. It's precious to watch."

"I don't suppose he'd be interested in doing something similar to our backyard," Janine said. "I'd be happy to pay him to beautify our yard. It's so plain and uninteresting."

Lynda Lee smiled.

"I'm sure he'd be delighted to do it," she said. "He has a special talent, an almost spiritual connection, with plants and gardens. He can work all day and never tire of doing it. He's a very special boy when it comes to plants."

"Well," Janine said and took another sip of her coffee, "perhaps he's found his calling early in his life."

Lynda Lee sliced some of the bread Janine had brought.

"Shall we have a piece?" she asked.

"Sure, but put it in the oven for a few minutes and toast it with some butter on top. Do you have some jam or preserves?"

"Sure," Lynda Lee said as she slid the toasting pan into the oven and set the timer. She reached into the fridge, took out the jars of raspberry and strawberry jam, and set them on the table, along with two saucers. When the timer dinged, she took out the toast and put two pieces on each saucer.

"How's that?" she asked.

"Looks yummy," Janine said as she helped herself to both jams.

"The bread smells delicious, Janine," Lynda Lee said. "What kind is it?"

"It's my first try with sourdough," she said. "I do hope it tastes good."

Lynda Lee took a bite with some strawberry jam.

"Oh, this is really good. The bread is tangy, so the jam goes with it perfectly."

Janine smiled.

"I'm a bit proud of myself for tackling the bread making. Husband Sam is a bread lover, so he'll be happy I've finally decided to try my hand at it. And goodness knows, I want to keep him happy. Things are not good at our house if he's not happy."

"Really?"

"What a temper he has! But keep this just between us, okay? He's already knocked three holes in the walls with his fists. Of course, they've been repaired, but still. I try not to say or do anything that will make him angry."

Lynda Lee could barely swallow her bite of toast but managed to get it down.

"I had no idea, Janine. Sam seems so quiet and gentle."

"As a doctor, he's the very best," Janine said. "But at home, he takes out all his frustrations with his fists."

Lynda Lee stared at Janine.

"Does he hit you, Janine?"

"He never hits the children, Lynda Lee. Never," she said and took a sip of her coffee and then a bite of her toast. "This is so good."

Lynda Lee pushed her saucer aside.

"That's not what I asked, Janine. Does Sam hit you?"

Janine took another sip of her coffee.

"He's a doctor, Lynda Lee. Doctors are always under a lot of stress. I can take a slap or two if it helps him feel better."

Lynda Lee took her saucer to the sink.

"And how long has this been happening?"

"Since the first week we moved here. I'm used to it by now."

Lynda Lee sat next to Janine and took her hands.

"Janine, this is not acceptable behavior. No man should hit a woman. Ever. He is your husband, yes, but he is not supposed to be your tormentor. I can get you some help because this has to stop."

Janine got up and took her saucer to the sink.

"I appreciate what you're trying to do, Lynda Lee, but it isn't necessary. I live in a beautiful home. I have everything I could possibly want or need, and I have a husband who is a respected doctor among his peers. A little slap now and then is nothing, so please, just let it go. And please respect our friendship by keeping quiet about it. It's no one else's business but mine and Sam's."

"Please, Janine, you don't have to put up with physical abuse."

Janine chuckled.

"And what would I have without it? If I told anyone, Sam would divorce me and then what would I have? Nothing. I'd have nothing, not a house, not a car, not anything and most of all, no money."

"Don't be absurd. Sam is the father of those children. He'd have to support them. And he'd have to pay you alimony, too. So, you won't be walking away with nothing. I can promise you that."

"Walking away to where, Lynda Lee? I've nowhere else to go. And I certainly don't want to tell my parents. They'd be all over Sam. Besides, they live in Maine. The last time I saw them was when the kids were born. Sam was on his best behavior then. My parents have money, but I don't want to leave my home, my friends, this community. Look, forget I opened my big mouth. I really need to get back home now. Keep the bread. I have another loaf at home."

And with that, she was out the door and gone.

Lynda Lee watched as she crossed the street, stood still for a moment and straightened her hair, then turned and waved, but she couldn't quite manage a smile.

Chapter 55

When Ray came home that evening, a little earlier than usual, Mark was still out in the garden and Julie was at the stove making mashed potatoes. Lynda Lee opened the oven and pulled out four beautifully-cooked steaks topped with a hint of barbecue sauce. They were still Ray's favorite. One by one she took them off the pan and laid one on a large square of Saran Wrap topped with a paper towel.

"Julie, if you're finished, would you plate these for me?"

"What's Mark going to have? He still insists that he will never eat meat."

"Oh, we have plenty for him: green beans, potatoes with gravy, homemade biscuits, and a fresh salad."

"And I made a chocolate cake. It's a new recipe, so I hope everyone will love it."

"I'm sure they will. You're an excellent cook, Julie," Lynda Lee said and winced.

"Your headache is back?"

Julie deposited the steaks on the plates and grabbed one of her mother's pill bottles from the corner shelf.

"Here you go, Mama Lynda. Maybe if you take the meds now, the headache won't be so bad."

Lynda Lee popped two pills into her mouth and washed them down with water. Then she smiled at the way the children called her Mama Lynda.

"Thank you, my sweet girl. You're always so thoughtful. Now, let's get this table fixed. Will you call Mark in for me?"

"I've washed up all the pots and pans and put them away," Julie said, "just the way you do. We won't have many dishes to wash after we eat."

"I should probably use the dishwasher Ray bought for us, but I'm so accustomed to hand washing that I rarely think of it."

"Let's give it a try next week," Julie said. "It can't hurt to try it just once."

As soon as Julie called, Mark came running in the back door.

"I just need to wash my hands," he said as he headed toward the bathroom. "Then, I'll be clean enough to sit at the table."

"Something smells mighty fine," Ray said after he'd changed into casual clothes. "Is that steak, perhaps?"

"Your favorite," Julie said. "Mama Lynda has once again cooked them to perfection."

Ray moved toward Lynda Lee and gave her a quick kiss on the cheek.

"Thank you, dearest, for slaving over a hot stove to make my dinner. I appreciate it."

"You're quite welcome," she said and kissed his cheek. "Now, take a seat while we finish up here."

Ray walked over to the dining room table and took his seat just as Lynda Lee put the last dish on the table.

Mark bounded into the kitchen and went immediately to his seat.

"I'm starving," he said, "and all this food looks great, smells great, too."

"As I recall," Ray said, "you live in a perpetual state of starvation, even though you eat three hefty meals each day and have a snack before bedtime."

"Mama Lynda says I'm a growing boy and I need all the nutrition I can get so that I'll grow up to be big and strong, and that's what I want to be, big and strong, like you, Papa."

Ray laughed.

"Well, yes, I'm big. I grew to this height when I was fourteen, bigger than all the other kids in my neighborhood. But as to the strong, I fear that my occupation hasn't encouraged much strength-building."

"You're plenty strong. You've helped me in the garden when I couldn't lift things that were too heavy for me, but for you, they seemed like feathers."

"Mark, eat your dinner and be quiet," Julie said. "You can talk after you eat."

Lynda Lee glanced at Ray who raised an eyebrow.

"The same goes for you, my dearest," he said. "You haven't eaten very much at all. You can't stay healthy if you don't eat, Lynda Lee."

Lynda Lee smiled and took a bite of her mashed potatoes, then a bite of her salad.

"I think she's waiting for dessert," Julie said. "She loves my desserts."

"Ah," Ray said. "And what delicious surprise do we have tonight?"

As she swallowed, Julie asked, "Should I tell him, Mama Lynda, or let him be surprised?"

Lynda Lee took another bite of mashed potatoes.

"Go ahead and tell him. I'm not sure his heart could take it if he didn't know. He's getting older now."

Everyone laughed.

"Papa, I've made a double chocolate raspberry cake, my first attempt, so I hope you'll all like it."

"It sounds just wonderful, Julie. I'm certain we'll all love it."

Julie smiled and finished the food on her plate and took it to the double sink, one side already filled with hot sudsy water, the other filled with clean rinsing water. A dish drainer stood on the countertop beside the sink.

"I'm on dishwasher duty," she said, "so when you finish, just scrape your plate and give it to me. Keep one of the forks for the cake."

"I really don't understand why you won't use your new dishwasher. It's the very best of its kind and it would save you so much time."

"Julie and I decided that we would try it next week. I promise," she said as she got up and went to the cabinets.

In a matter of minutes, the dishes were finished, and Lynda Lee took the dessert plates out of the cabinet and put one at each place.

"Plates are ready," she said to Julie.

"Dessert forks?"

"They're ready, too."

Julie set the cake in the center of the table, removed the lid, and listened as everyone gasped.

"It's a masterpiece, Julie."

"Thank you, Papa. I hope it tastes as good as it looks," Julie said as she carefully cut a wedge of cake for him.

She handed it to Mama Lynda.

"It's for Papa," she said. "The man of the house is served first."

She sliced another, much smaller piece for Mama Lynda and handed it to her.

"Please let me know what you think of it. Your opinion is very important to me."

"Hey, what about me?" Mark asked.

Julie sliced him a rather large wedge of cake and handed it across to him. Then she sliced a small piece for herself and sat down.

"Julie, this is absolutely delicious," Mama Lynda said. "It's so smooth and chocolaty. I love it."

Julie smiled.

"I'm not a chocolate lover like your mother, but this cake is just delicious," Ray said to Julie. "I love the raspberry filling. It's both tart and sweet. Marvelous."

"So, Julie, what do you think of your new creation?"

"I think it's one of the best cakes I've ever made," she said as a broad grin spread across her face. "It's so much tastier than I imagined it would be."

Lynda Lee sat back and put her napkin in her lap.

"Perhaps if you work on it and make it several times, perfect it the way you want it, this might become your signature dessert dish!"

"Oh, Mama Lynda, that's a wonderful idea. I'd never have thought of it."

"It seems to me," Lynda Lee said, "that if you're serious about wanting to be a baker, then you should begin a portfolio of your signature dishes. Don't you think so, Ray?"

"A marvelous idea," he said. "We'll get you a binder so that you can begin to fill it with your favorite dishes to make. We'll take photos of each dish and put them in your binder with your special recipes. Would you like that?"

"Oh, I would love it. Just think, my baking featured in a binder all by itself."

The smile spread all across her face.

"And then," Ray said, "when the various neighbors call and want you to make something for them, you'll have the binder to flip through. And remember, you must charge a fee that is appropriate but also profitable for you."

"A fee?"

"Yes, Julie, a fee for your services. It's time you started charging for these sumptuous desserts and meals that you make for the neighbors."

"But they're our neighbors," Julie said. "It doesn't seem right to charge them money. I'm just a teenager, not a real baker."

"Okay, well, let's try something," Ray said. "Get a few plastic plates, three or four, and put a slice of your cake on each plate. Then wrap them with Saran Wrap. Go ahead. Do as I say."

Lynda Lee got up and helped Julie finish each plate while Ray busied himself tearing strips of paper and writing on each strip.

"We're finished, Papa," Julie said.

"Bring the plates over here," he said. On each plate he taped a small piece of paper that had $1.00 written on it.

"Now, you two head down the street to the neighbors. Pick the ones we know fairly well and ask whoever comes to the door if they'd like to buy a piece of your Double Fudge Chocolate Raspberry cake. It's just an experiment to see who is willing to pay for this wonderful cake."

When Lynda Lee and Julie returned after completing the experiment, they showed Ray the results. Between them, they had ten dollars.

"The people paid us ten dollars because the cake was so pretty," Julie said. "I can't believe it, and two of them asked if I would make similar cakes for them."

"You just haven't learned your worth yet, my dear," Lynda Lee said, "but soon enough, you will."

Chapter 56

As they each climbed into bed, Lynda Lee said, "Ray, could we talk for a bit?"

Ray lay on his back, adjusted the covers, and pulled her close to him.

"Is something bothering you?"

"Yes," she said. "Something is bothering me. It's about Janine."

"Tell me all about it," he said and yawned.

Lynda Lee braced herself on an elbow so that she could see his face.

"What impression do you get about Sam?"

Ray turned toward her.

"Well, he's a fine doctor. He cares for his patients, but sometimes, when I hear him talking, his voice is a little loud, and occasionally, I've seen him lose his temper, but he never really does anything. I can just tell he's angry. But all in all, he's a helpful person to have around in an emergency. Why do you ask?"

Lynda Lee said nothing for a few seconds.

"Tell me, honey. Tell me what's wrong. What is it that you know about him that I don't know?"

Lynda Lee sighed.

"He abuses Janine. He has a violent temper at home. She said he's never hurt the children, but he's put holes in the walls and when he's very angry, he hits her."

Ray sat up.

"What?"

"It's the truth, Ray. He's a wife abuser at home. Janine is terrified of him. She says she has to be careful about what she says and does around him because if he's unhappy, then she's the one who pays for his anger. If word got out, it could ruin the reputation of the hospital. No one wants a doctor who is a wife abuser."

"Are you sure about this?"

"Janine wouldn't lie to me. She brought over some freshly-baked bread this morning and we talked for a while. I noticed a bruise on her face and even though I didn't say anything, she said that she had to be careful around Sam." Lynda Lee brushed at a stray hair on her face. "She has to watch everything she says and does. She said she had to keep him happy or pay the consequences."

"I've seen evidence of his temper, but I had no idea he was hurting Janine. If, indeed, he is a wife abuser, we have no room for him on our team. Should I have a talk with him?"

"No, no, I promised Janine I wouldn't tell anyone, but she can't expect me not to tell my own husband."

"But your husband, my dear, is his boss. It's my responsibility to keep our team emotionally stable for our patients. Tomorrow, I'll go through his patient manifests to see if there have been any complaints lodged against him. Then, I'll go to the real source: the nurses. They know everything that goes on, literally everything. There is one in particular I have in mind. If she knows anything, she'll tell me and she'll tell me straight."

"What will you do?"

"I'm not sure, Lynda Lee, but I don't want our hospital and all the work we've accomplished in the Cardiac Care Unit to have its name besmirched by a wife beater. Sure, he's a fair doctor, but he isn't good enough to keep me from confronting him or going to a higher authority."

"Janine is stuck, Ray. She can't leave him because she has no money. She is entirely dependent on his income. So, she tiptoes around him trying to keep him happy so he won't explode and hurt them."

"Does she have parents?"

"Yes, they live in Maine, I think. But she hasn't told them about Sam. In fact, she talks to her mother and father only about once a year because Sam doesn't like her talking to them."

"Right," Ray said. "He's afraid she'll tell them how he really is."

"She told me in confidence that her parents were wealthy, but they haven't seen each other since the children were born."

Ray shook his head.

"I can't even imagine it. After all these years here on Weaver Street, we have a wife beater in our midst. All the parties they've hosted, the number of times we've been in their house, and there's not an iota of evidence that Sam is beating her."

"I really don't know what to do for her, Ray," Lynda Lee said. "How do you help someone who doesn't seem to want any help?"

"Don't worry yourself about it, sweetheart. Between my detective work and the nurses' gossip, we'll get to the bottom of this. Janine and her children deserve to live in peace, and Sam definitely needs some counseling. But to be honest, if he truly is an abuser, I'll have to fire him from the team. I can't risk that kind of negative publicity. Word will get out and if it's found that I knew about it and did nothing, then my livelihood is also on the line."

"Is there anything I can do?"

"Just keep being a friend to Janine. Invite her over more often. Perhaps she'll tell you other things that might be important."

"I can do that," she said and kissed Ray on the cheek.

"Thanks for listening, Ray. I just had to tell you."

Ray kissed her gently on the lips.

"You did the right thing, exactly the right thing. Now, let's get some sleep. I have an early appointment in the morning. But, don't worry. I'll see to it that the matter of Janine and Sam is handled discretely. I have to act on this now that I know, but I'll try to do it in a way that will be the least detrimental to Janine."

"You're a good man, Ray Rogers. I'm glad I married you all those years ago."

"So am I, sweetheart, so am I."

Chapter 57

Lynda Lee occupied herself for the next few days in her beloved weaving room. She hadn't done much weaving or sewing in the last few months, primarily because it seemed to make her headaches worse. But on this day, she felt better. The headache was just a gentle throbbing in the top of her head, utterly bearable.

The rug in the hallway was looking a bit shabby, so Lynda Lee decided that a new one was in order, this time done in a myriad of colors with fringe at the bottom ends. She had a color scheme in mind: blues, yellows, and greens all woven into a colorful rug.

As she wove, she found herself humming. She'd missed being at the loom and missed sewing for the children, even though they both wore mostly store-bought clothes now. But perhaps with her skill at weaving, she could make each of them a sweater or jacket that they would be proud of.

The colors for the rug finally began to come together. The blues, the yellows, and the greens looked handsome together, but they needed a touch of something, a red perhaps. So, she stopped her weaving and added a large spool of red yarn to the mix. It would take several days to finish, but she enjoyed the work. And she felt a bit of excitement at the way it would turn out. She could imagine it with all the bright colors and that image helped her keep going.

She wove all day until she heard, "Mama Lynda, we're home," Julie called and walked into her weaving room. "This is pretty. Is it a new rug for the house?"

Lynda Lee stopped her weaving.

"Yes," she said. "The one in the hallway is looking a bit shabby, don't you think?"

Julie shrugged.

"I really haven't paid much attention to it, but now that I think about it, you're right. So, we'll have a brand-new rug for the hallway?"

Lynda Lee smiled.

"Yes, my dear, a brand-new rug and when I'm finished, I'm going to make new sweaters for you and Mark. I have the designs stored right here," she said and pointed to her head. "Something quite feminine for you, something dressy, but something heavier for Mark since he's outside so much."

"Thank you. You're so good to us, Mama Lynda. We never lack for anything."

Lynda Lee smiled and got up from her loom, straightened the folds in her blouse, and brushed at her capris.

"I guess it's time for dinner," she said.

"Dinner is on me tonight," Julie said. "I want you to rest and take care of yourself. Just relax and let me fix dinner. Okay?"

Lynda Lee tilted her head.

"And what is it that you're going to fix?"

Julie cleared her throat.

"I thought I might make some spaghetti with meatballs and a nice salad. I noticed that we had that large loaf for French bread in the cabinet. And we have some Parmesan cheese. So, spaghetti with saucy meatballs, a salad and toasted bread?"

"Oh, that sounds yummy. Do you need help?"

"If you would make the salad, I can handle everything else. Is that all right?"

"Perfect," Lynda Lee said. "Spaghetti and meatballs is Papa's favorite."

"It's Mark's, too," she said and giggled. "Now, if you'll just do the salad, then I want you to go sit down and relax. You need some relaxing time before dinner."

Lynda Lee chuckled.

"One salad coming up," she said and gathered the things she needed from the fridge and the cabinets. "Radishes and little green onions or not?" she asked.

"Oh yes, I love them both, especially the little green onions. They'll be great with the spaghetti and meatballs."

Lynda Lee spent the next few minutes cutting the full head of lettuce, the tomatoes, green onions, radishes, and adding a handful of capers to the large wooden salad bowl. She sliced a few strips of carrots into the mix and then added a squeeze or two of lemon juice. She mixed it all together with a spoonful of mayonnaise and a bit of Dijon mustard. When all the ingredients were blended together nicely, she grabbed a Tupperware top and sealed it around the bowl.

"Done," she said. "Ready for the fridge."

"It smells delicious. You added a bit of mustard, didn't you?"

"I did. Read it in one of the cookbooks. It adds a little bit of spice to the dish. Now, what else can I do?"

"You are dismissed from the kitchen, Mama Lynda," Julie said and smiled. "Papa won't be home for another hour, so it's time for you to rest. Just rest. That's all. Do you need your pain pills?"

The headache which had begun only as a gentle pulsing had morphed into a very painful throbbing from front to back.

"Yes, thank you," she said to Julie. "Two please."

Julie handed her the pills and told her to go and rest.

"By the way, where is our Mark? I haven't heard a peep from him."

"He'll be here shortly. His friend Johnny from the Botanical Gardens picked him up at school and took him out to the gardens to help him plant some new roses. I told him it was okay, that you wouldn't mind. Did I do the right thing?"

"Yes, that's fine with me. We have to encourage Mark's passion for gardening and learning new things. I think he's found his calling with gardening, so I want him to get all the experience he can. But, next time, he needs to ask me before he makes arrangements with Johnny. I'll be sure to tell him when he comes in."

"He hadn't planned on going out to the gardens. I think he was surprised to see Johnny, and he did ask me if I thought you'd mind if he went."

"Okay, well, I'll be kind, but I'll mention it to him. I think I'll take a short nap before dinner. Be sure to wake me if you need me."

"Go," Julie said and made a shooing motion. "Rest. You'll feel much better after a rest."

Chapter 58

Lynda Lee climbed onto the daybed and adjusted the pillows. She took off her shoes, let her hair down, and pulled the lightweight blanket onto her lap. Then she lay back, snuggled against the pillows and fell sound asleep.

The dream came immediately and she found herself once again struggling to get up the rocky precipice that led to the old Irish weaver. She brushed her way through dense growths of bushes and thick-leaved trees with thorns that cut her each time she took another step. But she kept going, so strong was her desire to see the old weaver and perhaps Scaylee. On her hands and knees she crawled through an opening that led her to the spot she sought. The road was smooth on her bare feet, her long blue sequined gown pushing trails of dust behind her.

But there was no one there.

She looked up and down the road. The old Irish weaver wasn't at her loom outside the cottage, and there were no crowds of people gathered to hear one of Scaylee's stories. She wandered up and down the smooth dirt road looking for signs of them. She saw the cottage with the door open, so she stuck her head in, but it was empty and no fire burned in the fireplace.

Lynda Lee began to panic. Her heartbeat quickened, her pulse raced, and her headache throbbed.

"Where are you?" she called. "Scaylee, Maman, where are you?"

She sat on the dusty road and cried.

Her dream place had vanished. It looked the same, but the people were gone. They had all but disappeared.

As she wiped the tears from her eyes, she thought she heard a sound, a baby, perhaps. Again, she looked around but saw no one. So, she got up and followed the sound, and as she walked down the road, dust cropping up underneath the hem of her blue sequined gown, she saw a child standing on the road by himself, a little boy of five or six years old.

She walked toward him.

"What is your name?" she asked as she approached him.

"Are ye lost?" he asked.

"No, I'm not lost, but the people who are supposed to be here are gone. I can't find them. They're always here. It's why I come here in my dreams. I come to find them and talk to them."

"Maybe this is not your dream," he said. "Maybe you're in someone else's dream."

Lynda Lee frowned.

"You can't be in someone else's dream, little boy. That's not possible. This is my dream and I've come to find the old weaver and Scaylee, the storyteller."

"They've already left," the little boy said.

Lynda Lee brushed the hair from her face.

"Left? To go where?"

The little boy shrugged.

"They wouldn't leave, not without letting me know."

"They've gone already. I told you."

"Gone where?"

"To the other place."

"What other place? I've been visiting here in my dreams for years and years. If they were going away, they would have told me. If they've gone, why are you here all alone?"

"I'm waiting," he said.

"Waiting for what?"

The little boy shrugged again.

"But I ain't scared," he said. "They'll come get me when it's time. You must have been gone for a long time 'cause I don't know nothin' but I know more than you."

Lynda Lee put her hands over her ears.

"This is not right," she yelled. "This is not what it's supposed to be. I need to see Scaylee and I need to talk to the old weaver."

"Lynda Lee," the voice called. Ray shook her shoulder. "Dinner's ready and it's time to eat. Wake up, sweetheart."

Lynda Lee opened her eyes. Tears streamed down her face.

"What's wrong, Lynda Lee? Why are you crying?"

"They're gone, Ray. The people, the weaver, the storyteller. They're all gone."

Lynda Lee put her hands over her face.

"I can't take it, Ray. If they're gone, then I am lost, utterly lost."

Ray lifted her up and hugged her close to him.

"You're right here where you need to be, Lynda Lee, with me and the children."

"But my dream," she sobbed. "They've all disappeared. The people I cherish in my dreams have disappeared. I couldn't find them anywhere."

Ray hugged her again.

"Maybe this was a different dream, sweetheart, one you haven't had before."

Lynda Lee took her hands from her face.

"A different dream? That's what the little boy said."

"The little boy?"

"Yes, all my cherished friends were gone, but there was a little boy who said he was there waiting."

"What was he waiting for?"

"He said he wasn't afraid because they would come get him."

"Sweetheart, this is getting a bit too complex for me to follow. Maybe after you've eaten and showered you'll feel better. Then you'll be able to sleep soundly for the night. And who knows? Maybe you'll have the right dream this time, the one you don't like to wake up from."

"But the dream's no good without the old Irish weaver and Scaylee, the storyteller. It's just no good. It's terrifying."

"Don't cry, sweetheart. You're exactly where you should be right now. Here with me and the children. It's home, Lynda Lee. Our home. We're all here, safe and sound. A dream is just a dream. It has nothing to do with reality. So, go get washed up and let's have a nice dinner, okay?"

Lynda Lee got up from the daybed and went to wash her face.

She whispered, "Scaylee, Maman, please come back to me. Please.

I can't make it here without you. When I dream tonight, please please come back to me."

But even though she fell asleep quickly that night, the dream did not come.

Chapter 59

When Ray woke up, he found Lynda Lee's side of the bed empty and smooth as if she hadn't even been in bed. He showered, dressed and walked down the hallway, through the living room, and into the kitchen.

He found her sitting at their little table by the window with a cup of coffee that seemed untouched. She was staring out the window.

He walked over and kissed her atop the head.

"You're up early, sweetheart. Did you sleep at all?"

Still, she stared out the window.

Ray sat down at the table and took her hands in his.

"It's just a dream, Lynda Lee. Those people you've seen in your dream are not real. Dreams are just that, dreams. They're what our brains imagine when we sleep, but they are not real, honey."

She didn't respond.

"Lynda Lee, look at me!"

Lynda Lee turned and looked at him, her face expressionless.

"You are where you're supposed to be, Lynda Lee. Right here with us in our home. We have everything, a house, a car, two beautiful children. We love each other and want what's best for each other. Isn't that true?"

"I can hear them calling to me," she said barely above a whisper. Then she opened her pill bottle and took two more pills. "This headache is going to kill me, Ray, and I can hear them calling."

Ray leaned closer to her.

"That's just silly, Lynda Lee. A headache is not going to kill you. No one has ever died from a stress headache. If you're so worried about the headaches, why don't you come into work with me today and we'll find another specialist who might know how to cure them. How would that be?"

Lynda Lee giggled.

"Or, we could admit you to the hospital for a few days and do some real testing. The children can take care of themselves just fine."

"Go to work, Ray. You don't like to be late."

"I don't want to leave you like this, Lynda Lee. You're not yourself today. I'm worried about you. I'd rather stay home with you than leave and go to work."

"But what about the device you're trying to create? It's important to you and to all your patients."

"It's a failure, an utter failure. I can't risk anymore lives with this device. But, I've laid the groundwork. Someone else will come along and study it, find the errors in my calculations, and fix them. It's out of my hands now. Apparently, it's too early for a heart pacer."

"One of these days, Ray, they will be commonplace. So, go to work and see if you and your team can fix it. I'll be fine here."

Ray got up, kissed the top of her head again, and asked her to call him throughout the day just to check in with him.

Lynda Lee giggled again.

"I can never reach you when I call, Ray. Don't worry. Everything will be okay."

Ray lowered his head and walked toward the door.

"I love you, Lynda Lee," he said. "And to me, you are still the Goddess of Weaver Street, the most beautiful woman in this town."

Lynda Lee looked at him and smiled a thin smile.

When he'd left, she got up and warmed her coffee then sat back down at the table and stared out the window toward the backyard and the lake. She was taken by the beauty that surrounded her. The lush gardens, the marble table, the bird fountain with its water spewing out, the plants and bushes that Mark had so carefully put into the ground to surround the house.

She heard a sound and looked to see two little chickadees at the bird feeder. They glanced in her direction then kept eating.

Lynda Lee walked closer to the bird feeder and was surprised that the wee birds had not flown away. She reached out a hand and touched a tiny head.

Her heart skipped a beat when the little thing didn't move. He just kept right on eating.

She smiled and walked back into the house, brushing her fingertips together to savor the touch of the little chickadee. As she sat down at the table, the pain in her head grew so intense that she put her head down, covered it with her hands, and cried. She took several more pills, put her head down on the table and cried herself to sleep.

The dream came unbidden.

This time, though, she walked barefoot straight onto the dusty road, not in her blue gown but in a comfortable shirt waist, the newest one in her closet.

At first, she saw no one, and her spirits dropped. But as she kept walking and looking, she heard voices and saw a gathering of people. Someone in the crowd waved to her and came running toward her.

"Lynda Lee, you're here at last," Scaylee said and hugged her.

"But I was here only a few hours ago and no one was here, Scaylee, only a little boy who said he was waiting."

"A little boy?"

"Yes, he couldn't have been more than six years old, but he just stood there and said he was waiting."

"Oh, the little waiting boy. Yes, he's been here for a long time."

"What is he waiting for?"

"His mother," Scaylee said. "He's waiting for his mother, and shortly, his mother will be here to get him. He'll be so happy to be reunited with his mom. He's waited a long time for her. But we have many waiters here, all of them waiting for a loved one to come."

Lynda Lee smiled.

"A happy reunion then?"

"Yes, for both of them. Now, tell me about you. How is the headache?"

"Gone," she said. "It was so bad this morning that I couldn't do anything but cry. The pain was so bad that it blocked out everything else. I didn't mention it to Ray. He doesn't know what to make of these headaches. But I feel wonderful now that I'm here with you and Maman. Where is Maman, by the way. She wasn't on the roadside weaving."

Scaylee laughed out loud.

"That woman," he said. "She's at the cottage. We have plenty of clothes for the soldiers, but still, her place is at the loom and she stays there most of the time."

"May we go see her? I'm not sure how much time I have left here. Sometimes, it seems like I'm here for only a few minutes. Then Ray wakes me up and we're always late for some party or something."

He took her arm.

"Let's go see Maman, the old Irish weaver."

They walked down the smooth road. Lynda Lee wondered at all the beautiful trees, the bright blue sky, and for the first time, the myriad of birds flitting about.

"You'll never guess what I did this morning," she said to Scaylee.

"Tell me," he said.

"I was sitting at the table watching the bird feeder that Mark made for me. Two little chickadees came to the bird feeder. I went outside and got as close to them as I could and I touched one of them on the head. It didn't fly away. It just kept eating the bird seed. It was the greatest feeling, Scaylee, to touch one of these tiny creatures."

"I don't believe I've ever touched a chickadee."

"His little head was so smooth, like a tiny piece of velvet. It was a great feeling," Lynda Lee said and rubbed her fingers together.

"We're here," he said and called out, "Maman, you have a visitor."

The old weaver appeared at the door in the same clothes she'd been wearing before. Something about her seemed different, but Lynda Lee couldn't put her finger on exactly what it was. And then it came to her. Maman's face had a bit of a golden glow to it. It made the ancient weaver seem ageless and attractive.

The woman opened the door.

"Come right in."

"Maman?" she said. "Is it really you?"

"Of course it's me, Child. Don't you recognize me?"

"You look the same but different. Your face seems aglow and it's really pretty."

"Oh, hush now, Child. I haven't been pretty since my wedding day."

"Your wedding day? Oh, I wish I could have seen you."

"'Twas long before your time, Child. Long, long before."

"Where is your loom?"

"The loom is in the far corner back there. I'm told we've enough uniforms, so I have different work to do now."

Lynda Lee smiled.

"And what might that be?" she asked. "What other work is required of a weaver than weaving?"

"Come along, Child. I'll show you directly. Scaylee, why don't you take Lynda Lee down to the Center? I'm sure she'll love it. Then, by the time you get back, I'll show her the surprise."

"What kind of Center do you have here in Galway, Maman?"

"Oh, Child, we're far north of Galway now."

"Come on, Lynda Lee, let's go see the Center, shall we?" Scaylee asked.

He took her arm as they walked.

"It's quite beautiful here, isn't it?" he asked.

"Yes, everywhere I look I see something that almost takes my breath. Everything is so beautiful, lush, green, vibrant, almost glowing."

Scaylee smiled at her.

"I'm so glad you're pleased. The Center is just down this road. It is a sight to behold. There will be lots of people here, so hang onto my arm."

Lynda Lee stopped in her tracks and put a hand to her mouth.

Ahead of her, she saw a building called The Center. It rose high into the sky, the top disappearing in the clouds. But the lower building itself seemed to be made entirely of glass, a magnificent oval in the center of lush hill and fields.

"It's so beautiful," she said. "I've never seen anything like it."

"I thought you might like it. Now, let's go over here so that we can sign your visitor card."

"I have to have a card?"

"Yes, you do. We all do."

"Do you have one?"

"I do, yes."

"I'll never be able to keep up with a card, Scaylee. Maybe I should just wait for my next visit and get one then. Besides, I really need to brush my hair and straighten up."

"Okay, just go right into that room. You'll find a brush and anything else you need."

Lynda Lee walked into a large room filled with other women who were checking their hair, putting on lipstick and making adjustments. She picked up one of the clean brushes and ran it through her long hair. After giving it a good brush, she patted her face with cold water, wiped it with a clean white towel, and grabbed a lipstick from the myriad of colors available.

Then, she stepped back and looked at herself, the shirt-waist looking clean and crisp, the minimal makeup seeming just right.

"How do I look?" she asked as she walked back out into the Center.

"Amazing," Scaylee said. "Now, let's get your card."

Scaylee guided her to a table where several attractive women sat with smiles on their faces.

"And what is your name, dear?"

"I'm Lynda Lee Rogers," she said. "I'm visiting today."

"Ah yes, here you are," the woman said as she scanned the pages of a thick book.

"My name is in that book?"

"But of course it is, Child. May I see your right arm?"

Lynda Lee held out her arm as the woman ran some sort of light right above her wrist. It was warm but didn't hurt at all, and when she was finished, the woman asked, "How was that?"

"Just fine thank you."

"Well, we're pleased to have you with us, Lynda Lee."

As she and Scaylee walked out into the bright sunshine, Lynda Lee said, "Scaylee, my mark is gone. What happened to it?"

Scaylee chuckled.

"It's not gone, Lynda Lee. You just can't see it unless it's under a certain light. But it will always be there."

"I should be getting back now, Scaylee. I've been gone awhile and I don't want Ray and the children to worry if they can't wake me up."

"First, I want you to see what Maman has prepared for you. Okay?"

Lynda Lee smiled.

They walked briskly down the road until they came to a more modern version of the cottage Maman had. It had appeared while they were gone ... right next to Maman's cottage.

Maman stepped out of the doorway.

"Here it is, Child, just for you. Come and see."

Lynda Lee walked into a bright cottage with a large fluffy bed, a dresser, a standing mirror, and a small kitchen with a refrigerator full of food. The inside was all white but decorated with murals of vivid flowers and little birds.

"What is this, Maman? It's a beautiful cottage. I just adore it."

"It suits you, Child. Don't you think so?"

"It's so pretty I might never want to leave," Lynda Lee said.

"Well, that is good because this is your new cottage, right next to mine," Maman said. "Whenever you feel tired, you can take a nap or if you're hungry, you can fix a snack. But I haven't shown you your big surprise. Come with me."

Lynda Lee followed her into another room, just as bright but a little smaller. It had big windows and plenty of light and at its center sat an old loom.

"For your weaving, Child. You have all sorts of fabrics to work with, all sorts of wools to loom. I hope you'll have everything you need to enjoy your job as weaver for our residents."

"My job? I have a job here?"

"Well, someone had to take over my job as weaver, and I knew just who could do it."

"May I start when I come back? I really need to go check on Ray and the children, but I won't stay long. Is that all right?"

Maman closed her eyes. Scaylee closed his, took a deep breath, and said, "It's time, Maman. We must show her."

Scaylee took Lynda Lee's arm and guided her to one of the large windows. He snapped his fingers and Lynda Lee saw ... she saw them, Ray and the children standing beside a grave. All of them wiped tears from their eyes, but there they were: Ray, Julie, Mark, and many others standing at the gravesite.

Lynda Lee's eyes filled with tears.

Scaylee hugged her and said, "We'll look again in a little while and see how your precious family has fared."

"I can look whenever I want?"

"You can look whenever the window will allow it. It's all up to the window. It's what on earth you would call magic. Here, we call it a miracle."

"Let's have a cup of tea, Child. It will relax you."

Lynda Lee stumbled to the table and sat. Scaylee sat next to her and Maman across from her.

Before she took her first sip, Lynda Lee said, "I'm dead now, Maman?"

Maman put her hand over Lynda Lee's.

"Yes, Child. On Earth, you are, but here, you are alive and well. The window will let you check in on your family, and soon, you'll adjust to life here and be happy again."

"But, I will never see my husband or my children again," she said as tears rolled down her cheeks.

"Why not?" Maman asked. "Years pass quickly here, Child. You'll see them all in time. You won't age here, so you will still be their Goddess of Weaver Street. You just have to be patient."

"Truly, I will see them again?"

"You will, Child. You will."

Chapter 60

Lynda Lee adjusted to her schedule quickly. She helped some children learn to read. She visited other people who were new and needed help putting their lives together. She went along with Scaylee when he came to tell his stories. Without the headaches, she was completely free to do what she wanted to do.

She most enjoyed looking into the miracle window, as Scaylee called it. Sometimes, the window came on by itself and showed her something about her family that she would never have imagined, like Julie using their kitchen as her own successful bakery. She watched as Julie interacted with the people who came in, how kindly she treated everyone, and the little extra treats she would put in the bag for the children. She had grown into a caring and talented woman.

Every now and then she used the trick Scaylee had taught her. She could, at times, blow into the window. When she did, her family would get a brief whiff of her favorite perfume, Diorissimo by Christian Dior. She had worn it every day on earth and she wanted her family to at least have a whiff of it to remind them of her.

Every time she did this, her family or family members would all stop and breathe it in.

"That smells just like Mama Lynda's perfume," Julie would say. When Ray got a whiff, he simply closed his eyes and savored it. And when Mark smelled it, he would always say, "Thank you, Mama Lynda. I miss you and I love you."

Lynda Lee loved her days at the miracle window. On those days, she felt alive and still a member of her family. She knew that they still loved her and that they hadn't forgotten her, and it filled her heart with gladness.

She heard a soft knock at the door.

"Scaylee, come in," she said.

"Someone is here to see you, Lynda Lee."

"To see me?"

Scaylee nodded.

He turned to the woman and said, "Here she is."

Lynda Lee couldn't place her at first. She was an attractive woman, nicely dressed, healthy, and then an image came into her mind.

"Janine? Is that you?"

The two women hugged.

"I've just arrived," Janine said. "He finally did it, Lynda Lee. He finally hit me so hard that it killed me, so here I am."

Lynda Lee led her to the mirror.

"But look how pretty you are now," she said. "No bruises, no cuts. Your face looks perfect."

"Oh, I was so afraid that I'd be scarred and bloodied forever," she said.

"Come along, Janine," Scaylee said. "Maman is ready to show you the Center, but don't worry, you'll see each other again."

With one last hug, Janine was gone.

Lynda Lee smiled. She was so happy that Janine was out of her painful situation at last. And she knew that Janine would adjust to their new world. There was just so much to love about it. Beauty and miracles everywhere.

When Scaylee returned to escort her to the Center to work with the children, she turned to him.

"Where exactly are we, Scaylee?

"We call this place The Crossroads."

"You hadn't told me that before," she said as she straightened her hair and then brushed at the skirt of her dress.

"It didn't really matter before, did it?" Scaylee asked as he opened the door for them. "You always thought you were in Galway. That's where you wanted to be."

"I asked Ray once if we could go to Galway. He said no because my dream people wouldn't be there and then I'd be disappointed."

"He was right, wasn't he?"

Lynda Lee smiled.

"Yes, he was right. I'll give him credit for that one, but at the time, I thought he was just making fun of me. He always thought that my dreams, this place, you and Maman were just some people and places I'd imagined. He never really believed that I was telling the truth."

"Sometimes it's hard for humans to believe in an afterworld. It goes against logic and reason. Here, we understand that, and then there are people like you, Lynda Lee, who believe in the miracle of what's awaiting them with no reservations at all."

"Well, I was innocent. I thought it was Galway, a place I'd love to be."

"But you listened to my stories, you learned what Maman wanted to teach you, and you never doubted either of us."

"I'm content here, Scaylee. I wish I could stay here forever."

"You can stay here as long as you want, Lynda Lee."

"Really?"

"Yes, as long as you want. This is your home now."

"Scaylee, will you tell me a little about yourself. I know you, but I know nothing about you and I'm curious."

"What would you like to know?"

"Have you always been here?"

"No, of course not. I was born in Galway, like Maman."

"Then how did you come to be here and why do you tell stories?"

"In Galway, I was a teacher. I told stories to my students, and they seemed to like them. In fact, my first job was as a storyteller and a musician. I sang then, and I would sing stories to anyone who would listen. Sometimes, I could draw a crowd. I loved my students and I loved Galway, but inside, I always felt that I was supposed to be doing something more."

"And how did you come here?"

"The same way that you did, Lynda Lee, except that I was riding my horse and I wanted her to jump a fairly high fence. We'd done it before, so I was sure that she could make it without hurting either of us. Well, she made the jump, and I woke up here."

"Were you ever married, Scaylee? Did you leave behind a wife and children?"

"No, I never married. Somehow, I just felt that it wasn't the right thing for me."

"But you had family, didn't you? What did they think?"

"My parents had died from an outbreak of smallpox that hit Ireland."

"I'm sorry," Lynda Lee said. "How old were you when they died?

"I was only a boy, about seven or eight. Now, I can barely remember them."

Lynda Lee leaned forward, closer to him.

"Who raised you, Scaylee? You couldn't have made it on your own."

"No, I didn't make it on my own, Lynda Lee. Maman raised me."

"Maman?"

Scaylee nodded.

"Maman is my great grandmother. I grew up under her love and care. She taught me so much, and I will always love her. Now, I'm going to leave you to your work because I know how busy the children and students keep you. But if you need anything, let me know."

"One more thing, please, Scaylee."

Scaylee nodded.

"How long have I been here? I've seen Julie and Mark grow to very happy and productive adults, but the miracle window never shows me Ray. For some reason, I can't make it focus on him."

"I think in Earth years, you've probably been here ten years or so."

"Ten years?"

"Yes, and as to Ray, I can't answer that. I'm not sure why the window won't show him. Shall I make some inquiries?"

"Please do, if it's not too much trouble."

"Consider it done."

When Scaylee left, Lynda Lee went back to work. She went to her loom and envisioned a soft green gown for Maman, one with a full skirt but not too full, and comfortable enough to work in. She looked at her fabrics and chose a bright green sateen fabric, not too dressy and very comfortable to wear. She chose the softest linen and wool underskirt that she could find: thin, soft, and smooth.

"I can hardly believe that Maman is Scaylee's great grandmother," she whispered. "I'm so happy that he told me his story."

Lynda Lee looked at the fabric and ran her hand across it, pleased with her budding creation. Perhaps one of these days, Maman would find an occasion to wear it.

Chapter 61

Lynda Lee worked for several days on Maman's new outfit, and when it was finished, she hung it up to let the wrinkles fall out. She opened one of the backroom mirrors to let in the early morning mist to help those wrinkles fade. Then she imagined Maman wearing it with pleasure and a smile crossed her face.

Now, she was ready for a short nap so she lay on her fluffy bed and went to sleep, a sound sleep uninterrupted by dreams. She had no idea how long she had slept when a hand touched her shoulder and a male voice said, "Lynda Lee. It's time to wake up,"

She opened her eyes and saw Scaylee sitting on the opposite side of the bed.

"Sorry to wake you, Lynda Lee, but you have a visitor."

"A visitor?"

"Yes, someone has come looking for you."

Lynda Lee wiped the sleep from her eyes and went to the mirror. She ran a hand across her hair and it straightened out beautifully. Then, she ran her fingers over her face and it was perfectly made up, just the way she liked it. She put a finger to her lips and gave them some color.

"Thank you, Scaylee," she said. "Just one more minute and I'll be ready."

She walked toward the door and held up her hands.

A very light mist of lavender spread across her and dried instantly.

"I'm ready," she said. "A visitor, after all this time. I wonder who it could be."

"I think you'll be surprised," Scaylee said.

When she and Scaylee walked out the door, she stopped and could hardly believe her eyes.

Ray stood at the edge of the road. He looked confused, almost dazed. He had lost weight and most of his hair.

Lynda Lee walked up to him.

"Ray?"

"Lynda Lee," he said and hugged her so tightly she could hardly breathe. "Lynda Lee. I thought I'd never see you again."

"It's all right, Ray. You're safe here," she said and when she looked at him, he looked exactly as he had when they first met. Tall, handsome, strong ... the old Ray had returned to her.

"Come," she said. "Let's go inside and talk for a bit. Then we'll take care of some of the things you need to do."

As they were walking in, Ray said, "Lynda Lee, please forgive me. Forgive me for not taking those headaches more seriously and for making you feel silly about those dreams. But most of all, I want you to know about your headaches. The doctors, on autopsy, found a slow-growing tumor deep inside your brain. It's what killed you, and I will never forgive myself for not suspecting it all along. There are some tumors which cannot be detected by an MRI, even at an advanced medical facility. Yours grew so far underneath the brain tissue that it was hidden from all of our testing methods."

"All those earthly things are forgiven, Ray. Everything. You're in a different place now, a place where love is the most important gift you can give to those around you."

"Thank you. It's been a tough burden to carry all these years. Knowing that I'm forgiven gives me hope."

"Sit down and rest, Ray. You look tired."

"I am tired, Lynda Lee. I recovered from a mild heart attack, but then another full-blown one came right after. It was painful at first, but it didn't last long. I went to sleep and when I opened my eyes, I was standing on the edge of this place when a man who rode a horse and had on a cowboy hat came and brought me here. He knew my name even before I told him, and he said, "Welcome to The Crossroads."

"That was Scaylee," she said. "He rounds up strays and lost ones and brings them in."

"I'm grateful to him. Do you have some water? I'm awfully thirsty."

Lynda Lee got a glass and held it out the window where it quickly filled with sparkling water.

"It's the purest water you'll ever drink," she said.

Ray emptied the glass in one large gulp. Then he wiped his mouth.

"That's good," he said and sat up straight. He stretched his arms and legs and said, "I feel so much better."

Lynda Lee smiled.

"Just about everything here is designed to make you feel better," she said.

Ray looked around the room.

"So, is this your home? The home of my beautiful Goddess of Weaver Street?"

"No one calls me that here, Ray. And yes, it's my home. Do you like it?" she said as she put the glass on the counter.

"There's something very cozy about it. I love all the little knick-knacks you've found. You've done a beautiful job with it. But to be honest, when I look out the window behind the bed, all I can see are clouds. Is that a mural or a painting?"

"No, those are clouds, real clouds," she said.

"Then how does the house stand by itself? There's no foundation."

"Oh, there's plenty of foundation," Lynda Lee said. "It's just different from what you'd find on Earth. Ray, how are the children?"

Ray stood up and walked around the room inspecting each little thing.

"The children are lovely, just lovely. The bakery is so successful that Julie has opened a second one in downtown Tuscaloosa. All the students at the college have given her more work than she can handle. But, she's quite the business woman."

"And Mark?"

"That boy. He's doing so very well. He loves his job and earns an excellent salary as the head of the gardening division. He's been a staple at the Botanical Gardens for years now, and he loves his job. He's received write-ups in the newspapers about his gardening skills and he has had one promotion after another. He's become a fixture at the Botanical Gardens."

"Did either of them marry?"

Ray turned to her and smiled.

"Julie married about two years ago. In fact, she's just had a baby daughter who she named Lynda Lee, after you. She's never quite gotten over the loss of you. She wears your clothes, she uses your makeup, your perfume. She is the spitting image of you, Lynda Lee."

"So, life has treated them well," she said.

"Yes, those two are unstoppable. I imagine that Baby Lynda will be the same way. They don't need us anymore, Lynda Lee. They're fully functioning adults who've made the very best of their lives."

"Then we were right to adopt them," she said. "I often wondered about it."

Another knock sounded at the door.

"Come in, Scaylee," Lynda Lee said.

"I've come to get your husband for a while. We'll get him signed in and introduce him to some fine people."

"Aren't you coming?" Ray said to Lynda Lee.

"No, I'm covered. It's your turn now."

Before they left, Ray turned to Lynda Lee.

"In my eyes, you will always be the Goddess of Weaver Street, Lynda Lee. I just want you to know that."

When Scaylee and Ray walked out together, Lynda Lee felt a lightness that she had never felt before. She had always thought that she knew what her dreams were, what she wanted to do, how she wanted to look, what she needed to be happy. She thought back to all the work she put into those beauty pageants, all the money and time that went to making herself beautiful and smart, and all the trauma she suffered from her mother because of it.

Now, she thought of them as wasted years, years filled with nothing but trauma and vanity. But then she remembered that if she hadn't had those years, she would never have met Ray.

She chuckled at the thought of the many cans of Spam they'd eaten, the no-name cookies in a clear plastic bag. Ray had given her a wonderful life, but something seemed to be missing. She had never been able to find out what kept her from being happy and content. But then, perhaps it was the brain tumor eating away, devouring the happiness she should have felt.

But now? Now, she felt that lightness of spirit, that happiness that she'd heard so many people talk about. That happiness was hers now. It was hers and it was here in this place called The Crossroads.

Chapter 62

Lynda Lee and Maman sat side by side at their looms, Lynda Lee making a very soft cloth for the many children who came here while Maman made heavier clothes for the "boys" as she called them, those who wandered here after being fatally wounded in battles of some sort. Maman had always had a soft spot in her heart for the wounded soldiers.

As they wove, they hummed a song they'd heard Scaylee sing not long ago. Lynda Lee didn't know the words, but Maman sang them in Irish Gaelic, and occasionally, Lynda Lee would recognize a word or two.

"Do you miss being in Ireland, Maman?"

"I had a whole lifetime in Ireland, Child. I'm busy here, and I don't dwell on it because when I look around or when I use my window, I can be back there in a second. It was a lovely place to grow up, to marry and have children. There was always beauty all around me, natural beauty, the trees, the rain, the grasses, the ancient stones, always something beautiful. The scent of it alone made every day special."

"I wish I'd been able to visit there," Lynda Lee said wistfully.

Maman looked over at her.

"You can visit any time you like, Child. Just use your window. It will take you there."

"But I would only get to see it. I wouldn't be able to feel it, smell it, walk in the rain, or look at the natural beauty of it."

"That's nonsense, Child. Do you use your window very much?"

"Hardly ever," Lynda Lee said.

"Then that is the problem. Your window was created especially for you, Child. It will show you whatever you want to see, and despite what you think, you won't be just looking. The window will allow you to feel everything you see. I must reprimand Scaylee for not letting you know."

"I don't use the window much because I feel so far removed from the things I see. I check in on my children, of course, and sometimes," she said and leaned closer to Maman, "I purposely leave a bit of my scented lavender spray on them so that they won't forget me."

Maman smiled.

"I used to do that, too, but later, after a time, I stopped and let my family get on with their business. The memories they have of me should be sufficient for them to remember, and if they don't, what's the harm? People deal with loss in their own ways, Child."

"My daughter, Julie, named her baby after me. That's sweet, isn't it?"

"You should be proud. You were a good mother. But Julie has to forge her own path now without you and her papa. And because you taught her well, she'll do it. But I know how it feels to just peek in every now and then. I do it myself, but don't tell Scaylee I said that."

The two of them chuckled until Lynda Lee heard a voice and saw a hand grasping the edge of the road.

"Someone needs help, Maman."

"Yes, go, go and help. Someone took a wrong turn. Go, Child. Help them."

Lynda Lee knelt at the edge of the road and put her hand down until she grabbed hold of the other person's hand.

"Don't worry," she said. "I've got you. Just calm down and let me help you up."

The woman was able to drag herself up. She bent over and dusted herself off. Then she straightened and looked at her rescuer.

"Lynda Lee? Is that you?"

This woman was elderly, frail, and had no teeth. Her hair lay in thin gray strings almost plastered to her head.

"It's me, Lynda Lee. It's Beth. We lived on Weaver Street together until John and I moved away."

"Beth?"

"Yes, it's me, Beth."

"I'm sorry, Beth," Lynda Lee said. "I didn't recognize you. Why are you here?"

"Old age," Beth said. "My liver and heart just gave out. Can I have a hug?"

Lynda Lee stepped forward and hugged her, but still, she didn't recognize her.

"This is my friend, Beth, Maman."

"Hello, Beth. Do you weave?"

"Sort of, but mostly, I'm better with a sewing machine. Lynda Lee used to have a beautiful antique loom. She showed it to me once. We were close friends until my husband moved us away. But I've never been happier than when I was close to her on Weaver Street. It was a very special community."

Lynda Lee looked at the bent old woman in front of her and saw no sign of the gregarious, happy woman who'd lived beside her on Weaver Street.

"What is that I hear?" Beth asked. "A horse?"

Lynda Lee smiled as Scaylee trotted toward them on his fine white horse, the horse that never aged. He pulled beside them and climbed down off his horse.

"Hello, Beth," he said. "Welcome to The Crossroads. I'm Scaylee, the storyteller."

"You don't look like a storyteller, sir," the frail woman said.

"We are not always what we seem to be," he said. "Lynda Lee, Beth seems as if she could use some recovery time. Will you find a bed for her? There are extras down the road a bit."

"Yes, of course," Lynda Lee said. "Here, take my arm, Beth, and we'll find a place for you to rest. It's not far away."

Lynda Lee took Beth a few steps away to another cottage and told her to lie down and rest.

"I'll check in on you later," she said. "The rest will help you recover."

Lynda Lee walked back to her place beside Maman.

"It happens sometimes," Maman said. "People we know come here, but they're changed and we don't recognize them right away. Just give it a little while, Child."

"What did Scaylee mean when he said that we are not always what we seem to be?"

"Oh, Child, that would take an age to explain, but there will come a day when you will look at Scaylee and he, too, will be changed, but you will know who he is. It is the way," Maman said, "here in The Crossroads."

Lynda Lee went back to her weaving. She mumbled to herself, "It is the way, here in The Crossroads."

A smile lit up her face.

Suddenly, she felt that lightness of spirit, that she'd heard so many people talk about. That spirit was hers now, and the thought of it made her laugh out loud.

It was hers and it was here in this place called The Crossroads.

She was no longer the Goddess of Weaver Street, but for the first time, she was happy.

The End

www.ingramcontent.com/pod-product-compliance
Lightning Source LLC
Chambersburg PA
CBHW020415260626
47156CB00007B/2392

* 9 7 8 1 9 5 4 3 3 2 5 3 9 *